A MORGAN HAWKE STORY COLLECTION

BY

MORGAN HAWKE

Some of these stories were previously published and have been compiled into one volume that includes two new stories WARNING: These stories contain explicit material.

Molly Coddle
Molly is a brash robber with a taste for the family jewels. He's a handsome lord with just what she's looking for.

Queen of Dragons
The Wyvrn is a mythical creature of legend, a sorceress with enchanted dragon-scaled armor, or so the War Duke believes.

Phantom Highwayman
Bess conjures up the ghost of a highwayman . . .

Night Waitress
Lilli is a waitress in an all-night diner. Bruce is a dangerously attractive man that won't take no for an answer, even if it's for his own good. What's a succubus to do?

Wolf Moon — Snow Moon
Heather had a wild fling with a dark handsome stranger, but now that stranger is back saying that she's contracted a very rare sexually transmitted disease — Lycanthropy.

Temple of Lillith
It's been quite a long time since the goddess Lilith's last summoning by a mortal, and she has every intention of taking advantage of the situation — to their mutual pleasure.

The Pirate's Pixie
Everyone knows that a child's laughter makes fairies, but Captain Houk comes from a far older century and he remembers what breaks them: Carnal Knowledge.

A Morgan Hawke Story Collection
Copyright © 2019 Morgan Hawke
ISBN: 978-1-4874-2747-4
Cover art by Martine Jardin

Published by eXtasy Books Inc or
Devine Destinies, an imprint of eXtasy Books Inc

Look for us online at:
www.eXtasybooks.com or www.devinedestinies.com

Molly Coddle

Highway Robbery
Autumn 1764

"Dammit, Molly, you're always spoiling the pretty lords,"
growled the huge highwayman from amongst the
night-dark trees. He was practically invisible on his massive
black horse. A second black charger tugged on the reins knotted to his saddle. The six powerful coach horses chomped at
their bits and stamped in impatience as they stood sweating
and blowing from the failed escape attempt.

"Christ's cock, girl," he continued to snarl. His pistol was
primed and pointed at the coachman as Molly dealt with the
passenger of the imposing conveyance.

"Is there something you wanted to say?" Molly asked. She
smiled, showing her perfect white teeth. With one hand, she
swept her feathered cavalier's hat from her head. Her red-
gold curls tumbled across her shoulders and down her back
in wild disarray.

The young man they referred to replied with a muffled
"Mmfftt!"

"Well, I do suppose it is rather difficult to say anything in
your position." He was face first in her ample bosom. Molly's
arm was locked around the back of his neck with her gloved
hand knotted in his long, neatly bowed queue to keep him in
place. The silky tail of his overlong golden mane looked so
pretty against the black leather of her riding gauntlets. She
had tied his wrists together behind him, so he really had no

1

way of coming up for air.

"So, now will you surrender your valuables, or do I need to get rough?" She pulled back on the fine silk of his tail, lifting his face from the deep valley of her bosom.

"That was unfair," he wheezed as he gasped noisily for breath. The moon silvered the fine perfection of his face, the cupid's bow of his delicious lips.

Molly pouted prettily. "Well, I did say *stand and deliver*, milord." She tightened the grip on his hair then bent lower until her full lips were almost brushing his cheek. "Oh, come on, give it up so I can be nice to you," she purred. "I can be very, very nice," she breathed, then brushed her lips against the fine shell of his ear.

"Well, all right," he said softly, then moaned as she rewarded him with an exciting touch of her tongue on his ear. Molly stood up abruptly and the handsome young lord winced as she pulled him up from his knees by his hair. "Hey!" he protested.

"All right, now tell my rather burly assistant where you've got the jewels stashed in your rather impressive coach."

"You mean your vastly large and abundantly well-armed assistant highwayman?"

"Mind your manners, milord." She tugged his hair in annoyance, and he yelped.

"I thought you were going to be nice!' He winced, his aqua eyes flashing in annoyance. He bit his lip as she tugged again.

"We'll get to that presently. Where are the goods?" She pushed him up against the coach, which rocked from the impact. She pressed her cool length against his, breast to breast, broad chest to incredible bosom.

"Be reasonable. Just who is getting robbed here, anyway?" He was once again surprised by her height. She was staring at him eye to eye. Her legs were so, well . . . long in her boots up to the thigh and tight man's breeches. Her doeskin-clad hips writhed against the silk of his breeches, and he felt himself leap to sudden and profound attention. He choked as his thoughts traveled straight down to the warm vee in her parted thighs that was cradling the heat of his erection.

"The jewels are in a compartment under the driver's seat," he said breathlessly.

"That's my good boy," she purred, then brushed his lips with hers.

He leaned to kiss her more fully and was surprised when she met him halfway. Her red lips parted, and her tongue swept in to parry with his. She tasted so fresh, so sweet, like a cool glass of spring water. He moaned and shook as lust took over his body.

"Mmm." She sighed, breaking their kiss.

"Can we untie my hands now, I'd like to . . ." he stopped as he gazed down at the expanse of exposed bosom so tantalizingly close. He desperately wanted to hold those abundant creamy globes in his hands, then peel them from her half-undone waistcoat and draw her nipples into his mouth.

"I have a better idea," Molly whispered.

"What?" He felt her palms against the silk of his breeches, then busy fingers on his trouser buttons. His mind churned to a sudden halt and leapt in panic. "Right here? In front of your, um, assistant and my coachman?" It was getting very difficult to think. All he could concentrate on was the feel of her gloved fingers inside his breeches, then along the contours of his rigid flesh.

"And your two footmen as well," she chuckled. "Mustn't forget them. Don't worry, I've got a floor-length greatcoat on, they won't see a damned thing."

He watched in fascination as she caught the fingertip of one glove in her white teeth and pulled, peeling the leather from her hand. They both sighed as she slid her bare hand into his pants and along his heavy erection. She snuggled up tight against him. He tried to make room for her by getting his hands over her head, but she wouldn't let him drop his hands around her. He ended up holding them high. They struggled for position a bit more, but he so very wanted to touch her, and his hands and elbows kept getting in the way. If he hadn't been so fucking hard, he would have laughed at the situation.

She grunted in frustration. "It seems that you're right, doing you up against the coach could get problematical, seeing as your hands are tied," she conceded.

"You could untie me," he whispered invitingly as he nuzzled her perfumed neck under that incredible mane of red waves. He rocked his hips and his cock against her palm.

"That would take the fun out of it." She giggled and pulled away.

She gripped the lapels of his frock-coat and he gasped. "What?" He was tugged forward, then pushed back.

"Into the coach, my fair lord, I'm gonna fuck you on your seat-cushions," she growled.

He sputtered in alarm as he was shoved onto the leather bench of his own coach. Aggressively, she tugged his cravat from his neck. Her lips found the column of his throat, and shivers raced up his spine as her tongue made magic on his skin. Diligent fingers undid his breeches the rest of the way, releasing his aching flesh from its painful captivity. It rose firm and unrepentant against his flat belly.

"Now that is a lovely sight," Molly purred, her eyes locked to his erection. She licked her lips and pulled away, dropping her greatcoat on the opposite bench. She opened her waistcoat the rest of the way and parted her shirt.

His mouth dried in appreciation. "That is a magnificent pair," he choked. The uncertain light of the candle lamps in the coach gilded her skin warmly. Her nipples were a soft rose and pronounced, rising from generous areolas.

"Why, thank you," Molly said softly, then skinned out of her leather breeches.

His eyes slid down the muscular length of her long legs, then back up to the soft red nest of curls at the joining of her thighs. He licked his lips in anticipation. She grinned cheekily, then straddled his thighs with her knees up on the seat. She sat up and brought her delicious breasts to his lips.

He dove, rubbing his cheeks and lips against the silken softness of her voluptuous breasts. He delighted in her resulting moans. He bared his tongue, tasting, sucking, licking, nipping and partaking of her flesh as though she were a dessert he would never be permitted again. She whimpered and pulled suddenly away, her engorged nipple slipping from his lips with an audible wet smack.

"What? Oh!" He sputtered as her mouth descended onto his. She slanted her lips over his for a better fit, then swept in with her pointed tongue, showing no mercy. She wriggled over him as she positioned herself. He worked his hands, but the knots were too tight around his wrists.

He jerked as he felt a cool hand between their bodies, then on his hot erection. She captured his length and tugged it, stroking its firmness. He felt the swollen head of his cock being rubbed against wet heat. His buttocks clenched as his body felt the entrance to moist haven. She dropped and engulfed him in her snug wet sheath. Their moans filled the coach as she sank to his balls.

"Umm, that is a very nice fit, milord," she sighed them pressed forward, her nipples raking across the silk of his shirt.

"Since we are now on more —" He swallowed. " — more intimate terms, you can call me Beau." He grunted, then moaned as she rocked forward onto his cock. She was so wet that he could feel the trickle of liquid down his balls.

"Mmm, I like Beau. Thank you, Beau." She rocked back, then forward to please herself and him in the process. "You'll forgive me if I hurry," she panted.

"I'll forgive you anything," he groaned as he strained up into her moist depths. "Just tell me your name."

"Call me Molly," she said, hissing as her body clenched around him with rising pleasure. She rocked atop him, gripping his shoulders, her thighs holding him captive. She thrust hard down on him, fucking herself on his rampant cock.

"God, Molly," he grunted as his crisis became painful, "fuck, fuck, fuck," he chanted, trying to hold on and wait for her. She was very close—he could feel by the way her body was trembling around his cock. She stilled. She threw her head back and began pumping up and down on him, her cunt squeezing him so tightly he was convinced she was going to milk him dry.

"Beau!" she moaned, her mouth open as she violently came.

He shouted as ecstasy suddenly ripped through him.

Molly abruptly dismounted, and ropes of his cum spurted forth to spatter across her.

Beau fell back against the padded seats of the coach in exhaustion, delighted with his release and the luscious view of Molly's bountiful breasts decorated with his cum. Pearls of creamy liquid hung on the tips of her nipples and across her throat.

"Remind me to give you pearls in honor of this occasion," he said softly. She actually blushed, then picked up his cravat and wiped at his cream, smearing it across her flesh.

Molly smiled. "I'm afraid you'll have to catch me first."

"Oh, I will." Beau sighed and smiled. "Give me time." He leaned forward on the seat. "You are just too magnificent to forget." His smile broadened. "Sooner or later I will find you, and then it will be my turn to tie you up."

Molly froze momentarily at the sight of his confident smile and hurried into her doeskin breeches.

A shout came from without. Molly grabbed her coat, then dove out of the coach, her shirt open and breasts still bare. They gleamed wetly in the starlight. She disappeared into the shadowed, rustling, woods surrounding the road. Fading hoofbeats filled the night.

Beau bent down and angling carefully, pulled a throwing dagger from his boot. In seconds he was free. Quickly and efficiently, he put himself away and tidied as much as he could with his handkerchief. His cravat, sticky with his own spending, was quite beyond help. He sat back to wait.

Long minutes later, a full troop of uniformed horsemen wearing his personal household livery appeared. They came galloping down the road to intercept the waiting coach. The troop's captain reined in his gray gelding, then bent over his saddle to peek into the coach window from the back of his sweating horse.

"Well, Lord Rushford, what do you think of our highwayman problem?" asked the captain.

"I have met the enemy, and I am determined to catch her." Beau's aqua eyes gleamed with the challenge as he stepped out of his coach. "I can also see why she's been given the name Molly Coddle." He straightened the lace at his cuffs. "For a hardened thief, her form of persuasion is rather gentle," he said with sarcasm. "And vastly unique to say the least."

The captain frowned. "Her persuasion is gentle?"

The mounted troops behind the captain looked at each other in confusion.

"This is the first thief I've ever run across that doesn't use knives to pry out information." Beau tugged at his cuffs and blushed.

"I, uh, see. So, do you think you can catch her?" queried the captain.

Beau looked up. "I was Spy-Master in Paris during our last war on the continent. I excelled at finding and apprehending enemy spies for years. Now that I'm home from the war, I should be able to catch one little thief," he scoffed.

The troop captain saluted Lord Rushford without a word. He straightened in the saddle and motioned his garrison down the road. In a well-ordered mass, the mounted troops paired up, then cantered down the dark road, leaving the coach alone on the rutted highway.

Beau turned and stepped back into the coach. He settled in his seat as his coachman whistled the horses forward into a trot. The coach picked up speed as they cantered homeward.

"Oh, yes, I'll catch you, my Mistress Molly Coddle." Beau chuckled. "And then it will be my turn." The perfume from their sexual frenzy scented the coach's interior. "Pearls," he whispered softly to the night. "Long, thick ropes of creamy white pearls."

QUEEN OF DRAGONS

Sorceress Seduction

A blue and gold banner emblazoned with a clawing white lion snapped in the wind above the War Duke's head. From the height of the ridge, his golden eyes watched the carnage of the battle that had shifted from the ridge to the valley below. His great black war-horse shuddered under him, excited by the scent of blood and death. The massive stallion pawed the bloodied earth, jingling his bit, his armored sides heaving. The horses of his accompanying troops shied nervously under their armored riders as they stood arrayed about him to either side.

The War Duke's eyes were drawn to the opposite ridge of the blood-drenched valley, where a woman battled ferociously atop a screaming fire-red stallion. Even in her crimson armor with its fanged dragon helmet, there was no mistaking the feminine curves. She lashed out at her attackers with uncanny speed and deadly accuracy.

The War Duke pushed his helmet visor up to get a clearer view of the woman. She looked like a red dragon in female form, the gilded scales of her armor glittering in the dying sunlight, her scarlet cloak flying about her like wings. Her sword flashed with the unmistakable glint of blue steel. The hilt was set with a stone that caught the dying sun's light and blazed crimson. No one could stand against her. Obviously, an artist had made that scaled suit of steel for her alone. It hugged her curves and moved as easily as flesh.

The War Duke whistled as he sat atop his restless stallion. "My God, she's magnificent!"

"Where in the seven Hells did the Boar find her?" one of the captains exclaimed.

The War Duke narrowed his eyes. "I can't tell what family she comes from. Her shield is too smeared with blood to see what's on it. She has to come from good family, though, I think that's a ruby in her sword. Nothing else would glow that bright in sunlight."

"God in Heaven! She just cut that soldier in half!" said another.

"That's not a woman. That's a she-demon conjured from the pits of hell," said a grizzled older captain. "Look at her, she fights with more than the strength of a man."

"I heard that the woman is supposed to be a sorceress called the Wyvrn, a fell creature born of magic, both woman and dragon," remarked one of the War Duke's lieutenants. "Her armor is made from the enchanted skin of a dragon."

"I heard that she was conjured by a powerful sorcerer during the Age of Legends." One of the War Duke's younger captains nudged his stallion closer. "I also heard tell that the Boar struck a deal with a devil for her."

"A sorceress wearing a dragon's skin for armor?" He laughed. "The Wyvrn is a creature of myth." The War Duke smiled grimly. "This woman is just a formidable warrior in a clever suit of steel." The War Duke looked about at his doubtful captains. "I will hear no more talk of sorceresses."

The armored roan the woman rode trumpeted a challenge, then reared on his hind legs, pawing the smoke-tainted air with bladed steel-shod hooves. The woman moved in perfect time with her infuriated mount. Her sword struck like lightning at the tide of men surging all around her. The roan suddenly spun in a circle, hooves slashing and teeth snapping. Horses bucked, fighting their riders, trying to get away from her inhuman fury and her demonic stallion.

The War Duke felt a stirring in his breeches at the sight of her dancer's grace and exquisite control over her screaming mount. His mind filled with images of himself wrapped in her powerful thighs, battling to ride her to submission.

"When we win this battle, I want the woman brought to me if she still lives," the War Duke ordered his men.

They rolled their eyes but saluted their obedience.

Smoke shifted across the battlefield, obscuring the War Duke's view of the sword-woman. He snapped his visor down over his face and shouted to his troops. As one unit, they charged down the embankment to join the battle, trumpets blazing and the flying hooves of their mounts a deadly thunder.

The War Duke awoke to a pounding headache. He groaned as torchlight speared into his eyes. Shifting away from the glare of the torch, he suddenly realized that it was full dark, and his wrists were tightly chained behind him. Lying on his side, he still wore his armor, though his helmet was nowhere to be seen. With great difficulty, from the sheer weight of his steel plate, he sat up against the wall. With a groan, he shook his head to clear his long black hair from his face. The back of his head throbbed in time with his heart.

In shock, he looked about him at the milling troops and realized that the red and gold banners of the Boar surrounded him. Walls of mortared stone rose all around him, surrounding him. He was within a castle somewhere. He squinted in the uncertain torchlight, looking for a door, an escape, anything.

"Bring the prisoner," he heard someone call.

Two fully armored, burly men-at-arms lifted him by the elbows and pushed him to his feet. His steps hampered by chains, the War Duke's spurs jangled on the stone floor as he was shoved forward.

"Where are you taking me?" he shouted. "What happened? Where are my men?" In stoic silence, more armored soldiers came forward. He struggled against his captors, swearing in three languages, his questions ignored by the guards. He took some measure of pride in that they had to use four men to hold him, even chained.

He was pulled and forced down a long, narrow stone-walled corridor, then shoved hard to his knees. His grieves squealed sharply on the floor. Mailed hands held him down by the plates across his shoulders.

The sound of steel-shod boots swiftly approaching came from the corridor before him. He could hear the voice of the Boar growling to his dukes about the morrow's battle.

A group of fully armored knights, still spattered with gore from the recent battle, stopped ten paces before him. The crowd parted, and suddenly, the dragon-helmeted woman was standing before him in all her scaled glory. At her throat, a huge ruby seemed to glow with uncanny fire. He had thought her armor red. He smelled the strong taint of copper and crimson dripping from her entire suit. The red was blood, smeared across her as thickly as paint.

Her body flowed like silk and water. Her armor was so exquisitely crafted that the scales shifted, flexing with each step as she moved, expanding and contracting with each breath. He watched as she turned to the man next to her and said something softly. Suddenly, he could see her back. Her arms and spine were ridged with razor-honed overlapping spikes. Her gauntlets were tipped with sharp claws and armed with daggered spurs to the elbow. The artistry of the armor was perfect in every detail and gilded with silver even on the tiniest edge. The fanged helm appeared to be joined to her suit seamlessly. There was nothing to show how the helm was attached to her shoulders or how it was to be removed.

Her magnificent body looked naked but for the carnage-spattered scales that covered her completely. The vee of her woman's flesh was delicately outlined by her armor, and at eye level. The War Duke felt the blood pound to his manhood as he gazed at her.

"Yes," she said, her voice hissing from within her dragon helm. "This is the one." Her horned dragon helm turned ruby eyes to the Boar standing a pace away. "He is mine. You agreed." She wasn't asking a question.

The War Duke could not believe his ears. Hers? He was her prisoner?

"I agreed, witch. Him, you can have with my blessing." The Boar let out a filthy laugh. He looked directly into the War Duke's eyes. "You poor bastard. You should see what happened to her last one."

"Where are my men?" the War Duke snarled.

"Without you, they'll fall to my troops at dawn. If I were you, I'd be more worried about her tender mercies." He laughed again, then strode away with his knights.

So, the War Duke thought, *they have me but not my army. If I can escape . . .*

"I must be prepared for the battle before me," the woman said to the War Duke, interrupting his thoughts.

He could feel an odd tingling in his head as she spoke to him. The helm parted seemingly by itself at her throat, and she pulled it from her head. Hair, the color of blood, fell in a scarlet cloak to her hips. Her face was that of an angel, with wide-set onyx eyes and full lips made for kisses. The white line of a scar slashed across her cheek. Rather than marring her perfection, it added incredible character.

"You are not like the others," she continued.

No longer distorted by her helm, she spoke in a voice that seemed to reach inside and stroke him from within. He was enchanted.

She cocked her head to one side as she gazed at him, eyes narrowed. "I have no time for little mysteries or for niceties. I have need of your strength."

Looking into her black eyes, he thought he saw the crackling of distant lightning deep within. There was power and a touch of sadness. *For him?*

Handing her helm to one of the waiting guards, she gestured, ordering them to strip him of his armor.

The War Duke had no idea what was going to happen, but he wasn't going to willingly submit to anything. They unchained his wrists, then held him down, arms spread wide as they unbuckled, then peeled the separate pieces of his steel armor from him. Even on his knees, he fought them every step of the way.

"Stop," the woman said sharply.

The guards froze, and so did he. They had his chest-plate and the bulk of his armor off him. His gorget, his gauntlets, and bits of his armor littered the floor. He still wore his shin-protecting grieves over his doeskin trews and spurred boots. His padded gambeson, worn under the steel chest-plate hung open, baring his naked chest.

Like a great cat, the woman moved toward him. He could smell the raw copper of blood on her armor. His captors held him firmly as she reached out a gauntleted hand. She touched his breast, and her clawed fingers raked only lightly. She splayed her fingers and placed her palm over his heart. He couldn't stop her from feeling its pounding. His breath shuddered in his chest. *What the hell is going on here?*

Warmth flooded from her palm, and he looked up at her, startled. Her eyes were intent, locking onto his. He felt himself drifting, falling into her bottomless black gaze. He forgot the guards; he forgot the battle. He only saw the woman before him.

"Release him."

He heard her voice as though from far away. Fascinated beyond thought, he watched as she came closer, filling his vision with her violent and threatening beauty. She bent closer; then her lips were touching his in a feather-light kiss. All thought stopped as he felt the warm silk of her soft lips moving over his.

"Desire me."

Her breath brushed against his mouth, and her voice rippled straight to his loins, bringing the fine hairs of his neck to attention. His heart hammered violently in his chest, and he felt his blood surge powerfully into his groin, filling him with overwhelming and burning need. Pressing forward, he sought closer contact. His mouth opened to taste her, to take possession of her. She let him within, her tongue stroking his, and he shuddered with violent passion.

She rushed forward into his arms, and he found his hands released to take her, and his ankles free as he rose on one knee to meet her embrace. His arms closed around her, and the edged scales on her back and spine seemed to fold away their sharp edges under his bare hands.

He grunted as her full weight fell onto him. Her armor-plated body was as heavy as anyone wearing plate mail might be, but the armor was surprisingly warm and moved fluidly, very unlike steel plates, as she let him hold her.

With surprising strength and ease, she knocked him back on the hard, stone floor, straddling his hips. His manhood was aching, trapped against the leather of his codpiece. He almost cried out in his sudden need to bury it in her warm flesh. She rose up on him; her clawed fingertips raked gently across his nipples and down his stomach scoring him with livid marks. He shuddered, and a fierce moan of pleasure was startled out of him.

She placed her hand on the glowing ruby at her throat, then slid her hand down. The ruby began to glow, spilling bloody light over her skin and his body, and seemed to beat in time with the pulse he could see beating in her throat. The brilliant red stone appeared to be lodged at the base of her throat, grafted into the skin.

He watched as her armor split, shifting apart as though it was retreating into her skin. *My God,* he thought in alarm, *she is a sorceress . . .Only magic can explain this!* The parting scales revealed her full perfect breasts, topped with rosy and hardened nipples. He swallowed. *Sorceress or not, she is incredible.*

The armor continued to separate down the center of her body, spreading until he could see her smooth belly and the shaven mound of her female flesh nestled against the leather of his codpiece. Oddly, her powerful thighs remained scaled by her armor as she straddled him.

The War Duke's mouth dried as he gazed on her sleek alabaster perfection, her muscles rippling under generous curves. She leaned down over him, pressing her naked breasts to the wall of his chest. Her clawed fingers slid through his long black locks. Suddenly her hand locked in his hair, gripping him mercilessly. She looked deep into his eyes, covering his mouth with hers in a searing kiss.

Mouths locked together, he sat up with her in his arms and grunted with the effort. *This is no feather-weighted maiden,* he thought. His mouth slid from her lips down her throat. He captured a breast in his hand, bent to bring his lips to the hard nipple that crowned it. He stroked against it with his tongue, then sucked hard, bringing a moan from the woman. He slid an arm around her scaled back to hold her in place as he ravished her breasts.

He snaked a hand under the curve of her buttock to touch her intimate flesh. Her hips writhed as he found her and slid his finger into her moistness. He explored her, and her excitement dampened his fingers and palm. Searching far within her depths, he discovered the soft fleshy mass that was her passion's trigger. He pressed against it, flicked it lightly in a steady rhythm.

She shuddered in his arms, and her hips bucked as she rode his hand, eyes slitted, biting her lip. He gripped her tightly, holding her while sitting upright, as she chose her rhythm and began panting her way toward ecstasy's release. She stopped at the very edge, snarling, and vibrating with unreleased tension.

In sudden temper, she released his hair to tear at the ties on his codpiece.

He spread his legs wide to avoid the spines and spurs of her gauntlets, then hissed as his flesh was released to her palms. He felt her close her clawed fingers around him with unexpected gentleness. Her eyes locked to his, she slowly stroked his shaft and brought her lips down, opening wide to sheathe him.

The heat of her mouth was incredible. He groaned and panted as her tongue swirled and licked at the swollen, sensitive head. His hips bucked into her mouth for more. She took him deeply, sucking hard, her tongue stroking from within. He moaned, mouth open, eyes rolling back from the exquisite, intense pleasure. His hands tangled in her blood-red hair. She rose, stroking him with her lips, grazing him gently with her teeth as her palm cradled his balls. She fell, swallowing him whole. He could feel her throat closing around him. She pulled back, then sucked him back down her throat, and he gasped.

He grunted, sweat gleaming on his chest as his hips bucked without control. He watched his flesh wet with her saliva sliding in and out, fucking him with her mouth until he was ready to burst. His neck muscles stood out in relief. He fisted his hands in her hair. He was so close, just a bit more and he would spill himself in her mouth.

She released him, and he cried out in frustration. She

shoved him until his back was flat against the stone floor. Her hand wrapped around his shaft again, taking possession of his flesh. He looked up from where he lay on the stone to see her poised above his hips, holding him in position at the damp red mouth of her cunt, her ruby mane in wild disarray about them both.

She sat, plunging herself down onto his rampant shaft. He bowed up from the floor as she took him deep into her body. She grasped him powerfully from within, then rocked forward, leaning down over him, her clawed fingers splayed on his chest. She leaned, then nipped lightly at his nipples.

Without thought, he grabbed her scaled hips and lifting, surged up into her. His spurred heels raked the cold stone of the floor as he dug for purchase. She rocked, riding him as he bucked up into her heat. The muscles of his arms stood out in whipcords as he anchored her hips to keep her locked against him as he laid full length on the stone. He grasped her breast with one hand and brought her to his mouth, determined to bring her to release. He sucked hard on her distended nipples and felt her shake with violent passion.

She moaned, long and low. He could feel a light sweat start on her hip under his palm and the trembling of her body around his cock. He recognized the signs. She was close, almost there. He was on the brink of his own climax, and he didn't know if he could hold out much longer. Curling his hand around the curve of her buttock, he pulled, rocking her hard, grinding her against him while working to angle his shaft against that soft fleshy mass that was her hidden trigger. She cried out as he found it, and her cunt grabbed hold of him. His cock felt as if it was being sucked into the very depths of her. He gasped in mind-numbing, ecstatic euphoria.

She shuddered hard, vibrating around him, and he realized that she was beginning to climax. The screams of her mounting ecstasy echoed strongly in the empty stone hallway.

Suddenly he felt the tightening of his own imminent release. He groaned, and she shoved him hard, dropping full length and heavy upon him, pinning him to the floor under her considerable weight. She writhed and moaned as her climax thundered through her. He choked in pleasurable pain as her powerful inner muscles gripped his cock like a steel vise and shuddered around him.

Her arms locked around him, claws digging deep. He could feel tiny trickles of blood running down his ribs. He locked his arms around her as he worked to pump himself into her heated depths, not caring if her armor cut his flesh to ribbons. He hissed as the pain of her clawed fingertips intensified his orgasm as it arched through him in a glorious blaze. In mindless rapture, he felt his shaft and balls tighten, trembling on the very edge, then explode to fountain into her, filling her with his body's essence.

Through the fever of his pleasure, he saw the corridor filling with a blinding and bloody light that seemed to be coming from her ruby. The light of her ruby swelled to a glaring intensity. Suddenly the War Duke felt the light burning into him, blazing with intensity and glory that wrapped around his body and swallowing him whole.

Renewed passion violently blazed through his mind and flesh as he felt his life, his soul, being drawn into her body.

Suddenly her pleasure slammed in a brutal red wave through his mind, then burned in a heated wave into his soul. Ecstasy echoed back and forth between their shared thoughts, magnifying to a tidal wave of screaming rapture. His howls joined hers as the pleasure went on and on, washing over them in wave after wave.

Without warning, her armor rippled under his hands. He gasped. What was happening? Through the red haze of shrieking pleasure, the War Duke struggled to move out from under the woman as her armor came to virulent life and writhed over them both. She wasn't wearing a suit of gilded armor; it was an enchanted skin.

"By all that's Holy—let me go!" He fought to get away, but she held him pinned to the floor with her uncanny strength as the scales stabbed into him with a thousand tiny claws. It was quickly grafting itself to him, scale by painful scale.

"I cannot," she said softly and clung tighter. "I need all of you."

He shouted as he felt himself being wrapped to her body with incredible speed. "What is happening?"

"My enchanted dragon's skin is sealing us together," she said softly. "It will soon be over."

"But why?"

"I am the Wyvrn, and you are mine."

He froze in astonishment. By all that was Holy, he was indeed taken by a sorceress; she really was the Wyvrn! A woman more than half dragon, conjured by a powerful sorcerer long ago. But that was only a legend, a myth.

Struggling anew, he discovered that the armor had sealed his body to hers; he was trapped in the circle of her powerful arms. He felt a kind of betrayal as he realized that he was still hard from wanting her.

The skin covered both of their bodies with amazing speed, then suddenly encased both of their heads together, smothering him in absolute darkness. Fear gripped his heart in a vise. The sound of her pounding heart filled his ears. He couldn't breathe.

"Surrender to me," a soft voice was saying over and over, as though from far away. "Give me your strength, your fears, your soul," the voice whispered. "Be of me."

He opened his mouth to scream, and her lips covered his. Air was forced into his straining lungs, and he found he could breathe. Through the ripping pain of the enveloping skin, he could still feel the moist heat of the woman wrapped around his man-flesh.

"Yield, and have your revenge on the Boar," the voice continued, stronger, clearer. "Open, let me in. Yield, and live," it commanded in a ringing voice that seemed ageless and ancient.

In a way he could not fathom, he could feel that it was her voice, speaking directly to his soul. He couldn't speak, her mouth covered his completely, but his soul screamed, "I yield!"

The doors of his mind slammed wide, letting in an inferno of flame. He felt a burning at the base of his throat. A firestorm swept into and through his blood, searing into his frantically beating heart. Wrapped in her unyielding embrace, his body shuddered and trembled with unspoken shrieks of agony and splendor as passion blazed through him. A second powerful wrenching climax consumed him from within. He felt his soul tear apart in a howling red tide of flames. Flame closed in on him and smothered him into red-tinted darkness.

"Body to body, soul to soul, heart to heart. Be one with me," whispered the ancient voice. "Rise and be reborn, child of my flesh, my soul, my heart. My love."

The War Duke shuddered suddenly awake. She drew away from him and stood. He stared up from where he lay sprawled on the stones, surprised that he could see. Surprised that he lived. He had been convinced that her fire had torn him asunder. There was an echoing surprise in her onyx eyes as she stood over him.

The Wyvrn held her clawed hand out to him. "You are reborn, a Wyvrn as I am. More dragon than man."

He looked up from the floor as she towered over him. He felt an inner movement, a second self that was very old and very powerful. Something else was living around and within his body. In that moment, he knew that he was no longer merely human.

"I have much to teach you."

He saw a shimmering beauty within her that he hadn't noticed even in the throes of lust. He felt a powerful aching emotion roar through his heart.

He took her hand and discovered that his own hand was gauntleted and spurred as hers was. With ease, she pulled him to his feet. He found that he was entirely covered in scaled armor from throat to foot. His body was encased in glittering black scales. The scales of her armor were shining silver and clean of all traces of the blood that had painted her completely.

"You're clean," he said softly.

"It is the blood that feeds the dragon's skin. After a long battle, the suit must be fed and fed well." She looked him over, her hand warm against his black scales.

Power surged through his limbs, and he stretched, reveling in his newfound strength. In astonishment, he found that his armor seemed weightless and completely unrestricted, allowing him to move as smoothly as though naked.

He looked at his scaled arms. "Does it come off, or am I sealed in here forever?"

She smiled. "The skin can be shed, but the ruby is what connects us to our dragon's soul. The skin responds to the ruby."

He lightly touched his throat and discovered a stone lodged there.

"That is your dragon's eye, the seat of your soul," she said. "I have never seen anyone receive one. You are the first to survive my embrace." She tilted her head to one side. Anguish touched her eyes. "All of the others died in flames, burned to dust."

Around him, a light dusting of ash lay scattered on the floor. There was a scent of burned cloth, leather, and scorched metal. They were the remains of his clothes and his own plate armor. The guards were nowhere to be seen.

"The trappings of your mortal body," the Wyvrn said softly. "The guards have fled, having seen the remains of my last lover." There was sorrow in her eyes. "I am not truly sure why you survived to be reborn when others have not, but I suspect that part of you wanted to be as I am." She cocked her head to look at him.

"To be powerful? To be a creature of magic and legend?" The War Duke flexed his muscles, discovering a new strength and an odd hunger he couldn't quite identify. "To be more than merely human?" He smiled. "Somehow I just don't understand the attraction." He raised a brow sarcastically.

"Come, I have promises to keep, and a need to see the color of the Boar's blood." Her smile was fierce and cold. "I am under gaes, an oath that forbids me to harm the Boar."

"How does the Boar have command of one such as you?" He could feel something strange and protective swelling in his breast. He could not imagine anyone controlling her will.

"There is a sorcerer you must slay to release me," she said gazing at him with a question in her eyes. She leaned over and picked up her dragon helm from where it had been dropped on the floor.

He took both her hands, "Your enemies are my foes. For you, I will slay them all." He dipped his head low to hide his fears and uncertainty from her. "For I find that now, I cannot live without you." He lifted his head.

"Beloved," she whispered.

He touched his lips to hers, and she returned his kiss with fervor, tasting him. She pressed her body to his, and he could feel her warmth and firm muscles under her suit undulating against him.

She embraced him, resting her cheek on his armored heart. "For you, I would slay the moon and the stars. We are bound, heart to heart, and soul to soul. Forever."

He pulled her close reveling in her warmth and scent. "I will need a weapon."

"Your sword is never further than your heart." With a smile, she pulled away from him. "Grip the eye of the dragon and pull. Carefully."

He touched the stone at his throat, and surprisingly it split, and a part of it came away in his hand. Lightning arced up his arm in a blaze of white heat, and the scent of ozone filled the hallway. In his palm was the hilt of a perfectly balanced blue steel sword. Ruby light flamed from the pommel and reflected up an edge as fine as a razor.

"I have never seen a blade such as this."

"Your weapon is made of dragon fire." She looked at her helm thoughtfully. "You conjure your helm as you do your sword, by touching your ruby."

"For the Boar and his pet sorcerer, I will need no helm." His voice deepened to a bass rumble. "I want them to see my face. I want them to know that I would slay anyone or anything for you."

"Come, it is time to blood your steel and feed the hunger of your dragon. Our enemies may be found in the castle library, secure in your defeat." The Wyvrn touched her own ruby, conjuring a sword like his own. Her black eyes blazed with fierce joy as she led the way.

There were no guards at the narrow door of the library. Politely, the War Duke knocked.

"This had better be important!" bellowed a voice.

The War Duke shoved, slamming the door open against the wall with a crash. He took two steps into the small room, his blade in his hand.

The tiny room was crammed with leather-bound volumes on wooden shelves. Tall candles under glass illuminated the room from all four corners. Maps and parchments littered a long table that was shoved against the bookshelves below an arching window.

"What the Hell? You're supposed to be dead!" shouted the Boar, still in full steel plate. He stepped away from a gaunt older man in shimmering red robes.

"The small man in the robes is the sorcerer," hissed the Wyvrn from beyond the doorway. "Kill him quickly."

The aged sorcerer rose from his stool by a tall narrow desk that dominated the room. He raised a hand writhing with black flames.

The War Duke grunted in reply then the world appeared to slow down. His sword flicked out, almost by itself, in the gentlest of motions. A thin line appeared at the throat of the robed man. The sorcerer's mouth made an O of surprise, and then his head flew away from his body. The rest of him crumpled in upon itself in a boneless heap with a hiss of silk. Blood spewed from the body and sprayed in a hot fountain across the War Duke's chest. He could feel each individual drop as it struck him.

The Boar drew his heavy sword out with a filthy curse and struck at the War Duke.

Without thought, The War Duke raised his own weapon to parry the Boar's blade. As though in a dream, he danced around the slow, clumsy strikes of the Boar. The blue steel blade sliced into the joints of the Boar's armor in long smooth slices without a trace of resistance. A joyous red haze slid across the War Duke's vision.

"Beloved?" whispered a soft voice.

The War Duke blinked and found himself kneeling in a pool of blood spreading thickly across the stone floor of the library. His was looking at a pulped mass of bleeding flesh gripped in his fists, his sword gone. He lifted his eyes, and the Wyvern's black orbs, glimmering with blue lightning, met his.

In silence, she dropped to her knees before him.

"And so, you have blooded your steel and ripped out the heart of the Boar. I am free," she said.

He could smell the blood dripping from his hands. In disgust, he pitched the wet mass of flesh against the wall.

"Now we must feed your hunger," she whispered.

He could smell the fresh copper of blood on her armor, on his own armor, on the floor, in the air he breathed. It was spattered in rivulets across the leather tomes and streaked the walls. His man-flesh swelled rigid with sudden cruel, and painful lust. He gasped with the strength of his body's virulent and overwhelming desire.

"I need you," he growled, his body pulsing with effort not to take her there on the blood-soaked floor.

"Take me," she whispered, only inches away.

"Wait . . . I am as you now." He looked at her with pained eyes, thinking of the men she had destroyed in her fiery embrace. "What if I kill you?"

"It is how we feed. It is the ecstasy that triggers the magic, but it is the blood that feeds the dragon. I believe that there is enough blood and death in this room to satisfy both our dragons, but if it should kill me, I would die gladly in the arms of my beloved."

"I . . . I can't take that chance." There was an inferno building up under his skin. Sweat started to drip from his face. A fine trembling erupted all through his limbs.

"You can. You must. If you don't take me, you will die here and now. Your dragon will drink your blood and slay you to be fed." She locked her black eyes on his. I cannot let that happen." A flash of blue lightning blazed in their depths, swallowing him whole.

Ravenous with need, the War Duke reached for her. He hooked his gore-coated clawed hands into her hip plates and pulled. The Wyvrn tumbled into his arms, and he rolled her easily beneath him. Her hair spilled in a bright skein of crimson silk across the dark maroon lake washing across the floor.

His lips captured hers, tasting blood. His tongue speared her mouth hungrily. His spine writhed as he mindlessly sought to work his hips between her thighs, spattering still warm carmine red over them both. A sibilant growl rumbled from his chest.

His clawed fingers pawed frantically at her suit. It split and shimmered apart under his palm, his fingers scoring her white skin even as his own blood-spattered suit split down his chest, releasing him. With a snarl he pulled her thigh over his, opening her wide. His shaft was agonizingly swollen and inhumanly hard, and his mind enslaved by ravenous lust as he worked to penetrate her softness. Her spurred heel dug into the floor, raising her hips. He found her, then plunged within without gentleness, practically screaming with voracious need.

With both clawed hands, he cupped her ass and brutally pulled her up to meet his thrusts. She was tight but wet and ready for him. He buried himself repeatedly to the hilt, then pulled back to slam back into her damp warmth. He pounded savagely into her heat as fast and as hard as he was able. The loud slaps of wet flesh against wet flesh defined every lunge of his hips as he tried to go deeper, to hammer himself through her, into her core.

Around him, he could feel her flesh gripping him in a welcoming velvet fist. She shuddered hard below him, her body climbing to violent surrender. There was a flare at the base of his spine, and suddenly he was dancing on the raw edge of climax.

There was a tightening of her body under and around him, then she froze, her mouth open. He stilled in awe as he felt a blaze of white-hot flame scorch up from the woman below him. She shrieked, and he felt himself tighten painfully in reaction, then let go in an unbearable fire-fall of release. He pumped fiercely into her as he strove to empty himself into her completely.

A white heat flared at his throat, stealing his breath then searing him through the heart. The room filled with ruby light as their pleasure cascaded into each other's mind and soul, consuming them both. He barely heard her cries of insane joy as he howled in glorious sated rapture, the copper-sweet taste of blood fading from his lips.

As the light from their pleasure dimmed, a light dusting of ash settled where the scattered remains of the sorcerer and the Boar had been, leaving not a drop of scarlet anywhere for anyone to find on either of them.

He opened his eyes to her smiling onyx gaze, and sobbed with joy, hugging her tightly.

"Remind me never to doubt you," he whispered, chuckling.

"Oh, I will beloved, I will indeed."

The Wyvrn, beautiful and sleek, rose from her candle-lit bath. Her long silky mane of blood-red hair fell below her buttocks as she waited for him. Firelight gleamed across the water droplets that coated her.

"Welcome to my home, wife," the War Duke said with tenderness. He wrapped a warm towel around her alabaster human skin, planting a gentle kiss, then a not-so-gentle nip on her shoulder.

She turned her onyx eyes to his topaz gaze. With soft fingers, she slid her hand through his waist-length raven tresses. Her finger traced the ruby that glowed at the base of his throat, the fiery light throbbing in time to his heartbeat.

"Husband," she whispered to him. "Never would I have dreamed that I would find you. I believed that I was destined to live alone, slaying all who would love me."

"Beloved," he whispered to her, brushing his lips across her brow. "I will be here to share your battles and guard you always. For we are bound, heart to heart and soul to soul. Forever." His lips touched hers, and her mouth opened beneath his in welcome.

Across the fire-lit room, a dragon's scale suit of armor sat on a mahogany frame, gleaming clean and silver in the sunlight that poured through the castle window of their home. A ruby-pommeled sword of blue steel lay in its own stand before it. Beside the silver armor, a second stand of mahogany held a similar suit of dragon's skin, dark and black with newness.

In time the second suit would gleam silver also.

A second blue steel sword completed the set. Side by side, they rested.

Waiting for the next battle.

PHANTOM HIGHWAYMAN

A Ghostly Thief of Hearts

A nd still of a winter's night, they say, when the wind is in the trees,
When the moon is a ghostly galleon tossed upon cloudy seas,
When the road is a ribbon of moonlight over the purple moor,
A highway man comes riding, riding; riding;
A highwayman comes riding, up to the old inn-door.

Over the cobbles he clatters and clangs in the dark inn-yard.
And he taps with his whip on the shutters, but all is locked and barred.
He whistles a tune to the window, and who should be waiting there
But the landlord's black-eyed daughter,
Bess, the landlord's daughter,
Plaiting a dark red love-knot into her long black hair.

The Highwayman by Alfred Noyes (Circa 1789)

NOCTURNAL PRELUDE

Bess was dreaming of kisses.

Masculine lips moved possessively over hers. A warm velvety tongue surged aggressively into her open mouth.

She could hear her own moans as she returned the caress with enthusiasm. The rich musk of aroused male wreathed her senses, making her body hunger.

A pleased groan echoed softly, making his gratification known. His hand on the back of her neck, gently but firmly held her locked mouth to mouth for his hungry onslaught. His other hand was curved under the weight of her breast, cupping her fullness. His thumb brushed lightly against her erect nipple through the thin chemise.

She arched and rubbed slightly against his palm, shuddering with flaring urgency.

His warm lips left hers.

Bess sighed with disappointment.

"Bess, my love, come down," a dear familiar voice whispered in a rich baritone. "Let's go for a ride in the moonlight."

Bess lazily opened her eyes and looked down. Her heart jolted powerfully. "Aimory," she whispered back with a smile.

The horseman stood boldly atop the saddle, gripping the window frame. Moonlight silvered everything, including his eyes as he wound his fingers in her long black curls. His full lips were curved in a smile simply full of wickedness. The long golden waves of his hair, caught back with a black velvet bow, gleamed under the moonlight and spilled over the shoulders of his wine velvet frock-coat. The frills of the Brussels lace jabot, knotted around the throat of his black silk shirt, framed his strong jaw. The dark tricorn hat he normally wore was hooked to his saddlebow.

Bess arched her brow at Aimory. "One day that horse is going to take a step whilst you're atop him and dump you on your arse."

Aimory snorted in derision. "Who, Blackamoor? Steady as a rock, he is."

The huge black as sin thoroughbred took that moment to toss his gleaming head, jingling his bridle with a snort.

Aimory's eyes widened briefly then he chuckled. "Are you coming down here or not, my beauty?" He tugged gently but insistently on her springy tresses. "Come down to me, my love, tonight I need more than just your kisses."

"You know I can't. If I'm found with you, My Da will skin us both!" She lifted her head and looked about for anyone spying on them. Perched as she was on the windowsill, she had a clear view of the stable-yard of the inn and the surrounding trees.

"Not if he doesn't catch us," Aimory smiled rakishly. "I need you in my arms before I go, Bess. I'm after a prize tonight, a royal prize big enough to finally retire on."

Bess bit her plump lip as an abrupt shiver captured and shook her. "Is this the one we've been hearing about for weeks? The one no one is supposed to know about?" Her heart thumped hard in sudden fear. "I have a bad feeling about this jaunt, beloved." She reached out and caught hold of his warm hand. "You know my feelings are never wrong, Aimory. What if the magic spell that sorcerer gave you doesn't work this time? What if the Thief-Taker finally catches you?"

"That's why I need to hold you, my love, to make sure nothing goes wrong with the spell. It's powered by your loving, remember?" He smiled to reassure her. "The spell the alchemist gave me makes me and Blackamoor here living ghosties; bullets can't touch us, and nothing can outrun Blackamoor." He took both her hands in a firm grip and began to pull, gently, but with determination. "Come on down to me."

"I can't! I've never done . . ." Bess began to tip out of the windowsill and tried to twist her hands from his firm grip. "Aimory, you're pulling me right out the window!" Her whisper rose to an alarmed pitch. "What if somebody sees us?"

"What's all the fuss over?" Aimory leaned closer to the window to angle for a better grip on her wrists. "I intend to finally ask your Da for your hand tomorrow, though God and the whole county knows I've set my spurs for you. Please, Bess, this is to be my last run." He leaned closer, his palms warm on her waist.

"Your very last run? You promise, Aimory, on your soul?" Her choice was about to be made for her—she was already leaning halfway out the window.

He reached out and wrapped his arm around her waist. "I do, my lovely Bess," he whispered hoarsely. "I promise. Give me your sweet body, just to make sure the spell won't quit and cost me my life at the last second. Grant me your first love. There's no need to wait any longer, I'm going to be your husband soon. After this last ride I'll have better things to do with my time than robbin.' I want to spend my days in your arms, raising Blackamoor's colts and our sons."

"I don't know . . ."

"Please, Bess? Come with me tonight, for my very last ride as a highwayman? Tomorrow, I swear I'm hanging up my pistols. I've already told your Da that I'll take up that job in the stables he's been offering me, and I've put a down-payment on the Widow Rushkin's cottage." He reached up and kissed her mouth possessively, then tugged.

Bess drowned in his kiss and felt herself pitch forward,

falling. Strong arms wrapped around her and pulled her to safety across the saddle, tight against a broad velvet chest.

"Maybe a small ride, my love," she whispered as she looked up from where she sat across his doeskin-clad thighs.

CONJURATION

Bess jerked awake from a dead sleep and groaned. "Damn, I hate waking up right before the good parts!" She sat up groggily in the narrow bed, hearing what sounded like fading hoofbeats.

She could feel the low sensuous hum of erotic force that powered her particular form of magic. She slid her palm down her oversized T-shirt. Her nipples were hard with frustrated sexual excitement. "Shit," she swore softly. "How the hell am I gonna discharge this energy?" One of the drawbacks of being a tantric sex witch, was that anything that made her sexually excited, such as her almost-wet dream, charged up her magical energy. She'd have to burn that energy before things started floating across the room.

"Alright, what little tart conjured me?" bellowed a loud, masculine and pissed-off, provincial British voice.

The sound of a teenaged girl screaming in mortal terror suddenly erupted from the next room.

Bess groaned. "Mother of us all! What has that little pest done now?" Ever since cousin Alexandra had figured out that Aunt Bess was a witch, it had been one little incident after another trying to get Bess to do or teach her magick. Alex's Mom was going to skin Bess alive for letting Alex even guess that Bess was a witch.

Bess thumped the bed with her fist, then threw the pillow on the floor. She rolled to get out of the narrow bed and tangled her feet in the blankets, nearly falling. With a frustrated growl, she yanked the covers off, then threw them across the bed. Her bare feet thumped on the hard wood floor as she stood.

The girl shrieked again, only louder.

"So much for my vacation in England," Bess grumped. She darted out her door and into the hall of the Bed and Breakfast, then burst through the door into the next room, where cousin Alex was staying.

Alex's room was good-sized, with wood trim and white plaster walls. The window shutters were wide open over the bed, letting in wisps of fog from the night. In the center of the room sat Alex's traveling trunk, surrounded by a huge chalked circle marked on the floor. Yellow candles burned in mismatched china saucers at the four points of the chalked circle.

A slender girl with straight blonde hair and cornflower-blue eyes ran about the room in flowered pajamas, yelling her idiot head off. Pandemonium was in full sway.

"What the hell have you done now, Alex?" Bess shouted above the screaming. Silence dropped like a hammer. The girl was in tears. Alex pointed to a corner of the room, where the ghost was.

A slender man stood, or rather floated, two inches from the floor within a smaller chalked circle. Bess swallowed hard, her brows rising in appreciation. The ghost was rather good-looking in a rough kind of way.

Tall, heavily scuffed horseman's boots armed with very nasty spurs encased him to very shapely athletic thighs, stretching his worn leather breeches. He was dressed in a full-sleeved, silver-buttoned, ragged frock-coat that must have been chocolate velvet in better days. A bedraggled red sash held his coat closed over a narrow waist.

Her gaze slid across muscular arms folded against a broad chest. The tattered remains of a silk and lace cravat, that might have been black once, were knotted at his throat. Sandy curls cascaded in a tail down his back held by a not particularly clean ragged ribbon. She gazed up at a stubborn, clean-shaven chin on a sharp face and into slanted emerald eyes.

Whoa, what a hottie, thought Bess to herself and blinked.

"My, my, you're a pretty puss . . ." was his comment. He smiled at her, or rather leered with his mouth open, then he smacked his lips together. Bess blushed as she realized that she had run in wearing just a T-shirt that barely came to mid-thigh. She wasn't even wearing panties.

"Oh, great, she's conjured a letch!" Bess muttered to herself.

"What'd he say?" Alex whispered, tugging on her arm. Bess blinked in surprise. In her fascination for the cute ghost, Bess had completely forgotten where she was.

"Nothing I'm going to share with you."

"Hey!" Bess said as she spotted a heavy leather-bound volume in the middle of the big circle where it sat on the trunk. "That's my Grimoire!" Alex had been with her when she had found the old tantric spell book last week in a curiosity shop. She'd done nothing but pester Bess about it ever since.

"What the heck are you doing with my new spell book?" Bess bent to retrieve her book and glanced down at the page. Oh gods, Alex had been experimenting with tantric magic—sex magic, never mind that Alex was supposed to be a virgin! *What is it with college girls and sex?*

"Nice view . . ." the ghost said as he bent to look down Bess's low-cut neckline. Her full breasts were clearly visible. She was sure he could almost make out her nipples. "What I wouldn't give for a flesh-and-blood cock right now," he said with a shake of his head.

"Do you mind?" Bess snapped in annoyance, standing up abruptly. She lurched back as she realized that his lips were but a kiss away.

"What? Don't you like compliments?" He was practically

drooling.

"That was a compliment? Are you always this charming, or is it just me?" Bess snapped sharply. She stalked stiff-leg-ged toward the cowering teenager who had run behind the bed.

"Wait a minute . . . You can hear me?" He dropped his arms in surprise. "You can bloody well hear me? Wait a damn minute, you're the witch?" the ghost shouted to her rapidly retreating back. He reached out to grab for her shirt and his hands struck the boundary of the chalked circle. A flash of blue flared up. The ghost hissed in pain, pulling back sharply. Swearing creatively in French, he shook his burned hands, then tucked them under his armpits. "Hey, you!" he shouted, "Come back over here!"

"What did I tell you about touching my stuff, and this book in particular?" Bess growled, ignoring the cursing ghost. The Grimoire was opened to a page showing graphically how to draw a man using masturbation to power the spell.

Teenagers! If Alex's mother found out what was contained in her own tantric spell book, never mind the newly acquired antique, Alex would be kept from her perverted aunt till Doomsday.

"It's just a book . . ." Alex flinched, blushing to her roots.

"Just a book, she says," moaned Bess. "You are not old enough to go looking through my spell books, never mind an antique like this one. You are definitely not old enough to be experimenting with sex. or anything else in my books, especially this one!"

"I only wanted to have a bit of fun before I had to go back . . ." she sniveled. "I just wanted to conjure up a boy . . ."

"With tantric magic?" Bess's toe tapped on the wooden floor. "Sex magic?"

"I'm old enough to do anything I want, I'm eighteen!" she snapped back. "That's legal age in America, too!"

"I told you before, I don't know where this Grimoire came from, and it could be dangerous! Sorcerers are famous for writing their spells wrong to keep nosy people out of their books." Bess threw up her hands, then narrowed her eyes. "Have you any idea how glad I am that your mother is taking you back tomorrow?"

"I didn't mean any harm!"

"Tell that to him!" Bess said angrily as she pointed to the annoyed ghost. "How do you think he feels about being yanked from his rest?"

"Well it's not as if I had anything better to do . . ." grumped the ghost. He pulled his hands out from his armpits and examined them. "Actually, I could use a witch . . ."

"I thought the spell was only a . . ." Alex started, dabbing at her eyes with a corner of her pajamas, then sniffling noisily, "a spell to attract true love," she finished, very quietly.

"Now, put him *back*!" Bess finished with a shout.

"But I, um . . . I can't."

"Why not? The recipe is in here . . ." Bess flipped through the pages of her book. "I saw it earlier . . ." She flipped through the pages, hoping against hope, that the release spell wouldn't have to be powered by anything sexual.

"She can't 'cause she don't know my name," interrupted the ghost. Bess looked over at him in surprise and he smiled rather smugly. "And I can't tell her 'cause she can't hear me; she's not a true witch. However, you can hear me just fine, 'cause you are."

"I, um, I don't know his name . . ." confirmed Alex between sniffs.

"How the hell did you conjure him in the first place?" Bess swept errant curls behind her ear. Nervously she made an effort to comb her fingers through the black hair tumbling about her hips in a riot of sooty curls. Sighing, she gave it up as hopeless. Her mane was a forlorn tangle from being wrapped in a towel and slept on. She'd taken a cool shower right before bed, because it had been sweltering all day and this Bed and Breakfast didn't have air-conditioning.

"Well, I uh, found this . . . and the spell in the book said I could use it instead." She held out a scrap of tattered fabric with a nasty stain on it.

Bess took it and examined it closely. It could have been brown velvet from a very long time ago.

"You mean you were in my books yesterday? Never mind. Let me guess, you got this fabric from when we were visiting the town cemetery yesterday." Bess sighed. She'd only gone across the street to get a sandwich and a drink. She must have taken all of fifteen minutes. "No wonder you conjured a ghost."

"Actually no, not in the cemetery," she said. "There was this dug-up area around the outside of the cemetery fence, way in the back. I found this caught in a bush."

"Which comes round-about to my story," interjected the ghost. He was clearly admiring the way Bess's hair swung below the hem of her shirt. "Somebody dug up my body and moved it. I'd really like to have it put back."

"You were buried outside the fence?" Bess asked the ghost. She crossed her arms under her breasts, unconsciously pushing them and her hemline higher.

"Um, yes." he said, guiltily looking up from her cleavage. "*Was* being the operative word here. My body has been dragged off." He openly ogled the view of Bess's rounded thighs, as if by staring, the hem would inch up just a bit more.

"Terrific," Bess said, rounding on her cousin in exasperation. "They only bury criminals outside of hallowed ground. Congratulation! Your love spell just succeeded in conjuring an axe murderer!"

"Hey!" The ghost called out in a thoroughly offended tone. "I was not an axe murderer! I was a highwayman! And I certainly didn't use an axe. I used a pistol or a sword."

"Oh, you were a highwayman?" Bess snapped, rounding on the ghost. "You killed people with a gun or a big knife instead of an axe? That makes me feel so much better!" she cracked at the exasperated ghost.

"Now there's no call for all that, it was a good profession," he called back, shaking a finger her way. "And I didn't kill anybody who wasn't trying to kill me first."

"What's a highwayman?" Alex wanted to know.

"It's like a car-jacker, only on a horse."

"Hey, you!" the ghost shouted at Bess's back, "they buried witches on the outside of cemeteries, too, you know!"

Bess whipped around to face the ghost. "Are you trying to piss me off?" Eyes narrowed, she raised a hand wreathed in blue foxfire.

Alex crooned in awe. This was the most magick she'd been able get Bess to demonstrate in four days.

"Actually, no . . ." Wide-eyed, he raised his hands in surrender.

"Fine," Bess, said to the ghost. Being careful not to smudge the chalk, she stalked to the center of the four burning candles. Setting the old book on the trunk she opened it, the parchment rustling as she flipped through pages. *Hmm, the return spell didn't take any actual sex, just a low level of excitement.* After the wet dream she had plenty of energy to fuel the spell, and she needed to burn it off anyway.

"So, what's your name, and I'll send you back?"

"I'll give you my name if you give me yours," he countered.

"Do you want to go back or not?"

"What I want is the bloody bastard who took my body. You did hear me say that somebody took off with it?"

Bess rolled her eyes and tapped her bare foot. "I don't know who took off with your body, and I really could care less, if you really want to know."

"I will settle for your name." The ghost crossed his arms in frustration. "Since you are not going to be of any bloody help," he continued in a mutter.

"All right, already," Bess growled. Names had power and giving him her name meant that he would have a part of her. She wasn't about to give out her magical name, which might give him command of her person and a key to her power. "My name is Bess, and I don't want to hear a single joke about being named after a cow."

"I wouldn't dream of insinuating that you have large brown eyes . . ." he returned with an innocent look. Her eyes were black actually, as black as her curling mane.

"Your name, highwayman?" Bess gestured impatiently and the chalked circle surrounding him began to glow with a warning shimmer of blue foxfire.

"Hey! Watch it with that stuff!" He flinched. "Now, come off it, witch, no cheating. Do you think you're the first witch to conjure me? Out with the rest of it," he said with a come-hither hand gesture. "I have to give you my first, middle and last name to get me out of this mess. It's only fair that I should have yours, too."

"You know," Bess ground her teeth in anger, "you really are a royal pr . . ." She glanced at the avidly listening teenager behind her. "Pest," she finished. "My name is Elizabeth Victorianna Merryweather, called Bess. There, are you happy now?"

"I'd be happier buried eight inches deep between your thighs . . ." the shimmer of blue climbed up to his knees. "Ow! Shit!" he yelped. "All right! All right! My name is . . . Wait a moment, Merryweather? As in, this is the Merryweather Inn we're at?"

Bess rolled her eyes at his stalling. "It's a Bed and Breakfast these days, but yes. I'm a distant cousin from America, so what?"

"I thought you looked familiar," he muttered. "Oh, so you're a Yank?" he said loudly. "Well, that explains everything," he said, throwing up his hands and shaking his head. "Anyway, I asked 'cause I used to have a . . . Well, I was going to marry the innkeeper's daughter as soon as I had enough blunt put aside. Her father's name was Merryweather."

"I can pretty much guess what happened to you. High-speed lead poisoning?"

"Yeah, well, she had an accident first." A look of stark pain and longing came over his face that was quickly shuttered.

"An accident?" asked Bess, curious in spite of herself.

"Yeah, an accident involving a Thief-taker General and a musket," he said bitterly. "I had the same accident later that day. Enough already, can we get on with it?"

"Anytime you're ready. Your name, highwayman?"

"I'm Aimory Stanton Plunkett." He crossed arms again, in extreme annoyance.

"Alrighty, here we go." Carefully shielding what she was doing from the teenager, Bess dipped her fingers into her damp cleft, gathering her feminine dew on the tips. "Say goodbye to Mr. Plunkett." Bess raised her arms, which lifted the hem of her T-shirt and gave the highwayman a view of her completely shaven mons.

"Hey, you haven't got any hair on your . . ." he called out.

With a brazen smile, Bess cut him off with a spate of Latin words involving his full name. With a sharp gesture she drew a sigil in mid-air with her damp fingers, which blazed with blue light. Mr. Plunkett disappeared from the chalked circle with an audible pop.

"Goodbye, Mr. Plunkett," Alex called out.

"Now clean up this mess and get back to bed. Your Mom is going to be picking you up first thing after breakfast," Bess sighed tiredly. "Which is not soon enough for me," she whispered under her breath.

"I'm really sorry," Alex said, sniffing. The girl bustled about wiping up chalk and dousing candles.

"It's okay, I took care of it. Let's just forget about it and get back to bed." Bess hefted the heavy book and opened the room door. "Please, no more excitement tonight?"

"Don't worry! I'll be good!" Alex assured her. "That was so cool," she whispered to herself.

Yeah, sure, but as soon as my back is turned . . . Bess really could not wait 'til after breakfast when she could resume her vacation. She stepped out into the hall and headed toward her own room.

"Is everything all right?" Bess about jumped out of her skin. The innkeeper's elderly mother stood at the top of the stairs in her pink night-wrapper.

"My cousin just thought she saw a ghost, Mrs. Merryweather," Bess said, telling the absolute truth. "She's going back to sleep right now. Sorry about all the noise."

"Oh," the elderly Mrs. Merryweather nodded to herself. "Well, in my day, there really was a ghost. He was a highwayman from King George's time." She sighed, then turned and began her journey back down the stairs, her hand trailing on the wall. "He'd come riding up on a big black horse to the inn looking for his lost love. She used to live here, you know . . ." the old woman's voice faded away.

Bess went back to her own room and stashed the Grimoire under the mattress. Picking up her pillow from the floor, she straightened her blankets, then fell onto the bed with a groan. Breathing a heavy sigh, she pulled the light covers over her head.

INCANTATION

The moon had fallen, and the sky was dark with only stars, when very slowly and very gently, the shutters over Bess's bed unlatched themselves and swung silently open. In the corner of the room, close by the open window, leaned a shadow deeper than the rest. The tiniest glimmer of starlight brushed a shoulder, outlining the ghostly form of Aimory Plunkett. He peeled the gloves from his fingers and put them in his coat pocket.

"Well, well, my Bess, it seems that you have fallen into my hands just when I need a witch . . ." he whispered very softly. He unbuckled his heavy leather belt and pulled the sash from his waist, draping them on a chair. "This time I'll find a way to keep you and your magick." With a shrug, his tattered velvet coat slid silently from his broad shoulders to the floor. The waistcoat followed. "One way or another . . ." The bedroom latch fell and locked all by itself.

Hovering by her bed, Aimory gestured with his fingers. Slowly, so as not to disturb the sleeping woman, the sheet and light blanket slid down, revealing Bess's coal-black curls falling in a cascade over the side of the bed to pool on the floor. The bow of her lips parted slightly.

"Mmm, mmm, the advantages of being a ghost," he whispered softly.

With a faint sigh, Bess stretched, both her arms extending under her pillow and over her head as though they were tied to the headboard. She moaned, then rolled onto her back. Her breasts lifted to high relief, sharply defined by the tautness of

45

her shirt, rising and falling in time to her breathing.

"Oh, Lord, Bess my girl, I don't remember you being built quite like that," the ghost whispered. Without a sound, he drifted to the edge of her bed. Biting his lip, he gestured again with two fingers. The wayward blanket drifted lower. The hem of Bess's shirt came into view, caught just under her full breasts. As her covers inched lower the strong line of her stomach and her belly button were revealed.

"In for a penny, in for a pound," he muttered to himself. The blanked slithered lower. There, unveiled to his avid and admiring gaze, was Bess's shaven mound.

"You really don't have any . . ." He swallowed hard. In his day, Aimory had heard that some high-priced Cyprians shaved themselves, but in all his living days, he'd never actually seen a completely hairless pussy. The soft pink of her inner lips pouted, slightly open and moist, peeking from between her parted plump thighs. She looked so naked. He licked his lips. She looked so . . . succulent.

"Bess, my lovely, do you have a kiss for me?" he breathed near her ear. "I want to taste those cherry lips," he whispered and sighed.

Bess moaned lightly in her sleep and licked her full lips. Aimory licked his own in anticipation.

"Let me touch you, my bold lass. Let me feel you," he whispered very softly. "Let me hold you . . ."

Bess moaned softly, then rolled her head to the side, facing Aimory, her eyes closed in sleep.

He took this to be a yes. Aimory moved to the side of the bed and knelt. Softly he moved his hand to touch the twisting curls of her blue-black mane. A spark of blue fire touched his outstretched fingers. He hissed and pulled back sharply, tucking his fingers into his mouth as though to salve them from a burn.

"Damn bloody witch," he muttered very softly. "Going to

play hard to get, the coquette, are you?"

"What can I use? What can I use to stroke my Bess with?" Aimory looked sharply around the room. His eyes fell on a feather quill stuck in its holder on the antique writing desk. "That ought to do nicely," he sighed softly. Raising his hand and focusing, the feather quill lifted from its holder and floated lightly across the room to his hand.

Inching as close to her bed as he could get without getting zapped by her unconscious protections, he softly gestured, and the sheets fell obediently to the floor.

Signaling with both hands, the hem of Bess's tee shirt slid up to reveal her full breasts crowned with pink nipples. Aimory whistled softly in appreciation.

Gesturing again, he levitated the feather to a rosy nipple. The feather brushed, flicking against her, back and forth. Aimory smiled as he noticed her nipple growing prominent. He increased the pressure with the stiff feather quill, and Bess moaned softly, her back arching upward into the feather's touch. The feather lifted, drifting lightly to her other breast, where it stroked her other nipple until it also came to attention.

"Well, this is fun, but I'm not getting any closer to actually touching her." Aimory tapped his lip with a long finger. The shimmer of aroused magick rolled from Bess's sleeping body, tingling along his phantom form. It gave him an idea.

"Hang on a minute, let's see if that old spell I got from the alchemist will do anything. Perhaps I can magick you into letting me in past your witchly protections. The old spell is supposed to make a man a ghost. Let's see what that spell does for a man who *is* a ghost. My Bess's kisses used to be enough to trigger it. You certainly look stoked enough to power it." Aimory moved as close to the head of the bed as he could.

"Now how did that incantation go?" Muttering a Latin phrase under his breath, he felt a drift of answering power move through the room in a sparkling breeze. "Whoa, oh yeah, she's got enough juice to power it," he muttered, glancing at her wet, glistening pussy. "Plenty of juice," he muttered.

"I call on you, Elizabeth Victorianna Merryweather," he intoned, using the birth name he had bargained out of her. "My sweet Bess," he added at the very end.

Aimory felt power surge in a tide appearing as a glittering fog. Concentrating on Bess's sleeping form, the spell fueled itself on the residual sexual energy. There was a brief flare of crackling blue and a slight smell of ozone.

"Hmm, that ought to do it," he whispered, rubbing his hands together. Using caution, he leaned forward. With tentative fingers, he reached out to touch the undefended silk of her sable mane. He smiled in satisfaction as the curls wrapped themselves around his fingers without a trace of her witch fire, then he leaned closer. His mouth hovered over Bess's, then he closed the distance and delicately touched his lips to hers.

His tongue stroked the softness of Bess's lips. Unconsciously she opened her mouth to his. Hesitantly, his tongue touched hers. He felt the lightest crackling of energy, then felt her power surge into his mouth. The tingling became a current, and his mouth was filled with sensations he hadn't felt in far too long a time. Her mouth opened wider, and he was sinking into the exhilaration of her taste and the sweet smell of a warm, willing woman. His arms gained weight and substance, pressing into the bed. His body gained flesh at an alarming speed, and suddenly he felt the urgency of an erection pressing tightly against the leather of his breeches. He inhaled, and his breath stole hers.

Bess jerked awake in total darkness as she felt her breath taken. She was being skillfully and thoroughly kissed. She stiffened as she felt hands shift on the bed to capture her shoulders, pinning her. Still muzzy from a thoroughly erotic dream, her body shook with passion and need. Sharply she pulled her mouth away. She couldn't see a thing in the room's complete darkness.

"Hot damn! I'm a man again!" said a far-too-familiar British voice. In a swift move, her assailant surged onto the bed.

"What the hell?" she squeaked breathlessly. Bess stared up into the darkness and found she couldn't sit up. Knees were braced on either side of her hips; long muscular thighs trapping hers. He was heavy. His somewhat cool flesh smelled vaguely of unwashed male, leather, and horse.

"Hello, my lovely," he whispered in her ear with a low chuckle. A skillful tongue swept the whirls of her ear and she couldn't help the resulting shudders.

"Get off me!" she snarled, raising an arm to throw him off. After a brief struggle he pinned her wrists above her head with one hand.

"What? Aren't you happy to see me?" he whispered in her ear. A hand slid up her waist to cup her naked breast and discovered her hard nipples. "Oh, I see that you are." He raised himself enough to slide partially to one side, pinning her legs under one of his.

"Who the hell are you?" she hissed.

"Hmm." said the familiar voice on top of her, "let's see if I'm still able to do my tricks." Several candles flared to life by themselves, bathing the room in soft golden light. Bess found herself staring up into the laughing, emerald eyes of a far too corporeal highwayman.

"Better?" he asked with a satisfied smirk.

"You!" she hissed, then blinked as she realized that she was sharing her bed with a ghost. Her eyes widened and she opened her mouth to scream.

Quickly the ghost covered her lips with his and swallowed the sound. His tongue slid in to stroke hers, and Bess's brain turned to mush. She returned the kiss without thinking; his kisses felt so familiar, so right.

"That's my Bess," he whispered against her lips. Her skin was soft and fragrant with the perfume of lavender soap and aroused female. "Never could resist my kisses."

Bess moaned as his mouth slid down her throat, nibbling and licking his way to the captured breast in his palm. Goddess, his mouth felt so damn good, she just couldn't find it in her to resist him. His wet mouth slid over her nipple. His tongue swirled and licked, then sucked it completely into his mouth. His teeth raked her sensitive flesh lightly and her breath caught. He suckled and nipped, savoring her like a starving man.

"Oh my God," Bess moaned and arched into his mouth. "What the hell are you doing? I thought I sent you back." Waves of pleasure surged from her nipples down into her damp cleft. His mouth thoroughly feasting on her full breast, she felt a surprisingly solid hand slide down her ribcage, and across her soft belly.

"I came back to finish what we started." His palm covered her shaven mound and explored her. A finger slid into her wet flesh, then tapped at her sensitive clit, making her hips buck in eagerness.

"What?" Bess couldn't think through her need. She hadn't felt this frantic and hungry for any man in ages. He slid his finger in deep and stroked her from within. He pressed and tapped a sensitive spot buried within her, and she found herself suddenly on the very edge of a powerful climax. Her thighs tried to open wide under his legs.

"Oh God, Bess. I can feel you wet and ready for me, my girl," he said with a panting breath. "I confess I can't wait; it's been too long." His hand left her saturated depths and the bed shook as he struggled to unbutton his breeches one-handed. He sighed as his painful erection slid from its entrapment. In a swift move, he released her captured wrists, then covered her with the full weight of his body. Bess's naked breasts pressed into the silk of his shirt. He drove his buckskin-covered knees between her thighs, spreading her wide.

Hard flesh pressed against Bess's softness. Mindless in her passion, Bess gripped his shoulders and arched her hips to brush her damp hungry opening against his eager hardness. She felt the blunt head of him press inward. His hips bucked, and he surged gradually into her. His moans were loud in her ear as he pumped slowly, deeper and deeper stretching her tender flesh to accommodate his girth and length. Her hips rose hungrily to meet his and he pulled away to surge hard back into her to the hilt.

"I've haven't had a fuck in so damn long, Bess . . ." He moaned. "I'd forgotten that it could be this damn good." He panted as he thrust himself into her moist depths; his pace and strength increasing as his excitement took over.

Bess felt his cock pressing and stimulating that sensitive inner spot his fingers had discovered deep within, and she was shoved with each thrust closer and closer to the edge. Her lips parted and she moaned, thinking of nothing but her urgency to reach that pinnacle. She lifted her hips, matching rhythm with his and bolts of pleasure rocked her body as she was pounded closer to climax.

"That's my girl, that's my girl," the ghost panted into Bess's ear. "Let it go, take your pleasure, fuck me darling, fuck me hard," he whispered in encouragement. His hands slid down and under to cup the firm muscles of her ass, raising her to meet his hard thrusts.

Bess's hips lifted hard against him over and over in increasing speed and power. Her hands slid from his shoulders, and her fingers dug into the hardness of his doeskin-clad buttocks to press him deeper into her. The sound of wet flesh slapping against wet flesh was loud in the room.

"Come on, come on. I'm almost there myself . . ."

Suddenly she froze. A searing bolt of pleasure howled through her in a waterfall of tremors. Her mouth opened to scream, and he again swiftly covered her lips with his own.

He hammered hard into her slick, trembling flesh, then felt the inner tightening of his balls. He was almost there, just a bit more. He thrust as deep as he could go, howling his own triumph into her mouth as he arched his back and poured himself into her. He moaned long and hard as he pumped his seed deep into her and was milked dry by her sucking inner walls. With a soft sigh, he fell atop her and they both collapsed, exhausted, onto the blankets. Aimory leaned over her and kissed her, gently but thoroughly.

"Now—sleep!" he commanded. Within moments, Bess was asleep. "Nice to know that little spell still works, too." Sighing, he carefully rose from her bed and collected his clothes.

"You were definitely worth the wait, my love," he whispered to Bess. He watched her sleep as he dressed. "Tomorrow is another day, and our adventures together have only just begun," he whispered to the sleeping witch.

"I've got a man's body again, hot damn," he whispered, jubilant. "Now that I know that the alchemist's spells still work, I can rejoin the living world and find out what happened to my dead body."

He eyed the window he had entered with grave doubts. "Guess I'll have to take the stairs," he muttered. The door unlocked with a tiny click, then swung open a few inches. With the softest of breaths, he slipped out the door. The candles winked out leaving the room doused in dim starlight that was fading quickly with the coming dawn.

VISITATION

Bess stood on the steps of the Merryweather Bed and Breakfast and waved goodbye to her cousin Alex as the car crunched out of the small gravel drive. Breakfast had been a quiet affair, and for that, Bess was truly thankful. Both Grimoires were safely hidden in the oversized handbag on her shoulder.

"Peace and quiet at last!" she announced to the empty parking lot. Sighing happily, she took a deep breath of the balmy air. The late morning sun was just beginning to get uncomfortably warm.

"Well the world has certainly changed since my day," announced a familiar voice from just behind her.

Snapping around, eyes wide in shock, Bess came face to face with the highwayman from last night. His wide grin and green eyes were only inches from her nose.

"Good morning, Bess, my sweet."

"What the hell are you doing here?" she squeaked. Bess leaped two steps off the porch in sheer surprise, then took a hard look at him. He appeared to have taken a shower somewhere and gotten a change of clothes. He was dressed in snug jeans and a short-sleeved T-shirt in forest green.

"Well, since you're here and I'm here, are you ready to help me find my missing body?" he grinned.

"I thought you were a . . ."

"A wet dream?"

"A ghost," she snapped in annoyance.

"Maybe I'm both?" he suggested with a leer.

"Maybe you're a pain in the ass?" she countered sweetly.

"Bess, I'm shocked!" Aimory said dramatically. "I had no idea you might be into that sort of thing," he purred with a lascivious grin. "There is always tonight!"

"What sort of thing? Oh! You pervert!"

"Quite possibly, but what has that got to do with last night?" The highwayman smiled as he stepped closer and lunged. His hands closed on her arms and he pulled her to him.

"You . . ." she began and was cut off as his lips captured hers.

"Yes, me. And I'm not letting you out of my sight 'till my property is recovered and interred." He wrapped strong arms around her struggling body to keep her still.

"I have no intention."

"Ah, but I have every intention of making you moan and pant."

"I'll have your ass arrested for assault."

"What?" he growled. "After a short while, I'll fade back into being a ghost and slide right through any jail I'm locked in. You can't stop me, and I'll come back to have you."

"I can stop you."

"You can't." His lips caressed her throat and Bess's breath caught as wanton shivers blazed down her body, hardening her nipples and dampening her panties. "Besides, you don't really want to."

"Why are you doing this to me?" she whimpered softly. She was powerless to control her lust.

"I need you to stay flesh, witch." He pulled her around the corner of the inn and behind some trees. With tender brute force, he backed her up against the wall of the building. "I can smell how much your body wants mine," he whispered.

Bess roused herself and shoved at the ghost's immobile shoulder. "I don't believe you," she growled.

"What can't you believe?" he asked as he nuzzled her throat. "That you were thoroughly fucked last night by a ghost, or that you enjoyed being thoroughly fucked by a ghost?" He was smiling. "Or that your body is looking forward to being fucked again by a ghost?"

"Oh!" she struggled unsuccessfully against the weight of his body pressing against hers.

"You were definitely worth the wait, Bess my girl." He pressed his hips against hers, letting her feel his hard length. "See how much I need you, feel how much I want you?"

"Wait? What wait? Get off me!" she tried rolling out from under him. He stopped her with a grip on her shoulder.

"Where do you think you're going?" He smiled. "We have a lot of catching up to do." he chuckled as one hand raised the hem of her dress, then skimmed up her thigh to tug at her panties.

"How the hell did you . . . Were we able to . . ." Bess sputtered. "Dammit, you're a ghost!" She pulled her skirt back down to cover herself.

"My name is Aimory. How were we able to fuck?" Pinning her with one hand he tugged on the buckle of his jeans. "Bess, you're a witch, remember?"

"What has my being a witch got to do with anything?" Bess protested as she tried to wriggle out of his grip.

He sighed as he freed his trapped hardness, shoving his jeans down, then went back to pulling her dress up and her panties off.

Bess opened her mouth to scream and his mouth captured hers in a fierce kiss, stealing her breath. Her scream became a moan. Without thought, she kissed him back, leaning into him. His body pressed her into the stout wall as he stroked her tongue with his. Bess felt as though she were melting. She found herself trembling for his touch as his mouth devoured hers.

His hands slid under her dress, then laid claim to her lace-bound breasts as he sucked at her mouth as though starved. Gently, he tugged her lace bra up and started pulling on her eager nipples. She gasped softly as her back arched into him. As though in a dream, she wrapped her arms around his shoulders and pulled him into her.

His hands slid down the wood of the wall to cup her buttocks. She could feel his erection hard against her stomach. With a groan he lifted her against the wall, then positioned himself. Holding her firmly, he let her slide down just enough to impale her on his cock. She grunted into his mouth as he possessed her, and he flexed his hips lodging himself firmly within. She rocked against him and he panted as he began thrusting in earnest. Her legs wrapped about his hips and she let out little whimpers as he took her against the wall of the Bed and Breakfast in full daylight.

"Mother of God, Bess, I can't get enough of you." he moaned in her ear, mindless in his lust. Their sweat mingled and dripped as he rocked her against the wood, sliding in and out of her wet passage. Damp from her excitement dribbled down his balls. The sound of wet suction and their soft moans wreathed about them as they mindlessly coupled, heedless of anyone passing by.

He moved his head and captured one of her nipples in his mouth. Sucking hard, he felt her flesh trembling around his aching cock, shudderingly close to climax.

Bess sobbed as her body screamed in raw animal need and rocked against him. She grasped him hard around the shoulders lifting and driving her body against his, rising and falling in complete abandon.

"That's my girl," he muttered to her. "Ride me love, ride me hard," Aimory whispered harshly as his own imminent climax made itself known. "Oh God, Bess, oh fuck . . . Oh, fuck me, my lovely . . ." Aimory slammed her against the wall hard as he buried himself again and again as deep as he could go. His balls tightened and he quivered on the edge of orgasm.

Bess took a deep breath as she felt the fiery rise of building crisis. She lifted and fell wildly on his heavy cock, digging her nails into his shoulders as pleasure snaked up with ferocity and blazed a path of glory through her.

Her mouth opened to scream and Aimory covered her lips with his, swallowing her cry of release as his own pleasure shuddered through him. She writhed hard on his iron-hard shaft and he felt his balls release to erupt into her warm and quivering depths.

"Bess, you are one hell of a fuck," he said letting her slide down his body to stand back on the grass. He took her mouth in a possessive kiss. He broke the kiss and Bess's eyes opened to see his cheeky grin. "As I was saying before, witches can give flesh to ghosts temporarily. All it takes is willing contact. All I had to do was convince you that you wanted to be touched by me," he said, completely omitting the incantation he had used.

"In your case, it was easy," panted Aimory from where he leaned against her shoulder in repletion and struggled to pull his pants back up. "You're a very passionate, lusty woman, my girl, easily swayed by seduction."

"Oh! I'll show you contact!" growled Bess. Furious, she swung a fist at him.

"Now, that wasn't nice!" laughed the ghost, ducking out of the way. He caught her wrist. "Now that we've gotten that over with, are you ready to go look at where I used to be interred and see what your powers can find?"

"You are an asshole, Aimory."

"We'll get to that later," he responded as he helped her get her dress together.

"Where are my panties?"

"I have them safe and sound right here," he said waving the scrap of cotton and lace. He shoved them in his pocket.

"Hey!"

"Don't worry your pretty little head about these, you'll not be needing them any time soon."

NIGHT WAITRESS

A Victim and His Unwilling Succubus

For Jazmin & Blue

It was four hours until dawn. The tiny diner I work in sits cheek-to-jowl with some old brick high-rises in the heart of the oldest part of the city. This used to be considered a decent part of town.

The diner was full to the brim with drunks that had spent last four hours drowning in over-loud dance music. The smell of ripe, sweaty bodies and sour beer-breath floated just above every Formica table. The noise level was appallingly loud as the club flunkies yelled back and forth across the tables to their equally deaf companions and shouted their late-night breakfast orders to the waitstaff.

With a damp rag in one hand and a coffeepot in the other, I swiped tables and refilled cups as I went. My black sneakers made tiny squeaks that I felt more than heard as I hurried across the linoleum tile. Light gleamed on the silver frames of my pink-tinted glasses, reflected in the plate glass mirrors that lined the walls. My long red hair, pulled back in a severe ponytail, poured straight down my back like blood.

"Hey, baby, what's a pretty girl like you doing here waiting tables?"

I stopped abruptly, sloshing coffee in the pot. Calling me pretty was like saying Fred Astaire could dance a little. It was not my fault—I had been made that way. Unfortunately for

59

me, I had been designed beautiful in the Victorian ideal, a delicate face, long harlot-red hair, full breasts, rounded thighs, a tiny waist, a pronounced ass and I was short. Very short, as in less than five feet tall.

Turning slowly, I looked at the long slim fingers that gripped my black polyester uniform. My eyes traced the fingers up a muscular arm onto a body that looked as though it had been pumped lean and hard by years of athletic machines. I stopped at crystalline-blue eyes framed in black lashes. His face was lean and well-made with a full, kissable mouth. His soot-black hair was pulled into a neat tail held by a silver clip that curled to his shoulders. He was dressed in a snug, short-sleeved silky pullover that showed off every bulge and curve of his sculpted torso. He had one knee out of the booth, so I could see the black dress-slacks he wore and how they showed his tiny waist to perfection. *Yummy.* My infernal appetite for handsome young men kicked in, making me salivate and moistening my panties.

"Hi." he said, leaning over to read my nametag. "Hi, Lili, I'm Bruce." He continued smiling, turning up the electric charm, all one hundred watts worth of perfect teeth. "You busy later on tonight?"

To use the modern vernacular, he was a hottie and I could tell by the smug way he was looking at me that he knew it. Guys that hunky always seemed to feel that they were entitled to harass any vaguely attractive girl in range. There was no way this cute idiot was going to let me go without attempting to charm me into having sex with him. How did I know? His hand was inching the hem of my skirt up my thighs, exposing the top of my nude stockings and the pins that held them to my garter belt. Terrific, just what I needed.

"I need to go back to work, sir." With a mostly clean hand I pushed my red bangs out of my eyes. Tipping my head forward, I glared into his eyes over the rim of my pink-tinted glasses. Apparently, Bruce was too drunk to notice the flame-red glints that my eyes tended to reflect under fluorescent lighting. That's what the tinted glasses were for, to hide that uncanny flicker of hellfire in their depths. I accidentally scare people all the time.

I felt like groaning in annoyance even as I assessed what I thought he'd be like in bed. I really was not in the mood to fend off another silly foolish man with a death wish he didn't know he had. He was probably convinced that I had been made with him in mind. Technically, my first master had hoped to create the perfect sex toy, and technically, he had succeeded. Unfortunately, and to his everlasting and rather fatal dismay, he gave me a hellish sexual appetite.

Bruce began pulling in earnest, probably attempting to get me to sit down next to him. I braced my feet and watched the muscles bunch in his arm. "Do you mind?" A deep growl rumbled low in my chest. He kept pulling and smiling. I guess he hadn't heard my warning growl. I don't think he realized that he was using as much strength as he was. I felt a few stitches pop in my dress. If we kept this little tug of war up much longer, my cheap uniform was going to rip.

Hmmm. I had two choices here. I could spill coffee on my assailant's head or put the pot down and backhand the idiot. Sighing, I did neither. He was just too cute to slap.

"What's the matter, sweetheart? I just want to talk to you."

I rolled my eyes as I put the coffeepot down. Smiling nastily, I took hold of his wrist. Applying a little pressure in just the right spot, his hand numbed and I was able to free my skirt from his white-knuckled grip. *I swear, doesn't this idiot have any survival instincts whatsoever?*

"Hey!" he yelped. "What the hell was that? Some kind of martial arts or something?"

"Nope." I smiled wider, flashing the white tips of my over-long canines. "Merely superior physical force, Bruce," I stated blandly. I skipped out of range of his hands and fled to the far side of the diner.

He stood up at his table and yelled. "Hey! I was talking to you!"

I blew him a kiss, then gave him a little wave from the far end of the diner. Sheesh, this guy really wanted to get himself in trouble.

Sam, a night cop and my occasional dinner date, was attempting to eat his ham and eggs in peace. After a few more shouts, Sam finally had to get up from his breakfast to explain to the cute idiot that he was disturbing the other diners.

Bruce settled down into sullen silence, ate his ultra-rare steak and scrambled eggs, then drank cup after cup of coffee. He stared at me the whole time while I pointedly ignored him. I suppose that as Bruce saw it, he was not done with me.

It was a full hour before dawn. My shift at the diner ended without any incidents other than the drunken cutie-pie hitting hard on me. Pulling my black sweater on over my cheap polyester uniform, I snuck out the back door.

Silent in my sneakers, I walked toward the passenger side of my battered car where it waited in a patch of oily darkness. My keys rattled as I pulled them out from my sweater pocket, then I caught the aroma of expensive cologne and male lust. I recognized the scent; it was the drunk that had hit on me earlier. I couldn't see him, but I could smell him. Apparently he was not ready to give up any time soon.

"Hi, Bruce," I said as I walked around to the driver side of the car. He was crouched low and leaning against the driver-side door. His legs were braced with his muscular arms loose and folded over his bent knees.

I pocketed my pink-tinted glasses. The night leaped into a gray twilight as my eyes adjusted. I swept a loose tendril of my blood-red hair behind my ear, peering at him through my red bangs.

"Hey, Lili. Let's go for a ride." He wasn't smiling.

I shook my head. "Nope, I have better things to do, Bruce." Like not killing someone because they were too stupid to realize the danger they were in.

"It wasn't a request, Lili." His voice was soft with a warning note in it.

It seemed that Bruce was not nearly as drunk as he had been earlier. "You gonna make me, Bruce?"

"Your pet cop isn't here to save you." He stood up in a single fluid motion, rather like a big jungle cat as opposed to the clumsy way most weight-lifters moved.

Perhaps all those bulging muscles had not been made in a gym. He towered over me, head and shoulders. Then again, at my height—or lack of it—everyone towered over me. You get used to it after a while. My guess was that he was somewhere well over six feet tall.

"I don't need anyone to save me, Bruce, I've been saving myself for a long time now." Bruce responded to my little comment with a smile so cold that it should have brought on an early frost. He took a step toward me.

"I'd rather not do this the hard way, Lili. I don't want to hurt you."

It was briefly there in his face. He really didn't want to hurt me. As if he could. I was made of sterner stuff, literally. I think I still have the recipe from my Master's old house somewhere, too.

"What exactly do you want, Bruce?" My smile never wavered as I raised a brow.

A look of hunger came over his face, then he buried it. "All I want is your undivided attention for an hour or so, then you go home. Story over."

His hands closed on my shoulders, and his fingers dug into me slightly, using a fair amount of strength that would have normally caused bruising. "Do you normally pick up dates by threatening them with physical violence?"

"Not normally."

That was there in his face, too. Not normally, but he did threaten girls into sex on occasion. Perhaps he deserved his fate after all. Besides, I was getting hungry, and I hadn't eaten well in a long time.

"Bruce," I said calmly. "Would it do any good if I told you that this is a bad idea?" He was not a nice guy; I wondered why I was still trying to warn him off.

"Afraid not," he said.

He was definitely sober, but still stupid. I shrugged. His hands relaxed on my shoulders. He smiled almost in relief, and held out his hand, motioning for me to give him my purse and my car keys. I handed him my keys.

He unlocked my car, put the keys in my purse, then signaled that he wanted my sweater.

"What do you want the sweater for?" I shrugged out of my sweater and handed it to him.

"Just wanted to be sure you weren't concealing anything under it."

I frowned. "Like what, a gun?" His brows dropped and his eyes went very cold. From the look on his face, apparently I'd made a good guess.

He placed my purse and sweater on the front seat and closed the door, locking my keys in the car. No big deal really, it wouldn't be the first time I had to break into my car.

I wasn't at all surprised when Bruce led me to an expensive sports car, all long black sleek lines. He was a complete gentleman opening the door for me. Once he closed it, I jiggled the handle. It didn't budge, and the lock was missing completely from the door. I wouldn't be able to open it from the inside without breaking a window.

"So what do you do for a living, Bruce?" I asked as we left

the parking lot.

"Security," he said without looking at me.

"I see. A hitman?" I didn't really expect an answer and he didn't give me one. "You must be good if you can afford a car like this one." He glanced over at me, dark and cold with the dead eyes of someone that had no problems killing. "I see," I repeated.

"Why aren't you a stripper or something?" he asked me. "You're pretty enough."

"Been there, done that," I quipped. I assumed that the *something* he was referring to was *why wasn't I some guy's expensive mistress.* Every guy I met seemed to think that since I was pretty, I should be a stripper or someone's mistress. "I don't like being someone else's property, Bruce, and as for stripping, the guys had a problem taking no for an answer. I'm sure you understand," I said with a mean little smile. He flinched. *Point for me.*

The drive was short and uneventful, ending at a very expensive hotel. He parked inside the hotel, hustling me into the parking garage elevator. No one saw us. *Good.*

The elevator opened directly into his living room with a balcony overlooking the tasteful part of the city. He had a suite all done in soft gray and mauve, all very tasteful and very expensive. With a gentle shove, I was pushed into the living room. To my right, I could see an open door to the bathroom and two more open doors revealed separate bedrooms. I turned and saw him code the elevator lock behind me. With a smug smile, he walked over to the balcony and pulled the drapes closed.

I strode over to a brocaded sofa, then kicked off my cheap sneakers, digging my stocking toes into the thick carpet. I turned around to watch Bruce strip out of his clingy shirt. His body was lightly tanned, rippling with intricate muscles. He radiated vitality and perfect health, inundating the entire suite with his delicious potency. My mouth watered. I knew my eyes were glowing slightly as my hunger began to surface fully. I caught the scent of my own special perfume beginning to drift from my skin.

"Bruce, are you sure you want to do this?" I tried again to warn him. "I'm not exactly —"

"Shut up and come over here." His face was closed, his eyes intent.

Stupid man. What he wanted from me was going to cost him big.

"As you wish," I murmured. I walked over to him, reaching for the buttons that went from my throat to my hem. I had a little less than an hour before dawn.

"Don't," he said hoarsely, "I want to do that." His hands closed over mine gently. He pulled my hands away from my buttons. His fingers were nimble as he started undoing the neck of my uniform to my waist, exposing my black lace bra and my snowy skin. I admit it, I like pretty underwear. He knelt on the soft carpet, then slid his hand into the front of my parted uniform to caress my softly padded ribs. He was very tall. Kneeling, his eyes were almost on level with mine.

"Your skin is so soft," he whispered.

I sighed softly. "The better to tempt you with, my dear." I don't think he even heard me.

He looked into my face, and I licked my red lips. Surrounded by the scent of aroused male, I took a slow deep breath and drank it in like fine wine. He gripped the edges of my uniform, suddenly ripping it open. Buttons popped and scattered all over the carpet. My black lace garter belt and matching panties made my skin look very stark.

His fingers dug into my firm ass, then he buried his face in my rounded tummy, rubbing against me as a cat would. I could feel the slight bristle of stubble against my hypersensitive skin. He opened his mouth and his tongue stroked across my belly in wet swipes, tasting me.

I pulled out the clip holding his smoky hair, freeing the silky length to sweep just past his shoulders, then tossed the clip onto the carpet. I slid my fingers into his mane. His hair was soft and very fine. My red nails scraped his scalp lightly in a caress; he moaned into my stomach in reaction. His head lifted, then he reached up to pull the elastic from my ponytail. My ass-length red tresses slid around us in a cloak of dark blood.

"Is this real?" he asked me as he ran his fingers through my harlot-red locks.

"It's not dyed, if that's what you're asking."

He responded by suddenly pulling my panties down to my knees. My mound was exposed to his view beneath the lace of my garter belt, showing neatly trimmed curls as red as my hair.

"See, the carpet matches the drapes," I smiled.

"Off, off," he growled, tugging my panties the rest of the way down.

I obligingly stepped out of them. His hands reached around me to unhook my bra. My breasts only sagged slightly as they were released. Not bad for a lady that was supposed to be in her thirties.

There was a hiss of in-drawn breath as Bruce got a good look at my cherry-red nipples. He flung the bra away, then cupped my full breasts in both hands. His fingers pulled slightly on my nipples, and they hardened from the attention. His arm snaked around my waist. Cupping my breast, Bruce yanked me forward onto his mouth and sucked, nursing hard on my nipples.

My body jolted in reaction as my hellish sexual appetite flared to brutal and demanding life. Suddenly it was too late, far too late to stop. The hunger rose within me in a firestorm of voracious longing. I could feel my eyes dilate, flaring to brilliant and telltale flames as I was overwhelmed by an appetite too long denied to even think about the consequences.

Panting in the throes of carnal greed, I found myself pressing Bruce's head to my breast. My stocking-clad thighs parted; I pushed my hips against him with a hungry moan, aching and throbbing in my need. I could smell my body's infernal perfume, a touch of brimstone and female in heat scenting the air.

He panted. "God, you smell so good."

"The better to seduce you with, my dear." My voice was a deep rumbling growl of pleasure. My hands slid all across his shoulders. I couldn't stop myself from reaching out to touch as much of his skin as I could, my nails digging in and scoring his naked back with livid red welts.

His mouth sucked strongly on me, then his mouth released my breast with the sound of wet suction. Sliding his hand up to cup my head, I felt an arm curve about my knees. I was suddenly flat on my back in the middle of the floor, Bruce's full length stretched over mine, his thighs trapping mine between them. I could feel a powerful erection pressing against my stomach. I averted my face, slitting my eyes to keep Bruce from seeing the flames leaping in their depths. He nipped my throat. In reaction, I dug my sharp, curved nails into his vulnerable back.

"Hellcat," he hissed in pain, then chuckled.

Surprising me, he captured both of my wrists and held them above my head with one hand. His free hand closed on the lace of my garter belt, and he yanked. The belt slid down my hips, then over my ass, pulling my stockings down. With a feline twist of his hips, he moved a thigh off me. In one strong pull, my garter belt and the attached stockings were peeled from me and flung across the room. With a satisfied sigh, he covered my bared body with his. His hips arched and he slid his trapped heat against my hungry flesh.

Dipping his head, Bruce kissed each nipple with great tenderness. I arched my back in welcome, pushing my breasts more firmly against his mouth. His lips slithered into the valley between my breasts, rising up he nibbled down my stomach. His tongue dipped into my navel. I sighed, pleased with Bruce's attention to details. My original master had been very proud of my navel; he'd worked very hard to get it just right. However, other parts of me were growing impatient.

"Your mouth, Bruce, I need your mouth on me," I said in a voice husky and deep with passion, then writhed my hips in temptation.

Bruce chuckled again as he continued to taste my skin with his tongue. I heard a metallic chink. I looked down watching as Bruce pulled some handcuffs from his back pocket. *Shit!* My heart thumped hard in my chest. *I did not need any more complications.*

"First things first, Lili," he said glancing up and smiling widely. I growled, then dug my heels into the carpet. Shoving, I bucked him off my stomach, breaking his hold on my wrists. I rolled out from under him, jumping to my feet. He snagged my ankle, and I hit the floor hands first. He chuckled, and it sounded nasty.

"Oh, no, you don't, the fun is just starting." He pulled me by the ankle, and I slid across the carpet on my hands and knees. The son of a bitch was stronger and faster than I had anticipated. I turned my head and hissed at him, barely stopping myself from baring my fangs.

I was expertly flipped over, then his full weight crashed down on top of me, his chest slamming down across my breasts. It should have knocked the wind from me; it pissed me off instead. I worked to buck him off again, but he was prepared for that move. I lunged to bite him, but he lurched out of the way. Breathing hard, he caught one hand above my head. I heard the rattle of the cuff closing over one wrist.

"Bastard!" I swore, swinging my free fist at his head.

"Bitch!" he snapped back, ducking my fist.

He grabbed my other wrist. The cuffs rattled again. "What the fuck are you doing, Bruce?" I asked with a snarl. I was fairly sure I could break the chain of the cuffs to free myself but wearing them still pissed me off. He grinned at me, the low-life shit.

"Ensuring my personal safety." He rolled to his feet, hauling me up by the wrists. "You're a lot stronger than you look." He panted briefly.

"The better to hold you with, my dear." I sneered as I said it. I could smell his arousal. The stupid bastard was getting turned on by my resistance.

"Are you a Goth chick?" he asked out of the blue. "I like the fangs," he continued. "But they look sharp and like permanent implants."

What the hell was a Goth chick? Oh, yeah, he thought I was part of the latest fashion craze with people running around pretending to be vampires. Some of them even had permanent fangs put in. Suddenly he made a lot of sense. No wonder he was so obsessed with having me in particular. Most guys take the hint that there's something a little weird with me and go away. None of my hints had worked on Bruce; in fact, all my hints seemed to have caught his interest more. Wonderful. I had actually run across a true weirdo. It seems Bruce had a vampire fetish.

Well, Bruce didn't know it yet, but he was about to get his wish. He was probably thinking the most amount of danger he had to worry about was getting bitten, and possibly losing a little blood. I was a succubus, an honest-to-Satan Victorian sex vampire, and now I was seriously pissed, and really turned on. Stupid, stupid man.

"There is no need for the handcuffs. I said I would fuck you." I snapped out a kick that he deftly avoided.

"Actually, no, you didn't." Ducking he caught me about

the waist, lifting me over his shoulder. I kicked out but he held my legs in an iron grip. "I just want to be sure I get what I want."

He rolled his shoulders to settle my weight and slapped my naked ass. I yelped, more in surprise than anything.

Cursing in three languages, I was carried into a bedroom, then thrown on the bed. His heavy body slammed on top of mine, making the bed squeak in protest and the air woof out of my lungs.

"Now how is it, that you speak French and a dialect of Arabic?" There was a strange glitter in his eyes as he pulled the leather belt from his pants.

"And just how did you recognize the languages I spoke, dear Bruce?" I countered. Deftly avoiding my attempts to kick him, Bruce wrapped the narrow belt around the chain of the cuffs, then buckled it to the headboard.

"That would be telling, Lilli." He leaned over me and licked his lips. "However, I should say that such things should never fall from a lady's lips."

Anger and desire were boiling in my blood, making my heart pound. "But, Bruce, dear, I never said that I was a lady." I lunged up at him, snapping my sharp teeth, and he leapt back.

He smiled and nodded. "But, sweet Lilli, I am counting on just that."

I was suddenly smiling too, but in avaricious anticipation. *The stupid fuck.* The skilled alchemist that had created me in the early nineteenth century had also underestimated my appetites and gotten me over-excited. As a succubus, I not only bleed my victims; I literally suck the vitality from them when they cum. Normally, I can control my desires and moderate my feeding, but accidents will happen. I planned to make this idiot figure it out on his own. Preferably, while writhing beneath my fangs.

"Now, where was I?" Bruce sighed. "Oh, yes . . ." With deliberation, Bruce unfastened his pants and writhing his hips and flexing his stomach muscles in wanton display, he slid out of them. His erection was heavy and thick, standing straight out from his thatch of dark curls. A nice full sack completed his package. His lean and well-defined legs were lightly furred with dark hair.

"For a prick, you are definitely yummy, Bruce," I said deepening my voice in its sexiest manner. My pussy was already slathering my thighs with appetite. His little show dried my mouth, so I licked my lips. "Why don't you come over here and do nasty things to me?" My teeth ached to bite down on his throat. My hips writhing, I undulated among the pillows. I spread my knees so he would have a good view of my unnaturally scarlet pussy. At the rate he was turning me on, I wouldn't have to bleed Bruce to kill him; all he had to do was cum.

"The best is yet to come, baby," he crooned back to me. Moving slowly like a big cat, he crept onto the bed. His hands caressed my feet, then traveled up my legs, spreading me wide. Bruce lifted my knees to work his shoulders under them. With a look of hungry triumph, he nestled himself between my thighs.

My infernal perfume released in his face. Bruce took a deep breath and I watched his eyes dilate with desire. His mouth brushed the softest part of my inner thigh. My body shivered in anticipation. He swept his tongue higher and higher until he was barely brushing my curls with his mouth. He took another deep breath of my scent, then I felt him brush the outer lips of my labia. He exhaled warmly, making me shiver, and he stroked my damp red flesh with the full length of his tongue.

I let out a breath I didn't know I was holding. It released in a loud moan. He moaned in return, then proceeded to drive me mad. The tip of his tongue brushed against my clit, swiping at the folds of my inner lips. Noisily, he sucked at my juices. His lips slithered across me tasting every fold, every crevice. He lapped at every pearly drop I released. The wet sounds of his mouth filled the room.

His hands held my thighs in a vice-grip as he tormented me deliciously. I writhed under him with gasping moans. Then, he focused his attack on my swollen clit. His tongue flicked, rubbing against my point of pleasure, his lips sucking delicately at first then with complete attention and devotion. He was trying very hard to make me cum. He was doing a damn fine job of it, too. Then his tongue buried itself in my starving pussy to an impossible depth.

My body arched in voluptuous abandon. I pulled at the handcuffs strapped to the headboard, my hips pumping themselves onto Bruce's mouth. Moaning, as I drowned in the building pleasure, I locked my thighs around his head and dug my heels into the mattress in an attempt to get a purchase for thrusting power. I could feel the fire-fall of pleasure beginning to wash over me in small waves, each growing in length and power. I could feel myself building to a powerful climax.

I looked down on Bruce with my eyes slitted to conceal their red fire. He looked back up at me. His eyes were slitted as mine were and glowing an inhuman heart-of-flame blue. My heart jolted.

"Bruce? Is there something you haven't told me?" I asked between pants. His tongue never stopped but he nodded, grinning slyly. "Bruce?"

He pulled his head up, licking his mouth with a long thin tongue no human ever possessed. *What the hell?*

He opened his blazing eyes fully, and I felt a definite pull. He was trying to roll my mind under with his eyes, the shit. He smiled widely; I noticed that he possessed an impressive set of canines to rival mine.

Fuck! He was a vampire! Well, shit, two could play at this game.

"Well, there's something I've been trying to tell you myself, Bruce . . ." I opened my eyes fully to let the red flames of my hellfire within blaze to full life. Using every drop of mental skill, I pulled at his mind. I was rewarded by a frown creasing his brow. Briefly his face went blank, his body freezing as I caught him, trapping his thoughts.

His fingers closed on me with sudden crushing force. Darting in like a snake, I felt his mouth, then his tongue on the softest part in the juncture of my thigh. I writhed suddenly but his tongue found the thick artery in my inner thigh, and he bit down. The pain was fierce. I rocked hard into a vicious screaming orgasm. My blood pumped into his mouth even as I wet the sheets with pearly drops of my pleasure.

Thank the unholy, he wasn't an incubus, a male version of what I was, or he would have sucked my vitality dry as I climaxed. Too bad for him.

I jerked on the cuffs, snapping the belt easily. Gripping his hair with both hands, I wrenched his fangs from my flesh. He howled in frustration, red spattering the sheets as though from a despoiled virgin. Still in the throes of lust, I locked my hands in his hair covering his blood-stained mouth with my own, kissing him fully.

He nipped at me, but I'd had centuries to perfect the art of kissing with and around incisors. The taste of my own blood on his lips and tongue fired my ardor. I growled a challenge deep in my chest. His arms locked around me and we embraced fiercely, kissing as though we were trying to devour each other. Which in a way, I guess we were.

I gained some purchase with my feet, then rolled him under me, my full breasts pressing against his rock-hard chest, my thighs straddling him.

He smiled. "Jeez, Lili, you're very strong."

I gave him a smile of my own. "The better to fuck you with, my dear."

"Good, because as soon as I finish fucking you, I intend to take that pretty throat of yours. I can't wait to see what you taste like."

Apparently he had no idea what I was up to. I rose up just enough to position myself over his rampant cock. "I don't know if you noticed, Bruce, but I'm fucking you." I thrust myself down hard onto him.

His mouth opened in a howl as I took him hard and deep. I rocked forward, then slammed back onto him with all the power I possessed. I was determined to pump the bastard dry.

He gripped my hips, rising to meet my downward thrusts. "God yes! Fuck me, bitch!"

I rode him with an enthusiasm I'd never dared to use before, and his moans told me that he was enjoying every second. "You're turn to cum for me, Bruce," I hissed, baring my teeth for good measure.

"Anything to please you, babe," he growled in return. His hips rose to meet me with killing force. "I love the taste of you, Lili, especially when you cum."

"You say the sweetest things, Bruce," I said panting. I raised my hands, pulling at the cuffs, and broke the chain with only a small show of force. Links sprayed across the sheets.

I dug my fingers into his shoulders, and he grabbed my long hair with one hand, holding my head from his vulnerable throat. His other hand closed on my hip, guiding my rhythm. I could feel his heart hammering in his chest. I increased my pace, lengthening my strokes. He writhed beneath me, his powerful thighs bunching as he lunged, bucking into me. I was very excited, and I was soaking him to the balls. His free hand slid up my body to cup, then grip my breast with bruising strength.

"Babe, you have great tits," he chuckled low in his throat,

and moaned.

"And you have a fantastic cock, Bruce," I replied.

I felt his climax begin to mount at a murderous pitch, the power of his building orgasm soaking into my skin. I moaned with the exquisite strength seeping into me. No human I had ever tasted possessed such delicious power. This vampire boy had to be old, really old to have so much vitality.

Lust gripped me as my own inhuman passion came roaring to the fore. At this rate I was probably going to kill him if he didn't pass out first. I could feel my eyes igniting to an inferno as I bathed in his energy. I was growing drunk with passion and impending release. I cried out as I felt him teeter on the edge of his climax.

"Oh fuck! Oh fuck, yeah!" he started wailing. Suddenly, he gripped my waist, then rolled me under his body to slam his pistoning shaft into me at full force, his cock impossibly large and rigid. I was shuddering with his impending climax. If he had been mortal, Bruce would have been dead by now.

Bruce threw his head up and lunged down, teeth bared. I gripped his neck with both hands to keep his fangs from my throat even as I rose to meet his thrusts. Crying out, he plunged his hardness deeply into my red flesh, then held himself burrowed as far into me as he could get. Suddenly, he came, howling as his balls released, spraying their load of cum into my waiting flesh.

I screamed, shuddering as I was dragged into an abyss of shrieking pleasure, drowning in Bruce's vitality as he poured himself into my body.

"Oh God, bitch, you are one hell of a fuck," he growled hoarsely, then collapsed.

"The better to eat you with, my dear," I whispered. I could see his vitality as an electric-blue mist wreathing around us both. It dissipated into my skin as I sucked the juice of his life into my hungry body.

"What," he moaned, shaking as he felt his life rushing out of him. "What are you doing?"

"Having breakfast," I quipped, while writhing in ecstasy. His life force scorched through my vitals in a joyous blaze. I could feel the essence that was Bruce touching me viscerally in ways more intimate than sex.

A rush from a second orgasm screamed through me and I cried out, shuddering and trembling beneath him. He moved feebly but couldn't summon the energy to even roll off of me. With a sigh, his eyes fluttered closed and he lay very still.

I shoved his inert form off me onto the side of the bed where he laid face up, eyes closed. I curled around his exhausted form almost tenderly.

"By the way, Bruce," I giggled, high from riding my second climax in a row, "my name is Lilith." I panted a moment. "As in the mother of demons." I laughed long and hard.

I took my time as I gently slid my needle-sharp fangs into his defenseless throat. He wasn't quite unconscious and flinched, then sighed in soft ecstasy as I took his blood. I only needed a sip or two; my actual needs had already been met. I was more than sated. Bruce was still alive, but just barely as I rose invigorated from his rumpled bed. Gazing at his collapsed body, I realized that I'd aged him considerably. He now appeared to be a sixty-year-old man instead of his seemingly twenty-four.

Well, damn, I guess I'm not the only true vampire after all. If they're all as tasty as this one, I'll never have to sip from mortals again, not when I can feast on immortals. Suddenly the future was looking much brighter.

I stepped out of the bedroom into the main sitting room. Passing in front of a wall mirror, I stopped in shock. My body had been transformed. I was no longer a mature thirty-something I was a sweet sixteen, possibly less. Bruce had to be old, really old, in order to have made me this young. I had never lost this many years without causing a death.

Piss. Now I'll have to quit my job.

I gathered up my clothes, shoving them into a pillowcase as I considered how I was going to explain my youthful self to my landlord.

Moving the curtains to the balcony, I saw that dawn was about twenty minutes away. I opened the sliding glass doors, smelling the city and the beginnings of morning rising from the pavement.

Stepping out onto the hotel balcony in all my naked glory, I gathered the stolen power that filled me. My scarlet locks lifted from my shoulders as the power coalesced and caressed me. I stretched out my arms and drew on the power to re-shape myself for flight.

My wings spread wide, the thin membranes stretched taut and sheer over the long elegant bones. I'm always amazed when I see them form from my body. Another advantage exclusive to the succubae vampires.

With a lunge, I leapt up and perched atop the railing of the balcony, clutching my pillowcase of clothes. The city night below me was quiet in those softest moments before dawn. The concrete valleys and cliffs of the city's tall buildings beckoned.

I vaulted from the railing into the soft gray of predawn, gliding on the updrafts, headed homeward across the sleeping city, laughing.

WOLF MOON: PART ONE

Ful Moon Rising

The werewolf drifted through the crowd of writhing dancers at the club, *Gothic Noire*, and scowled. Although the moon had yet to rise over the horizon, he could already feel its power calling to his soul right through the brick walls of the club. *I'll have to find someone to fuck soon, or I'll spend the next month locked in my wolf shape.*

In the smoked mirrors that lined the club's walls, his eyes glowed a brilliant predator green, reflecting in the club's low lighting. He turned his head, changing the angle of reflection. The glow winked out. Apparently, his eyes had started the shift from ordinary human hazel green to wolf gold.

He leaned against the wall in a dark corner to sift through the scents, searching for appropriate prey. With so many warm, sweating bodies rubbing against each other in multiple parodies of sex the aromas merely aggravated his hunger. He rose from his slouch, stretching to his full height and moved away from the wall.

He curled his lip in annoyance. Trying to find someone with enough passion to keep up with his appetites every full moon was a real pain in the ass. Unfortunately, nothing less than a woman's climax would give him enough power to keep control over his changes. Not having a woman of his own was his own damn fault, but he just couldn't see himself actually trying for a long-term relationship.

"Oh, hey, you're cute. And by the way, I'm a werewolf; is

that okay with you?" He scowled ferociously. *Oh, yeah, that'd go over real well. Then I'll have another freak chasing me cross-country with a shotgun full of silver.* Not that silver could do him any real harm. He smiled, revealing the gleam of sharp incisors. Not one werewolf slasher movie had gotten it right yet. Not that he was about to complain.

The clean, fresh aroma of blood drifted through the cigarette smoke and alcohol fumes.

He sniffed deeply to be sure, catching baby powder, soap and warm, frustrated woman. His cock rose to full erection, pressing uncomfortably against his snug leather pants and a smile curved his lips. *Perfect . . .* He followed the enticing fragrance to a tiny female leaning against the wall, completely alone.

He drifted past her, noting the waterfall of silvery-blonde curls that flowed past her shoulders to swing at her hips. Electric-blue eyes peeked out from under overlong bangs. Her full breasts were barely contained by the pearl buttons of her tight white blouse. The black lights made the lace of her bra glow fluorescent white through the sheer material that was tucked into a very short leather skirt.

She shifted her stance slightly, revealing a tiny glimpse of white panties glowing under the black lights.

He whistled under his breath. *That is one hot little package.* His rigid flesh pressing insistently against his stomach agreed wholeheartedly. He breathed in deep, studying the context of her delicate scent and was pleased to discover the complete lack of another male's scent. *So, she's not here with another guy, nor has she been touched by one recently.* A cunning smile curled his lips. *Good.* He walked past her through the door to the enclosed porch outside. *Now, how to corner her and get her out into the parking lot for a fast fuck?*

Heather leaned against the wall of the crowded Goth club and absently swept her long, silvery-blonde hair behind her shoulder. The harsh Gothic-Industrial music throbbed loudly, pressing against her flesh like hands, closing in on her.

In an attempt to look calm, cool, and collected, she took a sip of her Long Island Iced Tea and froze. Someone was staring at her. She could almost feel their gaze brushing like ghostly fingers across her body, lingering on her breasts and her far-too-exposed thighs.

Nervously, she dropped a hand to the hem of her leather miniskirt, tugging on it in a futile attempt to cover herself while looking around. She'd received a lot of curious looks because of her short skirt and tight blouse, but this was far more intrusive, almost aggressive.

No one seemed to stand out as the source of the gaze she felt.

Heather sighed and pulled at the buttons of her sheer white blouse. "I should've never let Lisa talk me into wearing her clothes. Everything's too damned small. I'm gonna pop a button any second." She tugged up the tops of the black seamed stockings that refused to hide beneath the hem of the leather skirt. The lacy straps of the snowy white garter belt showed every time she took a step. Unfortunately, there wasn't a damned thing she could do about it. Growling in frustration, Heather took another swallow of the sweet, potent drink and looked over at the crowded dance floor.

The huge orgiastic mass of dancers swayed and writhed to the heavy music in slow, exaggerated movements showing off their skimpy leather, vinyl, lace, and velvet costumes. Their faces, male and female, were practically disguised by heavy theatre make-up.

Heather winced. Despite how daring she thought her outfit was, compared to everyone else, she still looked like an innocent schoolgirl. She took a healthy swallow of her Long Island Iced Tea. *God, I can't win for losing.* And where the hell had her roommate gone anyway?

She straightened from the wall to look for her absent friend, and suddenly felt lightheaded. The bartender had apparently made her drink far stronger than she'd thought. She carefully set her glass on the narrow bar against the wall, determined not to drink any more. The last thing she wanted to do was pass out in this crowd. *Maybe I should go outside and get some air?*

With careful steps, Heather walked to the doorway of the enclosed outside porch without too much trouble. "Thank God I didn't wear those spike-heeled boots, or I'd be flat on my ass by now."

The tiny tree lights gave only a dim glow, especially after the harsh glare of the club's powerful strobes, but it was enough to see that the enclosed outdoor patio was practically empty. The crisp autumn breeze blew some of the fumes away, and Heather's mind cleared a little. Breathing deep, she smiled and looked up at the clear stars, then turned and promptly walked into a firm, hard-muscled body.

Strong hands gripped her upper arms, steadying her from their collision.

"Oh! Sorry!" Heather looked up—and up—into the eyes of a very tall and strikingly handsome man with fine, if sharp features and a pronounced five o'clock shadow. Dark brows slanted up over bright, yellow-green eyes framed by thick black lashes. The corners of his eyes tilted up to give him an exotic, feral look. Long waves of lustrous black hair fell over his shoulders.

Heather blinked at him. *He's so tall . . .* Her head didn't quite reach his shoulder. "Hi. I, ah . . ."

He pressed his finger gently to her lips for silence and a smile curved his lips.

Her lips tingled where he touched them. She licked them without thinking.

His smile widened, parting his lips slightly, revealing a

bright flash of white teeth.

Heather blinked. Are those fangs? *Oh, wait, this is a Goth club.* She smiled ruefully. Just about everybody wore fangs, and half of them really wanted to be vampires.

He reached out with fingers tipped in long, curved nails and grasped a thick lock of her blonde mane, letting the silvery strands slide slowly through his fingers. His eyes followed the path of his hand, apparently fascinated by her hair.

Intimate warmth curled in her belly. My *God. He's beautiful. I can't stop looking at him.*

His green-gold eyes locked onto hers and focused.

The fine hairs on the back of her neck rose. It honestly felt as though he was attempting to reach in to take hold of her soul.

He leaned forward slowly.

She shied back. *Is he trying to kiss me*? He was seriously handsome, but that didn't change the fact that she didn't know a thing about him.

He flashed a quick smile, grasped her hand, and raised it to his lips. Watching her closely, he softly brushed his lips across her knuckles, then brushed them fleetingly with the tip of his tongue.

She shivered visibly but didn't pull away. She'd never been kissed on the hand before.

He smiled and eased his hands into her hair, then very gently cupped her head. In a sudden move, he turned and pressed her tightly back against the wooden palisade wall.

Her eyes widened and she let out a small yelp of surprise. Her hands clenched in the lapels of his leather vest.

Leaning forward, he touched his nose to her ear. Slowly, he inhaled, then exhaled with a soft growl.

Long rippling shivers spilled down her spine. *Oh, God, what is this guy doing to me?*

Lightly, he touched his tongue to the shell of her ear tracing the curve, then dipped delicately into the sensitive center. He exhaled softly, creating a cool breeze against the damp flesh.

She trembled again, drew a ragged breath, then released a tiny moan. Her hands tightened on his lapels. The aroma of leather and his potent male scent curled around her. *He feels so good, he smells so good . . .*

His hand firmly cradled her head and his powerful body pressed against her, holding her captive against the wooden fence. He trailed his open mouth, nibbling lightly, along her jaw, and touched his lips to hers.

Shock rocketed through Heather's cloudy mind. *Is he . . . kissing me?* Her lips parted in alarm.

He swept in to stroke her tongue with his.

Holy shit! This gorgeous man is *kissing me!* He tasted only lightly of beer. Clearly, he hadn't had much to drink, unlike her.

He stepped closer, his erection pressing against the cradle of her hips, hot through the leather and heavy with intent. He deepened his kiss, slanting his mouth over hers for deeper penetration. His tongue stroked against hers in leisurely swipes, then he rolled his hips and pressed his entrapped cock against her softness.

Overwhelmed by the fierce sparks of pleasure deep in her belly, she felt powerless in his embrace, and oddly reluctant to do anything about it. She moaned into his mouth.

Slowly, he slid his hand from her silky hair down her shoulder and arm to press against her narrow waist. Carefully he skimmed his hand up her ribs. His hand closed over her breast through the blouse and he squeezed firmly.

She shivered, her nipple rising to a hot tingling point under his hot palm. She knew she should shove him away for his audacity, but she just couldn't summon the energy to do it.

His long nails tugged her hardened nipple beneath her lace bra.

A white-hot spark of pleasure seared downward to throb in her core. She gasped into his mouth and a shudder racked her body. A small moan escaped her throat.

He captured her soft moan in his mouth and inhaled deeply to steal her breath.

Want and need coursed urgently through Heather, washing away everything but the urge to get closer, to feel more, to feel him, to *touch* him. In a dreamlike haze, she pulled her hands from his lapels to slide them under his vest. She swept her hands over the silk shirt he wore and found that he was a solid wall of whipcord muscle. She swept her hands down his back, scoring him lightly with her nails, then dug in to pull him closer.

His growl of pleasure vibrated through her.

She wanted to touch his skin, but his shirt was tucked in. She hesitated. She couldn't just tug his shirt out; that would be rude. *Damn it!*

His thumb rolled her tender nipple under her blouse.

With a deep sigh, her spine arched eagerly, pushing into his hand. Her hips rose to meet his, pushing strongly against the heat of his erection.

He lifted his head to look at her with heated, hungry eyes blazing more gold than green. Licking his lips, his fingers unfastened the straining buttons to her blouse.

A warm hand slid inside her bra and his hand closed on her bare flesh.

The reality of a man's hand on her naked breast shocked Heather from her passion-hazed stupor. *Oh, God, I must be drunker than I thought!* Startled, confused, and alarmed, she tried to pull away, only to discover how firmly he had her pinned

His smile grew feral and he continued with the caress. He tugged sharply on her captured nipple.

Lightning bolts of liquid pleasure pulsed straight down, making her body jolt in time to his touch. She became aware of a slick wetness dampening her panties and felt something deep inside flutter with hunger and anticipation.

Heather turned away, her hands firmly planted against his chest. *Oh, God, I can't be doing this!* Biting her lip in sexual frustration and humiliated by her body's easy submission, Heather shoved him hard and rolled out from beneath him. She grabbed her parted blouse and bolted for the ladies' room inside.

Fearing to look behind her, Heather threaded her way through the crowd. *I can't believe I let that guy kiss me like that, I can't believe I was kissing him back! I hope to God nobody saw me kissing a total stranger like that!* She dove into the hall and headed past the stairs, only to find a line in front of the bathrooms halting her escape. "Shit." Heather felt a tug on her skirt and was turned around sharply.

The man she'd been kissing smiled down at her. His golden eyes were narrowed and intent. "Going somewhere?" Between one breath and the next, he imprisoned her arm in a powerful grip and bodily shoved her through a doorway and up a short staircase.

Heather very nearly tripped on the stairs, but his grip on her arm kept her from falling. "Hey, uh, I don't know you and I, uh, normally don't go kissing people. There's been a mistake, I didn't mean . . ."

He urged her into the dimly lit narrow room upstairs. "You didn't mean to kiss me?" His hypnotic voice slid over her like potent whisky.

Heather could feel her self-control slipping away from her reach. Her voice dropped to barely a whisper. "Not like . . . Not like *that.*"

He turned to look at her with eyes that were slits of gold fire. He licked his lips, the sharp points of his teeth gleaming in his predatory smile. "I have no complaints." He slowly backed her into a dark corner of the empty room. "In fact, I rather enjoyed it." The light from the solitary lamp etched his face with menacing shadows. "And I was under the impression that you enjoyed it, too."

Heather trembled in his grip. *Oh, God, oh, God, I think I'm in trouble!*

Abruptly, he turned and sat in the room's only chair, facing her. He tugged her closer. "I want you." His voice vibrated with unleashed passion. "I need you."

With him seated, their eyes were on the same level. Her traitorous body responded with a sudden and compulsive craving for his touch.

He released her arm to capture the back of her head, gently, but firmly gripping her by the hair.

Her mouth opened to protest.

He pulled, bringing her parted lips to his and his tongue swept inside.

Waves of hot and hungry desire washed over her and her objections faded into a long moan. She was lost in the firestorm of excitement that swept through her blood screaming in voracious desire.

He moaned into her mouth and his arm closed about her waist, his hand cupping her rounded ass. He tipped her toward him.

Feeling herself falling, she put her hands on his shoulders and gripped the leather of his vest.

His arm tightened pulled her down.

She fell forward to straddle his muscular thighs, pressed up against his body with her soft breasts crushed against the wall of his chest.

His fingers curled in her hair. Slowly, irresistibly, he pulled her head back, breaking the kiss. His moist tongue stroked her neck. Tingles followed in the wake of the caress.

Her eyes fluttered closed in erotic bliss and she moaned.

His fingers tugged on her buttons while the wet heat of his mouth closed on her throat. His sharp teeth grazed the delicate skin of her exposed throat. He nipped lightly.

Held still by his hold on her hair, a small hungry sound

escaped her lips. Heather felt the front of her bra open, releasing her vulnerable breasts to his mercy. Her nipples hardened powerfully in the cool air.

His hand closed about one full breast. He swept his hand over her pliant skin, nails biting lightly into her softness. A callused thumb slid over one sensitive nipple.

Small streaks of lightning raced downward and pulsed in her clit, as though his thumb touched here there instead.

The furnace of his wet mouth slid from her throat down her collarbone and onto the flesh of the breast. His mouth feasted on the delicate skin, with his tongue making damp circles. He took possession of a nipple, sucking softly, and then more strongly.

She gasped with the delicious pleasure that sincerely felt as though his mouth was far, far lower on her body.

His tongue flicked the nipple against his teeth, insistently shocking her with bolt after bolt of intense delight. He suckled strongly on one nipple and then the other, pulling on them until both were painfully erect.

Heat gripped her body in spasms of greedy desire, and she cried out softly in carnal lust. Barely conscious of anything beyond the powerful rippling sensations of hunger engulfing her body, she arched her back to lean into his mouth for more of his kisses.

He slowly spread his muscular legs between her soft thighs, irresistibly opening her legs wide. Her skirt slid up to her waist, exposing her completely. A hand splayed on the silk of her stockings, moving up in a slow heated caress to the flesh of her inner thigh. Suddenly his palm covered her heat, and he squeezed in possession.

She moaned in primitive fear and volatile anticipation.

A finger lightly caressed her panties, tracing the damp shape of her cleft through the snowy satin. The finger pressed deeper, becoming a long, slow rub against her excited clit through the pliant fabric. The finger wormed its way under the satin, seeking out her softness until he touched wet sensitive flesh.

She jumped.

Continuing his explorations, his fingers slid further under the white satin, parting her soft curls. He gently stroked the tender outer lips, then dipped into the mouth of her drenched cleft. The finger drove slowly into her moist depths, foraging deep, then deeper yet to caress her trembling inner flesh. He swirled his invasive finger to gather her dew and slid out. His mouth left her wet, exposed breasts and the sounds of him licking and sucking reached her ears.

She blinked, more than a little shocked. He was sucking the fingers that had been *inside* of her.

"Delicious, princess." The pleasure in his voice caressed her. Using the unrelenting grip in her silver-blonde hair, he tipped her head forward and brought her lips once more to his.

She opened her mouth under his and could taste herself on his tongue. She shuddered in reaction.

He pulled away to lock onto her eyes. Passion was written across his face like pain, his breath hard from panting. He spoke in a harsh whisper. "I want to watch you as I make you cum for me." Again his finger slid into her cleft, and another finger joined the first.

Her body clenched in wanton hunger to hold him within.

He withdrew his damp fingers to trace up her tender flesh and rub lightly against her clit.

The bolts of pleasure from his fingers jolted her sharply. Heather inhaled sharply.

He rubbed quickly back and forth against her.

Her lips parted and thighs tightened against the muscles of his leather-clad legs. She ground her hips onto him, begging for more.

He pulled her mouth to his for a hungry kiss, but kept his eyes trained on hers. He dipped his finger in her once more, sliding deeply to rub her inner flesh, then pulled them out, pushing in again, then pulling out in a slow fuck. Her wetness slid over his palm, and he rubbed at her clit with a damp thumb.

She whimpered softly and slid her hips forward onto his possessing fingers, wanting more, needing more, fucking herself on his hand.

He crushed his mouth to hers, capturing her soft cries in his mouth. He slid a second finger into her, burrowing strongly to find the soft, fleshy button buried deep inside. He pressed it with his fingertips, flicked it lightly, again and again in an insistent rhythm.

Her body rocked unconsciously against his palm until she edged toward the threshold of a crushing orgasm. Driven closer and closer, she let out soft, breathless sounds until she balanced right on the glittering edge. She let out a muffled scream of frustration that was swallowed by his mouth.

He gave her a smile that was filled with long teeth. "Yes, yes . . ."

Her hands tugged insistently at his lapels and her hips rocked against him in mindless lust. Harder and harder, she thrust against him, encouraging him to push deeper into her. His breath came in harsh pants

Eyes intent on her, he whispered. "I want you to cum for me, princess. I want to feel you. I want to taste you as you cum."

She arched, stiffened, then her mouth opened to suck in a deep breath and hold it. A powerful orgasm crashed through her, taking her in a howling, glorious blaze. She thrashed, crushing herself on his hand.

Firmly, he brought her lips down to meet his and he took her cries into his triumphant mouth.

Rapt in their throes of pleasure, neither noticed the couples that silently came into the room. Silently, intently, and voraciously they watched the elegant blonde and the rugged dark man in the chair, their eyes avidly devouring the scene before them. Clothing was loosened and hands roved and stroked, pleasuring each other.

In the mirrors, the blonde's full white breasts pressed into him while his mouth took hers, tongues working against each other ravenously. Her white panties were stark and visible in the dim light.

The dark man's eyes turned toward them briefly, wide open and brilliant gold then he returned his eyes and attention back to her, deepening their kiss.

The full moon was rising.

The werewolf could feel the moon's power vibrating in his bones, even behind the walls of cement that surrounded him. He had run out of time; he must take her now and damn the consequences. With the power of her orgasm singing through his blood, he could finally achieve one of his own strong enough to retain control over his ability to change at will. Without her orgasm to strengthen him, the full moon would force him to shift and lock into the shape of a wolf until another orgasm brought him back to his humanity.

With the sharp tips of his nails already extending into claws, he tore the delicate satin of her panties from her soft body with one hand, pushing them into a pocket. He released her long, silky hair and held her in a warm embrace while her after-tremors still shook her.

Her mouth locked to his in complete abandon, sucking on his tongue.

He ripped his trousers open to free his painfully hard flesh from its prison. Slipping a hand under her firm ass, he lifted and pulled her forward to impale her on his heavily erect cock, burrowing into her wet depths. Feeling her flesh giving way to accommodate him, he moaned harshly, his eyes losing focus with the intense pleasure.

Her eyes opened with a small cry of surprise. She looked around, apparently realizing they had an audience. She clenched around his cock in reaction. Clearly alarmed, she shoved at his shoulders, trying to pull away.

He almost smiled. It was far too late for second thoughts. He captured her hands and pulled them behind her, holding her wrists together with one hand. "Oh no you don't. It's my turn, princess." Personally, he could care less who watched. He needed her and he needed her *now*. Already he could feel his ears lengthening to points. He gripped her firmly with both hands and thrust up hard into her hot and tender flesh with a harsh grunt.

Her body shook with the impact and a soft cry escaped her lips. She closed around him like a moist fist.

His head spinning, he moaned. *Fuck, she feels good* . . . His booted feet planted firmly for support, he tilted his hips back to withdraw almost to the tip, then flexed his thigh and ass muscles to drive back into her wet depths, then again, and again . . .determined to bring himself to climax while there was still time.

Dampness slid onto his thighs from her excitement and the slaps of flesh against wet flesh were surprisingly loud.

Again and again, the werewolf thrust; deep, then shallow, then deeper, stronger and harder . . . Heat and pressure low in the back of his balls began to coil urgently. *Almost there* . . . He gripped her breast and took it hungrily into his mouth, sucking at the nipple to distract her, racing to beat the threatening moon swelling toward full strength in the sky.

A shudder wracked her body, a moan slipped from her throat. She leaned into him, her fingers tightening on his lapels, and started rocking into his thrusts.

He lifted his head capturing her frightened, but heated, gaze and smiled. "Good girl." Their panting breaths matched tempo. "Yes . . ." He felt the deep, tightening pleasure in his balls and he knew he was ready to spill into her hungry flesh. He was close, right at the edge. He growled in lustful pleasure. "Yes, yes, yes!"

She tightened around him with tiny spasms, her fingers clutching his vest. Her head tilted back, and her breath stilled, then a cry exploded from her lips.

She had cum.

Again.

He jerked within her, his cock swelling to excruciating hardness. He pulled her down powerfully onto his cock, her ass tight against his balls. With a wrenching howl of ecstasy and triumph, he spilled into her depths.

Trembling in aftershocks of carnal pleasure, and fighting for breath, he released her wrists and enclosed her tender body in a fierce hug. *Ah, yes!* The werewolf sighed deeply in relief both mental and physical. *Human for another month.* He could now seek his wolf form without losing his ability to return to being human. Gone also was the fear of being lost in a far more hideous form; a form trapped between man and wolf. *At least until the next full moon.*

She wrapped her arms around his neck, burrowing into him, openly seeking comfort. Tears slid down her cheeks.

He kissed her lips and then kissed her tears away. "It's okay, princess, it's okay." Gently, he lifted her from him and pulled out a black handkerchief to wipe his seed from her thighs. He helped her rearrange her clothes and closed his pants with a satisfied smile. He became aware of the sounds of the others in the room and remembered the audience.

The intruders were utterly oblivious to the two of them as they moaned and writhed, seeking their own pleasures.

Gently taking her still-trembling hand, he led her to the

stairs past a man moaning, eyes closed, gripping his lover by the hair as he pumped himself into her mouth.

Trembling on rubbery knees, Heather went into the ladies' room. Strangely, it was empty. Or perhaps not so strangely, considering just how many people had crammed into the upstairs room to watch them do . . . *that*. She felt both ashamed and strangely exhilarated. A minor tremor shook her, and her face burned. She used the sink to wash off the dregs of her make-up. *Two! I had two orgasms!*

Right in front of all those people watching.

Oh, God, does this make me a slut?

Too late to think about that now.

She grabbed a bunch of paper towels and wet them to wash the stickiness from her thighs. That's when she noticed. "Shit! My panties!"

Heather walked out of the ladies' room into the main room of the club wondering how she was going to deal with this . . .situation.

He walked over with a smile and handed her a drink.

She thought about running but discarded the idea. He'd already done his worst and she could really use the drink. Thirsty, she took the glass, drinking deeply. Alcoholic fire went straight to her brain. She winced. "Shit, I just chugged a Long Island Iced Tea."

He shrugged, a relaxed smile on his lips, and slouched against the wall. "That's what you were drinking before."

Heather looked into his lambent green eyes and scowled. "Yes, and look what kind of trouble that got me into." Memories of his body scorched through her and her face heated. She took another, smaller sip.

He smiled.

She frowned up at him. She could have sworn his eyes had

been yellow only a few minutes ago.

A slender, dark-haired girl came out of the crowd on the dancefloor. "Hey! Heather, where have you been? I've been looking all over for you! Did you hear? We missed the side-show going on upstairs!"

Heather winced.

The loud music and press of people closed between the werewolf and the spent blonde.

He slid away in the confusion and headed for the door. *So, her name is Heather.* He slipped out of the club and took a deep breath of the crisp autumn air. Cautiously he made his way to a dark corner of the parking lot where he'd parked his bike. *Perhaps Heather will still be around next month?* He pulled the scrap of satin that had been her panties from his pocket. *I have her scent now, so I can find her again.* Maybe he would seek her out before the next full moon. Perhaps he should consider taking her as his mate?

Heather looked around. The guy was nowhere to be seen. Ignoring her roommate, she ran out of the club. *Did he leave? That son of a bitch!* She looked about the parking lot and heard the thunder of a motorcycle revving up. *That sounds like my Dad's old bike,* she thought vaguely.

Looking toward the street, she spotted a classic Indian motorcycle.

The rider sped by in a distinctive leather coat and long dark hair whipped down his back. He looked back, smiled, and waved a scrap of white fabric that were quite obviously panties.

She didn't even know his name.

SNOW MOON: PART TWO

The werewolf watched the ponderous steel-colored clouds in the sky. Stepping from his battered red jeep, he lifted his nose delicately sifting the air for her fragrance. She wasn't here. *Shit.* This was the third week in a row he'd sought her out at the club *Gothic Noire,* and she wasn't here.

Night would be falling in an hour, but the snow-laden clouds washed everything with a muted gray light that defied the coming darkness. From the scent that floated on the breeze there would be snow tonight, a lot of snow, and soon.

The rising wind broke a small hole in the clouds, and he glimpsed the waxing moon floating in the encroaching twilight. It was more than half full with a bright shimmering ring of light encircling it. A Snow Moon, he'd heard it called. The hole in the clouds closed, hiding the moon away.

Closing his eyes, he concentrated, shutting out the odors of rubber, metal and gasoline as he stood amongst all the cars crammed in the parking lot. He closed his mind to all other human scents except for the perfume he sought; baby powder and woman, his woman. His steps brought him to where her vehicle had been parked. An old Mazda sat in the space, but her pickup truck had sat here, briefly and not too long ago. The scent was an hour old, but she had been here, then left.

His brows dipped in thought. *I guess it's time to hunt the old-fashioned way.* A warm flush of anticipation raced through him. He was finally going to see Heather again. Tonight.

He strode back to his jeep and shrugged out of his leather duster, then peeled off his T-shirt. The air was below freezing, but only the nip of the windchill registered. Sitting in the driver's seat, he pulled off his boots and socks. Yanking the thong from his hair, the loosened waves slid down his muscular back, but did nothing to keep the frostiness of the wind from his flesh.

He closed and locked the jeep, stashing the key behind the front tire. Naked but for his leather pants, he looked sharply about with eyes that saw better in the dark than in daylight. No one was watching, and no cars on the street. *Good.*

On the hardened soles of his bare feet, he jogged to a stand of trees and bushes in the next parking lot and hunkered down. Searching within, he felt for the sleeping power humming just below the surface. It uncurled from the base of his skull and swept over him in a wave of warmth and fierce joy. He felt the stretch and pull of muscle and sinew as his body shimmered from one moment to the next into another form.

A large rangy wolf in full winter coat of gray and white trotted out from the bushes. Nose to the pavement, the wolf cast about the parking lot for the trail he sought. To the wolf's nose, far more sensitive than in his man-form, the trace of the female's perfume became as clear and bright as neon. Head lifting, the wolf set off in a ground-eating lope to follow the aroma from the side of the road, tracking her scent by the vehicle she was driving. Time became meaningless in the now of wolf-thought.

Under the harsh light of the meat department in the grocery store, Heather found herself entranced by the sweet smell of raw flesh. Her mouth watered from the scent. Her panties were getting wet with eagerness even as her stomach cramped with appetite. Want, hunger and desire all fought for dominance while she stared unblinkingly at the plastic-wrapped ten-pound beef eye-roast on the refrigerated shelf before her.

With trembling fingers, she shoved her long, silver-blonde ponytail off her shoulder. She reached out with both hands to pick up the heavy piece of meat.

The rancid stink of sour beer-breath washed over her and a rough masculine voice snarled behind her. "Outta my way, I'm takin' that."

Heather glanced over her shoulder.

Behind her was an older, rough-looking man wearing a stained ball-cap and a battered coat, gripping a grocery cart loaded with snacks and beer. A gnarled hand reached for her prize.

Her lips pulled away from her teeth, a snarl boiling up from her as she eyed the threat to her food. "Mine!" Lunging, she snatched the chilled meat from the shelf, then turned away to hunch possessively around it.

The man snatched his hand back in alarm then bared blackened teeth. "I want that for my family, bitch!" He stepped away from his cart and took a menacing step toward her.

Heather gripped the roast hard, her fingers digging deeply through the plastic and into chilled flesh. A deep animal growl rumbled from her chest. If he tried to take her meat from her, she would . . . *I will bite him.* The thought shocked her and pleased her.

A hauntingly familiar masculine voice spoke calmly from behind Heather. "I think the little lady wants it for herself, mister. Why don't you have this other one on the shelf?"

Heather whirled to face the new threat, teeth bared, a growl still rumbling. She was forced to tilt her head back to look at him.

The man towered over her, two steps away, green eyes merry with humor. His long raven hair, pulled back in a tail, hung over his shoulder rakishly. A long, black leather coat swept the tops of his weather-beaten boots. His personal aroma of worn leather from his duster, soap, and potent male musk rolled over her in a wave. He smiled. "It's okay, princess, no one's going to take your food."

Heather's eyes widened. A powerful surge of memory tinged with lust washed over her. Images and sensations crashed through her mind of his hands on her breasts, his flesh buried within her, screaming as she came in his arms.

It was her seducer from the Goth club.

She took an unconscious step closer to him, then stopped. *Wait a minute, I'm pissed at him. He abandoned me at the club without telling me his name!* She cautiously stepped back.

His eyes narrowed slightly, and he breathed in.

She blinked. *He's smelling me!*

"Hey! the grizzled man bared his teeth at her tall seducer. "Butt out, shit for brains!" The guy turned to face Heather. "Hey, you stupid bitch, I said, I wanted that one for my family!"

Heather focused on the older man and tensed to attack. The hair on the back of her neck and the down on her arms lifted. *One more step and he's dead meat.* Her lips pulled hard back from teeth that were starting to ache. She felt a flare of heat at the base of her skull, then a bolt of fire raced down her spine.

The drunk bared his teeth and raised his fist. "You want some of me, bitch?"

The werewolf raised his brow. *Where the hell is this guy's instinct for survival?* Briefly, he entertained the idea of letting Heather take a hunk out of the brainless drunk. It might do the old lush a world of good to have a limb amputated by someone half his size. He sighed. *Then again, I really don't need another idiot toting a shotgun full of silver in my territory. Hmm, decisions, decisions . . .*

He took a step closer to the drunk. "I said, this one is hers." His voice, though reasonable, deepened to a bass rumble.

"You can have the other." He leveled his gaze at the old man, squaring his shoulders and straightening to his full height. The power of imminent change poured off his skin, whispering around him like a cloak and he knew damned good and well that that the depth of his eyes had flared with the gold of the beast within.

The man froze in place. Eyes wide, the drunk's mouth fell open and his face blanched to a sickly gray. The sour sweat stench of fear wafted from him.

He stared down at the older man, his slight smile unchanging, then took a single threatening step.

The grizzled man swallowed hard, snatched the other roast off the shelf, threw it into his wagon, then fled down an aisle, the wheels of his cart squealing.

He turned back to Heather. "Are you okay?"

She was staring at him with wide golden eyes that should have been deep blue. To his astonishment, tears trickled down her cheeks in silence and she hugged the huge roast to her chest, fingers still digging into the meat. "I . . . I don't understand what's happening to me." She sniffed and wiped her cheeks on the sleeve of her flannel shirt. "I'm normally a lot nicer than this, but I wanted to hurt him. I wanted to bite him for trying to take the roast. I could have let him have it and taken the other one myself . . ." Her voice dropped to a snarl. "But I just couldn't do it."

"It's okay, princess," he said softly. "Here, let me help you with that." Gently he pried the roast from her fingers.

With only a token resistance, Heather let him take her hard-won prize. "Princess," the werewolf said very gently, "how long have you been feeling like this?"

Her sapphire blue eyes flared golden briefly, with the fire of the beast.

"How long have you been needing to eat meat?"

"I dunno. I've been eating a lot of hamburger and steak

lately . . ." Her voice trailed off. She'd been eating a lot of hamburger and steak every night for the past week and a half. Sometimes snatching it from the microwave while it sat thawing, not even waiting until it was warm, sometimes twice in a night. She watched, as he appeared to be looking for something in her face and smiling in a sad kind of way.

"And I . . . I'm so hungry all the time, and for weird stuff." She sniffled. Heather had no idea why she was telling him anything. He'd fucked her in front of a bunch of people at the club, then left her to ride home with her roommate.

Taking a quick look around and seeing no one in the vicinity, the werewolf knelt and pulled out a long sharp blade from his boot. After peeling some of the plastic from the end of the roast, he carved a chunk off, handing it to Heather. Furtively, he re-wrapped the meat, wiped the blade on his sleeve, folded it and tucked it back into his boot.

The chunk was gone before Heather realized she'd even tasted it. She flinched. *Oh, gross! Why am I doing this?* Her brow furrowed as she realized that she was still hungry.

Kneeling before her, he peered deeply into her eyes as he handed her back the rest of the roast. "Princess, we need to talk. Let's go pay for your snack."

Heather dragged her heels but followed him to the checkout, cradling her roast.

The werewolf led Heather out to the grocery store parking lot, to where his jeep was sandwiched between a minivan and a battered station wagon. *God, how the hell do I start this conversation?* he thought as he helped Heather climb into his parked jeep. He climbed into the driver's seat, his keys heavy in his pocket.

"Let me see that," he asked, holding his hand out for her grocery bag. Heather passed it to him. In a smooth motion, he pulled out his boot-knife. He unwrapped the roast from the plastic again, then carved chunks off the roast. He passed them to Heather, who devoured them, barely chewing in her haste to feed her hunger.

Through his windshield, the werewolf watched the heavy steel gray sky pressing down. Only a few hours had passed since he had trailed her scent from the club to the grocery store. The freezing wind rattled the flimsy doors. Full night had fallen, and the snow would be coming at any time.

"Princess, where's your coat?" he asked casually as he continued to carve.

"I didn't wear one," she answered between bites. She was perfectly comfortable in her light flannel shirt and jeans. She took the chunk of meat in her hand and put the whole thing in her mouth.

"It's below freezing outside, and you didn't wear your coat?"

She chewed thoughtfully, then swallowed. "It doesn't feel like it's below freezing. I don't feel cold at all, but the wind is a little chilly."

The werewolf sighed. *She isn't noticing the cold and she's chewing bites of raw roast as though it's a cupcake.* He winced. He was not looking forward to this conversation.

I need to tell her what's happening to her, and that it's my fault. His sire had warned him that this kind of thing happened on occasion. Guilt was not something he was used to, but it was definitely guilt he felt. *Damn, this is going to be hard.*

"Princess, I have something to tell you. It's about me, and about you."

It took about twenty minutes to explain. She listened in total silence, eating the entire time. He thought it went rather well. She wasn't screaming.

"Do you have a name?" Heather licked some of the beef blood from her fingertips.

"Huh?" he asked, confused by the change in the subject.

He had become lost in the way she delicately licked each finger, then her palm with her tongue. When she popped her fingers into her luscious mouth to suck them clean, he felt himself harden violently. *I can think of a much better use for that tongue.*

"A name? Do you have a name?" Heather persisted. She turned her cobalt eyes to his.

"Uh, yeah, it's Rafe DuForet." He focused on her face and frowned. "Are you paying attention to anything I'm telling you?"

"So, Rafe," she said, tasting his name on her lips. "Basically, you are telling me that I'm turning into a werewolf? Like you?" Heather was smiling as she downed the hunk of eye-roast she'd been holding. "That's silly, there's no such thing."

"The reason you are craving and eating raw red meat—" he began as he handed her the last chunk of what used to be a ten-pound chunk of beef, " — is because your body is preparing for its first change. You need to eat because the change takes a lot out of you. If you don't eat enough ahead of time, you'll eat the first piece of meat you see. Even if it's walking around with a school-book-bag over its shoulder or sitting in your living room changing channels."

"And you're saying that I'm a werewolf because you . . . because we fucked?"

"When I, ah, took you—" He was trying to avoid the word fuck; he could see a dangerous gleam of gold building in her eyes. " — our auras, souls, energies, whatever, overlapped and it triggered your nature. You were what we call dormant, kinda like a recessive gene. I was so close to changing right then and there that my, uh, power shoved you out of dormancy, and now you're headed for your first change."

Heather could feel an uncontrollable anger starting to boil up. What was weird was that she could also feel a warm pool of heat dampening her panties. She couldn't seem to make up her mind if she wanted to hit him or kiss him.

The scent of her growing excitement was rolling over him in waves. He shifted in his seat, but he just couldn't get comfortable. "I'm guessing that one of your parents or grandparents was a were. Did one of your relatives take off one day and disappear?"

Heather's eyes went wide and her cheeks paled. He winced. *Shit, looks like I hit the nail on the head.*

"Uh, yeah." She turned to look out the jeep's windshield. "My Dad drove off on his bike, an Indian motorcycle like yours, when I was little."

"It was probably him."

"He used to have a leather bomber jacket with a big wolf painted on the back." Her voice cracked and she sniffed. "He used to take me for rides on his bike."

"Hey, hey, princess," he whispered softly, then wiped a tear from her cheek. "I'm there too, okay? Only it was my Mom who took off on me." He squeezed her hand in comfort and she smiled tremulously, squeezing him back.

"So, I'm gonna change into a werewolf at the next full moon?" Heather's eyes were wide. She swallowed the last of the beef and watched as Rafe tossed the plastic out the window of the parked jeep.

"No, in the next day or so." Glancing at the sky, Rafe saw the first flakes of snow starting to whisper out of the glowing clouds. "The full moon is more than a week away, and something else entirely."

Heather frowned. "So we don't change with the full moon?"

"Well, yeah we do, but it's different." Rafe cringed. *Oh, fuck, how the hell do I explain the effects of the full moon to her? That little talk is not going to be pretty.* "Anyway, once you've made your first change, you'll pretty much be able to control it. The stuff you've seen in the movies isn't true, not about silver and not about the change."

"So what am I supposed to do now?" Heather licked the last of the beef blood from her lips and leaned toward him as she stared at his lips. She had decided that she definitely wanted to kiss him. She wanted to touch all that dark hair, curl her fingers in it and hold him firmly to her mouth while she tasted him.

Rafe suddenly realized that the perfume of her female musk was growing decidedly stronger. Something was making her hot. He felt himself growing uncomfortably hard in reaction to her feminine perfume.

Breathing deeply, Heather realized that she could smell the aroma of a salty-sweet something that seemed familiar. Heather looked down and noticed the considerable bulge in Rafe's pants. The scent was coming from him. From his pants. A vivid sensual memory jolted her. His hot cum pouring into her writhing body, as his rich scent perfumed the air around them. The pungent scent had been on her own skin for days after he had taken her in the upstairs room of the club.

Rafe's brain turned to mush as she looked pointedly down at his painfully tight crotch. There was no hiding his interest or hers. Although the windows were wide open, her rich female scent seemed to fill the jeep to overflowing. His eyes focused on her mouth. Her tongue swept across the tender fullness of her lips. There was a definite lambent gold swamping out the blue in her eyes, matching the heat he knew was rising in his own gaze.

"Rafe?" she said softly.

"Yeah?" Turning in his seat, he breathed in deeply. The smell of beef blood and aroused female was overpowering. He leaned toward her with a creak of old leather from his coat; his mouth barely inches away from hers. From the corner of his eye, he could see that snow had started to fall from the sky in earnest, dusting the parked cars with silver, like Heather's hair.

"So, what do I do now?" she asked again.

"What do you do now?" he mumbled, swallowing hard and focusing on her tender lips. "Now you kiss me." With a lunge, he seized the back of her head and pulled her toward his mouth. Heather met him halfway, her hands closing powerfully on his forearms.

He angled his mouth over hers and her soft lips parted, letting him in. Their tongues met and stroked each other. He could taste the beef she'd been eating. His tongue explored her warmth, then brushed her teeth where sharp little incisors made themselves known. She was a hell of a lot closer to her change than he'd thought.

Shit! Shit! Shit! Rafe broke the kiss, his vision barely in focus from his lust. He wanted nothing more than to pull her onto his lap and pull her clothes off.

"Oh, no, you don't," Heather growled in frustration. With quick and determined motions, she shoved him back against his door, pulled the belt on his leather pants open, then undid his fly.

He froze, helpless to stop her. Lust and common sense short-circuited each other. Her hands dug deeply into his pants to find his rigid flesh, and she dove over his lap, her silver ponytail brushing his thighs.

"Jee-zuz! Heather, you're gonna get us arrested!" The wet warmth of her mouth closed on him, swallowing him to the root. Rafe swore, then threw his head back and moaned long and hard, closing his eyes in surrender. He leaned back and spread wide to give her room. He felt her tongue lash each ridge and vein along the base of his dick as she sucked with enthusiasm. He panted and his heart slammed in his ribcage. Without thought, his hands burrowed into her frost-colored hair to hold her in place.

Cracking an eye open, he noticed the arch of her spine where her shirt had pulled from her pants.

Heather felt Rafe lean over her. She moaned in encouragement as she felt his hand slide into the back of her jeans. His fingers slithered into the crack of her ass. She moved completely into his lap, her knees coming up on the seat, and felt him delve deeper into her jeans. He touched her damp, sensitive woman flesh with a finger. Using her free hand, she loosened her belt, popped her button and unzipped her confining jeans to give him access. He took the opportunity she gave him and buried two fingers in her heat. She moaned as she felt him caress her clit with a thumb, then slowly pumped his fingers in and out of her. She slid a foot to the floor, lifting and spreading herself wide to his inquisitive fingers.

Rafe's ass bunched and lifted, shoving his cock deeper into her mouth. His breath came in harsh pants as he put gentle pressure on her head to keep her in place. She sucked harder on him, as though starved for his cum. He gasped, and suddenly realized how close he was to spilling into her mouth.

The perfume of power assailed his nose. He was going to cum, and she was using his building orgasm to fuel her change. She was going to become a beast right here in the parking lot of the grocery store, where she would have her pick of meat to hunt, all of them carrying their own groceries to their cars.

"Heather," he hissed, "we've got to stop, we've got to stop now!" He was screaming with his need to pump himself down her throat. Gripping her by the hair, he pulled her off and writhed away from her mouth. She fought to reach him, her mouth open, her eyes golden and glazed with power and lust.

"Why did you stop me?" She bared sharp teeth and panted, shuddering.

"This is not the place for this." He gasped for breath, burning from his beast's nearness to surfacing. As he tucked himself away, he shook from the overwhelming desire to jack himself off the rest of the way, but if he came, even by his own hand, she would change. When she changed, her power would shove him into changing too. He could feel it in the lightning arcs down his spine. If they changed, then there would be two huge and hungry predators running through the parking lot. *Damn it! Frustration hurts.*

"Don't you want me?" Heather whimpered in painful rejection. Hurt bathed her eyes with unshed tears.

"God, yes! I want you, Princess." Rafe bit his lip as he saw the painful need burning in her expression. "I want you so bad I'm shaking." He lunged, gripping the back of her neck and took her mouth, sucking at her lips with all the pent-up frustration that swam in his gut. His tongue pushed and stroked against hers, tasting her in a lustful fever. He felt her reach for his hair, pulling him to her, sucking on his tongue and biting his lips, kissing him back for all she was worth. He reluctantly pulled away, his eyes glowing with urgency.

"Damn it, Rafe, why do you keep stopping?"

"I want to rip your clothes off and fuck you 'til you scream. I want to cover you in my cum and smear it all over your body and mine. But, I need to take you home, to my home, where it's safe." With shaking hands, he started the jeep, then put it in gear.

"Hey! Wait a minute! I can't just go with you. I have to go home!" Heather yelped.

"You have to go through your change," Rafe said as he looked behind, backing out of the parking space. "I'm taking you to my place where I can keep an eye on you."

"Oh, no, you're not!" There was a definite snarl in her voice, anger winning over tears. "You pushed me into having sex, then you pushed me away as soon as *I* wanted to have sex. Well, you've pushed me around one too many times, and I've had enough. Stop the jeep." Heather grabbed the handle on the flimsy door and shoved it open an inch or so.

"Sorry, princess, this is for both our own good," he said as he concentrated on the parking lot traffic. "I can't have a newborn werewolf eating people in my territory." The jeep made its cautious way through the parking lot to the exit.

"Eating people?" snapped Heather. "What the hell are you talking about? Do you know how crazy that sounds? Look, just because you tell me that my sudden appetite for raw beef means I'm going to turn into a hairy monster doesn't mean I'm buying your bullshit! I said, stop the jeep!"

"It's my fault, so I'm responsible for you." Rafe ground through clenched teeth. "So, you're coming home with me." He gunned the engine and the jeep picked up speed as it came to the exit onto the main street.

"Well, tough shit! You should have asked me, not ordered me around! She glanced over at her pickup, parked by the main doors of the grocery store. In a lunge, Heather flung open the door and tumbled out onto the parking lot. She landed on her hands and rolled over her shoulder, then dove between the cars. Heather stopped in surprise, hunched down between a pickup and a sedan. "Whoa, I've never done that before!" Her heart pounded with fear and exhilaration.

The sound of screeching brakes and Rafe shouting over horns announced that he was not done with her yet. Hunched over, she darted between cars and made a beeline for her pickup.

"Werewolves, my ass! That was the dumbest excuse for a date I've ever heard," she snapped as she ran crouched toward her truck through the maze of parked cars. "If he wants to sleep with me, he can just ask me like any other guy."

The last ten feet to her parked truck were open drive and swirling snow. Looking both ways for moving cars, she darted across the open space to the driver side of her truck. Reaching into her jeans pocket, she pulled out her keys. She flung open the truck door and climbed in, and slammed it closed, locking the door with a satisfied sigh.

Heather started up her truck and looked for the red jeep. She didn't see it anywhere, so she cautiously backed out of the parking space. Heather felt a niggling sense of disappointment that he hadn't tried to follow her.

The parking lot, crazy because of the sudden snow, was filled with people flooding out of the store and racing for their cars. A family of four staggering with groceries careened out in front of her moving pickup. She stomped on the brakes and slid a few inches in the snow. In fury, she rolled down her window.

"Okay, people, put your brains back in your heads before you get killed!" she snapped at the fleeing family. She rolled her eyes, then shook her head. "What the hell is wrong with me?" She rolled her window back up. "I never yell out my window."

Peering past the overworked windshield wipers, Heather made her way carefully out of the parking lot by way of the back exit. Cars were crawling everywhere and the yellow lines on the main road were disappearing fast under a carpet of white. The traffic lights swung slowly in a rising wind.

"Damn, this is one hell of a snowfall," Heather muttered. Carefully she exited from the main street, then pulled out onto the tree-lined highway leaving the lights of the small town behind. Snow obscured everything; she could barely see the road. The lines had disappeared completely under snow that was piling up fast. The glare of headlights suddenly filled her rearview mirror.

"What the hell?" she had time to yelp, then felt a hard thump on her back bumper, snapping her head forward. "Oh my God, he hit me!" Her heart leapt into her throat as her pickup wobbled in the slippery snow. She gasped. The idiot behind her was about to run her off the road! "Don't panic! Don't panic! Don't panic!" She glanced in her mirrors but could only see headlights. She couldn't tell what kind of car was behind her. She panicked and stepped on the gas to get out of the way, but that made her fishtail.

There was another thump as the car behind her bumped her again. She screamed in fright as her truck went into a slow spin. The truck skidded to the right sideways and thumped off the road. Her truck crunched off the edge of the road, then with a final slow turn, it slid nose first into a ditch filled with snow. The engine stalled.

Heather blinked, surprised that she was still in one piece. With an ugly curse, she started the truck and put it in reverse. The tires spun, throwing spumes of fresh snow. The truck rocked back a few inches, then rolled forward into the ditch. She was stuck.

"Goddammit!" she swore.

Something moved by her driver-side window. She yelped in surprise but couldn't see a damn thing through the falling snow. Then, her door handle was jiggled. Shuddering in fear, Heather grabbed for her door, then realized that it was locked.

Something came smashing through the window and she screamed in fright as glass sprayed into the cab. A gloved hand reached in to open the door.

Heather scrambled over to the passenger door. Flipping the lock, she threw the door open tumbling out into the snow-filled ditch. On her hands and knees, she desperately scrambled away from the road in panicked flight. She climbed the snowy hill as fast as her sneakers and clawing hands could get her. She was so scared her breath came in gasps.

She slipped and slid as she dashed up the embankment, then crashed through the brush. The snow melted from her touch so fast, she barely felt the cold, only dampness, as she tore up the hill. Her breath steamed as she bolted into the trees in her haste to get away from whoever was after her. Falling snow kissed her cheeks. Branches slapped at her face and tore at her flannel shirt as she fled uphill in the deepening snow.

She could hear nothing but the hissing of the falling snow, her feet, the snapping of branches and her own breathing as she fled. There was no sound of anyone in the brush behind her. She stopped and looked up the hill. *There has to be a house around here somewhere where I can make a phone call.*

Something grabbed her ankle and she fell to her hands in the snow. Turning, she raised her fists and snarled with her teeth bared. Rafe's dark head and gleaming yellow eyes met her terrified gaze. His hands were encased in black gloves, and one of them held her ankle.

"Come on, princess, we don't have time for this." He pulled on her ankle and she slid in the snow toward him. He reached up with his other hand and grabbed her thigh in a punishing grip.

"You son of a bitch! You pushed me off the road? I coulda been killed, you ass!" Now she was really pissed.

"Not anymore, you're a lot harder to kill these days. Now come on—before the roads close completely." He grabbed for her arm.

With a vicious snarl, she lunged at him, fists swinging. To her complete surprise, she caught him on the jaw with a satisfying smack.

In blank astonishment, Rafe raised a hand to his jaw, then his eyes narrowed grimly. "So you want to play rough?"

Heather suddenly realized that hitting him in the face had done nothing but make him angry. Not a good idea when he had delusions of being a werewolf. In sudden fear, Heather kicked out at his hand on her ankle.

With a muffled curse, he released her.

She rolled to her feet and scrambled back up the hill. *Oh my God, he's going to kill me!* She felt his arms wrap around her waist and she yelped in fright. She was slammed facedown onto the snow-covered ground, with Rafe's full weight on top of her. It knocked the breath from her, and his body was an inferno against her back. She did not want to think about what he would do to her now.

She screamed in panicked fury, then bucked, trying to throw him off. "Let me go!"

"Stop fighting me."

His powerful hands gripped her wrists and yanked them to the small of her back. She heard the metallic sound of a belt buckle being released and the sound of him pulling his belt from his pants. Was he going to beat her? Her blood turned to ice in her veins. She twisted her shoulders, but he held her fast.

She heard him panting as he sat up, straddling her with his thighs, his coat cloaking them both. She felt him wrap the belt around her wrists. *He's tying me up?* She pulled at the belt, but somehow he had it fastened so tightly she could barely move her hands.

Heather suddenly realized that she could feel and smell Rafe's massive erection pressing against the small of her back. The image of him pulling down her jeans to mount her from behind flooded her thoughts. She shuddered with fear and sudden violent lust.

"It's time to go, princess," Rafe growled. Heather's sweet scent of semi-aroused female and musky sweat from her proximity to her first change had him painfully hard. He tried breathing through his mouth to reduce the aroma, but quickly discovered that he could actually taste her heat on his tongue.

He could feel his own beast struggling to rise in response to hers. If he didn't get her to his cabin immediately, he was going to take her here in the snow. With his beast so close to the surface, this would be no gentle coupling. Using his weight, he held the struggling girl face down in the snow as he wrapped his narrow belt around her wrists, tying it tight.

"Stop trying to fight me, dammit," he growled even as his beast wanted her to fight. It was exciting him, urging him to take her brutally, here and now. As he held her pinned beneath him, the idea of possessing her and riding her to completion while in the throes of her change was intoxicating. The pent-up frustration from the aborted episode in the jeep earlier wasn't helping him control his temper, or his libido.

"Fuck you!" she snapped, spitting snow.

"My pleasure." He smiled grimly. *That's it!* She was going to acknowledge his dominance right here and right now. He knew he wasn't thinking very clearly, but at the moment, he really didn't care. His dick was hard, and he wanted it in her.

Sitting up in the snow, he flipped her over onto her back, her hands trapped under her body. Throwing his leg back over her thighs, he pushed his trapped hardness against her crotch. He then leaned over her, pressing his hips into her, yet holding the weight of his shoulders on his elbows, his long leather coat cloaking them both from the falling snow.

Licking his lips in anticipation, he pressed his face against the softness of her breasts, nuzzling against the hard nipples that were trying to poke through the snow-dampened flannel of her shirt. His lips closed on a prominent nipple rising under the flannel. Nipping and sucking, he pulled it and the fabric into his mouth. Using his teeth, he closed on the hard nipple and rolled it, tugging.

"What the hell are you doing?" She gasped, then moaned. His teeth and lips were making the hair on her scalp rise. She couldn't decide if it was fear or excitement.

Slowly and deliberately, he slid his trapped erection against her heat, back and forth, making her feel his need. He hissed with the incredible pleasure, then began to unbutton her flannel shirt.

"I'm taking you up on your invitation, Heather." His voice dropped octaves lower, a voice barely human. "To fuck you."

"What?" She shook her head. "No, damn you! Let me go!"

Ignoring her protests, his gloved fingers fumbled at the

buttons. In sudden impatience, he pulled the damp flannel apart and buttons sprayed across the snow. The shirt parted, revealing her lacy white bra. Her soft stomach rose and fell with her heaving breath. His leather-encased fingers slid possessively across her over-warm flesh. His lips followed, tasting the creamy skin his fingers had explored. He tasted the whisper of power rising from her skin. Her beast was close to awakening, and he could feel it under his tongue.

She felt his hand slide down to her belt. Heather shifted in disbelief. "What are you doing?" He wasn't really going to take her in the snow, was he?

He tugged the belt open, then free. "I already told you what I'm going to do." The button to her damp jeans followed.

"Rafe, don't do this." Her zipper being drawn down seemed loud in the winter silence.

"Heather, you started this, I'm finishing it." His gloved hand slid down into the opening in her jeans.

She gasped. His leather-covered palm felt hot against the roundness of her tummy. She felt her body stirring warmly under his touch. For someone who seemed to be about to fuck her in the snow, he was being surprisingly gentle.

With golden, slitted eyes, he stared down at her. His other hand went to his boot and he pulled out his knife. Her entire body tensed sharply. It opened with a loud snick. *Okay, now I'm really scared.* A small sound of fright escaped her lips.

He growled and his lips curled in a feral smile. "I suggest you lie very still."

She froze. *Oh my God! Is he going to kill me?*

The flat of the blade grazed her skin as he slid it under her bra. Pulling sharply, the delicate lace parted against the blade, releasing her breasts to his mercy. He licked his lips at the sight of her rosy nipples. They hardened visibly from the sudden exposure, crowning the perfect whiteness of her breasts and framed by the soft flannel.

"Dammit, Rafe! What part of *no* don't you get?" Heather snapped, primitive, feminine fear warring with her growing urgency. She writhed under him, struggling, secretly pleased that he had to use his entire body to hold her down in the snow. Something within her refused to back down, refused to give in. Refused to be submissive to his dominance.

"You have two choices," he said as he rubbed his cheek against her full breasts, breathing deeply of her delicious female scent. His stubble rasped her nipples. His golden eyes locked onto hers. The cerulean blue of her eyes was drowning in gold, becoming a rich sea green. "You can stop fighting me, and I will drive us both out to my cabin where we can fuck each other senseless in privacy . . ."

Heather shuddered hard beneath him from his graphic words. Lust gripped her vitals and her hips lifted against his trapped erection. She moaned with the pleasure.

"Or," he continued, breathing deeply, "I can take you now, right here in the snow."

Her body was very much inclined to let him take her right then and there. "I thought you said I have to go through some kind of change." She was stalling, confused by the potent mixture of her body's heated excitement at war with the panic that made her tremble. From the look of amusement on his face, she figured that he knew it, too. She was also trying not to breathe in too deeply, because the smell of his potent arousal was adding to her already overwhelming desire.

"Mmm, yes," he purred in reply, "the change."

As he pressed against her, she could feel the vibration of his deep rumbling growl against her skin.

His silky head dipped to her soft belly, where he rubbed his face like a great cat. "We're safe here. Or rather, the rest of humanity is safe from us here. There aren't any houses near here, so no people to draw us, and I live just over this hill. We can get your truck and my jeep tomorrow."

"Got this all planned out?" She could feel her temper trying to reassert itself. Was this all just a set-up?

He lifted his head from her belly and suddenly lunged up her body. "I do now." The hard wall of his chest pressed against the softness of her naked breasts and his lips were but a kiss away. "I guess you could say that doing you right here is a good way to burn off excess energy 'til I can take you out to properly hunt." He nuzzled the side of her neck, burrowing under her ear. He opened his mouth and dug his teeth lightly into the muscle of her neck, creating erotic shivers from her throat down.

"Hunt?" The fullness of his cock was pressing directly on her clit and it felt far too good. She licked dry lips. She didn't want to encourage this nutcase, but at the same time, she wanted to stay and have him bury his cock in her hungry body.

"Once you change, you will need to feed," he whispered directly into her ear. She could feel the tip of a damp tongue tracing the shell of her ear. "There are a lot of deer around here. Once you make your first kill, drink your first living blood, you'll be able to change whenever you like, so to speak."

Heather felt her panties dampen and a hard bolt of lust slam low in her belly at the thought of running down and killing a deer to eat it, still warm. *What the hell is wrong with me?*

His whispers brushed her ear. "Think about it. The fresh blood warm in your mouth."

She let out a small helpless sound in reaction to her warring feelings. She was a nice girl. Nice girls didn't kill animals, then want to eat them, to drink their blood as it pumped into her mouth from a still-beating heart. Nice girls didn't get horny over the idea, either. Nice girls didn't want to fuck in the steaming blood-spattered snow. *Why am I having these feelings?* To her dismay, she unconsciously rocked her hips up against him.

He chuckled. "I can feel your lust, princess." His words were barely more than a breath. "You want me to fuck you right here in the snow."

God help her, but he was right. *That son of a bitch!* All of a sudden, she wanted nothing more than to sink her teeth into the smug bastard. She wanted very badly to see the color of his blood, to taste it, warm and alive on her tongue.

Lunging upward, she snapped, reaching for his throat. With blinding speed, he lurched out of range. Her teeth closed on the collar of his coat. Using a palm for leverage, he shoved her back onto the ground. His eyes were pools of molten gold as he smiled viciously down at her.

"You're gonna have to be a lot quicker than that."

"Why can't you just leave me the hell alone?"

"It's far too late for that. What's your pick, my cabin, or right here?"

"Get off me, you!" she screamed. Digging in her heels, she bucked hard to throw him off.

"I guess that means right here, right now," he growled right back as he held her down with brute force. His mouth set in a grim line he threw his leather coat off onto the snow next to them. With inhuman speed he rose off her, then bodily tossed her onto his coat.

With her hands tied to the small of her back, she fell belly first. The air woofed out of her lungs from the impact. Before she knew it, she felt his knees straddling her calves, and his hand pressing on her lower back. Heather felt his gloved hands hook into the back of her jeans, then he tugged hard. He hauled her off the ground, then upright on her knees.

He wrapped an arm around her hips, pulling her ass into his kneeling lap, squarely against his trapped erection. He groaned in pleasure, grinding himself against her. His gloved hands slid up to cup the fullness of her breasts, pulling her up and back against his hard chest.

"You have no idea how glad I am that I don't have to wait," he whispered intimately in her ear.

Rafe wanted nothing better than to force her down on his coat and ride her to oblivion, but that would accomplish nothing but his own enjoyment, and might make her hate him. He needed her lust to overcome her fear. His fingers trapped her nipples and tugged. She shivered under his palms. "I didn't think I was gonna make the drive anyway."

In alarm, Heather lunged away, trying to get her feet under her. *Oh shit! Now what have I done?* Her breath came in gasps. His arms were steel bands around her, she wasn't going anywhere, and part of her was glad.

"Oh, no, you don't," he growled as he held her still. "The fun is just beginning, princess." Rafe clenched his gloved fingertip in his teeth and tugged, peeling the glove from one hand. With a sigh, he slid the naked hand down her belly and straight into the front of her panties.

Heather squirmed as his warm hand burrowed deep. She trembled as she felt him close on her, cupping her heat. A finger slid deep into her wet softness as he hunched over her back panting, his powerful erection tight against her buttocks. His other hand, still encased in leather, tugged and rolled her captured nipple with his gloved fingers.

She shuddered and moaned as he fought to burrow his hand deeper into her jeans to slide further into her more-than-willing flesh. Then he made contact with something soft and exciting deep within. He stroked it and she choked as she slammed to the edge of release. Her creamy honey slicked his palm. She gasped and moved against him, wanting him to touch her within again.

"More?" he whispered calmly though his breath came in harsh pants. His palm rode on her clit. He moved his hand, flicking his buried finger to stroke her inner pleasure point while massaging her clit at the same time.

She was jolted hard to the shimmering edge of climax. "Oh, God!" she cried out.

"More?" he asked again, his voice hissing with his own rising urgency.

"Yes," Heather sobbed. "God yes, more!"

With excruciating slowness, he stroked deep within her again, moving his palm against her. Her body trembled as she quivered on the very edge of a powerful climax, writhing on his hand. She was close, so very close.

With incredible speed, he pulled his hand out. In astonishment, she looked over her shoulder to see Rafe put his wet fingers in his mouth. His gloved hand clenched painfully on her breast.

"Damn, I love the taste of you." His eyes were narrow slits of golden flame as he sucked her honey from his fingers in delight. His tongue swiped his palm in slow deliberation, savoring her flavor.

Heather felt trapped with his arm tight across her chest as he gripped her breast. Faster than her eye could track, his bare hand reached out and cupped her chin, his fingers digging into her jaw without mercy. He turned her face away from him, pointing her forward, facing the trees in front of her.

He released her breast, wrapping his gloved hand around the silky length of her ponytail. Heather felt her chin released. Her head was pulled back with slow but irresistible force, baring her throat, holding her still. She gasped as his mouth closed on the side of her neck, his lips caressing the delicate skin, measuring her pulse as it pounded under his stroking tongue.

Without warning, his sharp teeth closed firmly on the muscle and skin of her vulnerable throat with bruising force. She could feel the points of long incisors digging in but not piercing her tender skin. She froze under his bite. If she pulled, her flesh would come away in his teeth.

She felt him let go of her chest to grip the back of her jeans in a fist, then pull. Her opened pants slithered down her thighs to her knees, taking her panties with it and trapping her legs together. His bare hand swept the white softness of her buttocks. His mouth released her throat while his gloved hand held onto her hair.

"Mother of the Moon, you have a nice ass, Heather," he growled out.

She heard him unbutton his pants, then his zipper being drawn. "Are you going to rape me?"

Rafe noted a thread of fear in her words. He felt a twinge of guilt at what he was about to do, but her beast was too close to the surface to ignore and so was his. His body was screaming to possess her, and he wanted to release it while he could still control his actions.

His fingers slid down into the seam of her buttocks. Using his grip on her ponytail, he tipped her forward enough for his fingers to dip back into her wet flesh. Unconsciously, her hips bucked wanting him to drive his fingers deeper.

"Can't rape the willing, princess," he said as he explored her. His chest heaved as he panted against her back. "And you just don't feel all that unwilling to me, babe." His hands shook as he stroked his hard shaft once, then pushed the purple head forward, nudging himself between her soft creamy thighs.

She felt the incredible heat of his hardness between her closed thighs rubbing up against her wet flesh. She could feel the curling hairs on his naked legs pressing tight against her. "Oh God," Heather whimpered, shuddering as lust wrapped her in white heat. She could barely think through her body's hungry demand, and trembled.

"It's all up to you, princess," he whispered in her ear, his breath heaving with suppressed excitement. "How bad do you want me? I'm right here, ready for you, waiting for you." His voice dropped to barely a breath of sound. "Open up and let me in . . ." He pulled back, stroking himself between her legs, his shaft rasping against her moist slit, the swollen head of his cock damp with precum and her honey, sliding against her hot and excited clit.

With a soft cry of surrender, she arched back against him, positioning his heat against the opening to her body.

Releasing a groan, his arms tightened around her in a vicious grip. He surged forward into her welcoming depths and impaled her on his heavily erect cock. She felt him stretch her wide to make room for his fullness. He pulled her body back hard; rocking her against him as he forged in as far as he could go, possessing her utterly.

Heather cried out as her ravenous body was filled to bursting.

"Oh, Jezuz fuck, Heather," the werewolf growled.

His eyes lost focus with the pleasure of her heat encasing him. He pulled out a little only to lunge in, seating himself firmly in her tender flesh. With frenzied hands he released her hair and loosed her wrists from his belt. Using his hips, he shoved her forward onto her hands, then hooked an arm over her hip. With heavy strokes, he fucked her in a swift brutal rhythm, her body squeezing and sucking him in on every stroke.

His fingers found her tender clit and stroked her in time with his pounding thrusts. His other hand gripped her thigh, holding her steady as she shoved back against him. He pressed his chest against her back and drove into her softness again and again. Her inner muscles squeezed and caressed him as he moved within her.

Heather felt a bolt of fire sear from the base of her skull down her spine and let out a whimper as she writhed against him. She could feel her body clenching and tightening. The heat of him, the smell of him, the raw force of him thrusting and thrusting into her wanton flesh overwhelmed her senses. She was close, so close, right on the glittering razor's edge. Lava pooled in her belly and spread to her shaking limbs. Pants became moans as the delicious warmth spread and blazed under her skin as sensual tension built at a fevered pitch.

The snow steamed around them from sudden heat.

Rafe smelled the scent of her climax building. The ripple of her power rose into a wave readying to burst in a flood. He could feel the pressure in his balls as he readied to spill into her heated depths. She was almost there, and he wanted to be sure they went together. His beast began to surface as hers neared its birth. He felt the fire in his bones as her power crested, feeding off his nearing peak, off his escalating power.

"Off, off." Heather heard him snarl viciously. Rafe suddenly stopped, pulling his hands away from her, and sat back on his haunches, still sheathed in her body. She swore viciously in frustration. The sound of ripping fabric reached her ears.

Startled, she looked over her shoulder to see him pulling the shreds of his shirt from his shoulders. Shoulders that looked larger, more menacing somehow. She caught his eye and gasped. His once-green eyes were molten gold in the gray snow light and glowing. He smiled, baring long canines.

Hands tipped in long curving claws reached for her and ripped her flannel shirt like tissue from her back, along with the tatters of her bra. With an arm around her waist, he stood up. He pulled her up with him still joined, his cock filling her. He was so tall that although he braced his legs wide her toes barely touched the coat they stood on. Violently, he tugged his pants down, ripping them, then kicking them off with his boots following. Her wet jeans followed, ripping under his claws, pulling her shoes off with her pants.

"Now," he growled in a voice no longer human in any way. "Now we change, skin to skin, you and I." His arms closed around her, his clawed hands raking down her lightly, scoring her breasts and stomach with red lines that didn't quite break the skin. Lifting her bodily, he cupped her mons, with his palm riding directly on her fevered clit. Holding her fast in his arms, his fingers digging in, his claws lightly marking her arms and body, he thrust powerfully into her again and again as they stood locked together in the falling snow. His muscles bunched and flexed as he strove to keep them both standing upright.

She moaned long and loud as she felt the fire sizzle up from her filled pussy, hammered to the brink of a crushing orgasm. The ball of fire at the base of her skull blazed outward in a firestorm under her skin to consume her. Her skin tingled and jumped as a streak of lightning blazed a path down her spine. She felt feverish and shaky, writhing against his hard body and harder flesh. Her mouth opened on a long, throaty, glorious cry.

"Let it come, princess. Let it consume your flesh and bone and blood," the werewolf snarled fiercely in her ear. "Cum for me," he groaned as he pounded into her.

She felt the crest of pure ecstasy, then screamed as she fell into glory. Fire blazed up her body in a joyous red wave. She shrieked with a pleasure so fierce it was closer to agonizing pain. She barely heard his screams as he joined her, suffering the throes of his own climax.

He howled as he released himself into her body, the power of her orgasm rushing through him in an inferno. Heat and rapture swallowed them both. Fire burned and writhed under their skin, power grinding through them, twisting and changing muscle and bone. Her triumphant howls joined his as they fell to the ground in the snow, still locked intimately.

She snapped awake, lying on his coat in the snow, her fur mingled with his as he lay beside her. His scent was warm and comforting to her sensitive nose.

Looking about, her sight seemed strangely dimmed, but the perfume of dormant trees and plants were strangely colored.

How can perfume be colored? she thought briefly, and then became distracted by the bell-chime sounds of wind pushing ice-rimmed branches against each other.

Her ears swiveled, and she heard the crystal tinkling of falling snow. The world was huge and crowded with sounds and sensations she'd never felt before.

His sleek wolf's head turned, and he regarded the silver she-wolf from golden eyes. Playfully he gripped her long muzzle with his powerful jaws in greeting.

She mischievously nipped his narrow shoulder with her sharp teeth. The glossy lupine head of her lover with its tall ears and white serrated smile was handsome to her new eyes. His black fur was thick and luxurious with its winter coat.

He nudged her shoulder to rise, and power surged through her new form.

She leapt in delight with her newborn body.

He jumped up and grabbed for her plumed tail playfully, his magnificent tail streaming out behind him.

They dashed off in the fresh snow, two wolves running side by side on paws that barely felt the ground.

Now we hunt, whispered through her thoughts.

TEMPLE OF LILLITH: LOVE IMMORTAL

For PsiVamp
Overture

"It's perfect, exactly what I need for my private ritual." The ceremonial magician grinned and pulled off his sunglasses to wipe his eyes with his sleeve. "A completely abandoned Egyptian temple out in the middle of nowhere, and nobody knows that I'm here." He tucked the dark glasses into his shirt pocket. Squinting his aqua eyes, he noticed how close the orange sun lay against the edge of the rolling dunes. "It's going to be really dark, really soon. No hunting around the outskirts of the temple for me. Looks like I get to set up camp right away."

He stopped the Range Rover just out of casual sight, parking it close to the crumbling mud-brick wall that bordered the temple yard. He frowned at the marks in the sand as he shut off the engine.

"The tire tracks in the sand are a dead give-away that somebody is here."

He climbed out of the rover and stretched; his shirt strained at the seams. *Hmm,* he thought while staring at the temple *I wonder why nobody's put a fence around this old relic to charge admission?* Pocketing the ignition keys, he pulled the battered fedora from his head and gave his hat a smack against his leg, knocking out the dust from the hat in a cloud.

There's no real road anywhere near. He scraped his hand through the military-short, sun-bleached, blonde spikes of his

126

hair and knocked the blown sand loose from his scalp. *Hell, the damn road ran out on me a long ways back, so, all those holier-than-thou Egyptologists could have missed it.* He firmly pulled his hat back on.

He watched as the sand curled from the roof of the temple to pile atop the dune behind it. *If this whole thing was buried in sand and the wind cleared it in the last dozen years or so, it could be that no one's found it yet,* he mused. The front of the roof was only a little higher than the back. If the wind had uncovered it, it was also possible that a sirocco windstorm could blow from the other direction and bury the entire temple overnight.

Raising his arm, he at wiped the sweat and grime on his forehead. "At the speed I was flying over the sand, I think I rattled a few teeth loose." He froze in mid-motion. "Oh shit, the violin!"

He took two strides to the back of the Rover and yanked open the trunk door. Carefully he pulled out the battered case of his violin. Flipping it open, he checked the instrument for damage after all the jouncing over the sand to get there. "Just fine." He whistled softly. "Not even dusty."

He stared hard at the waiting temple and frowned. "I have to make this fucking ritual work. I don't care if I have to raise Satan to do it, I will have my music back." He snapped the buckles to the violin case closed, then set the case carefully in the sand. "What's the use of being a musician that can't write music?"

With renewed determination, he went to get the rest of his stuff from the back of the battered Range Rover. Tossing his camping gear over his broad, muscular shoulder, he reached over and grabbed his heavy, red velvet, Magical Arte bag crammed with his ritual equipment from the passenger seat. He picked up the violin case, giving the vehicle's door a shove with his hip to close it.

He slogged across the heavy sand, stepped through the narrow gateway that was square and roofless, into the temple yard, then across more sand. He climbed the worn steps and glanced up at the towering lotus-capped pillars supporting the heavy stone roof. Traces of scarlet and indigo paint lingered in the deep grooves of the sculpted pillars.

"I didn't think paint would still be on anything sitting this long in the desert," he muttered in surprise. "I just hope to whatever god that the roof is still stable on this thing," he grumbled, stepping past the threshold and into the deep shadows of the half-buried temple.

Only a few steps into the entrance he was blinded by utter darkness. He dropped his pack on the floor to dig out his flashlight. Snapping the light on, the beam from his light tunneled back into deep shadow. He whistled softly under his breath. Big. The interior was much bigger than it looked from the outside. He focused the bright halogen beam on the walls. Brilliant animals, flowers, trees and nubile dancers leapt to colorful life under the torch beam.

"Damn, this looks like it was painted last week." He moved the light over exquisite birds and detailed antelopes cavorting in fields of reed and papyrus. "I haven't seen anything this well-preserved anywhere," he muttered.

He pointed his light up at the ceiling and took a startled breath. The entire ceiling was painted with constellations in a deep blue night sky. The whole mural glittered with stones embedded in the stone.

"I guess this temple hasn't been discovered yet." He smiled grimly. "The Egyptologists would have pulled the ceiling apart real fast." He hefted his backpack and violin, then strode deeper into the temple. His footsteps echoed as he crunched blown sand under his boot heels.

He discovered a doorway on his right. The brilliant beam of his light slid across carved dancing maidens, swooping owls and reclining lions framing the doorway. A white owl spread its lapis and mother-of-pearl wings over the doorway with eyes of solid gold set with onyx.

"Owls? Well, that's different." He pointed the powerful beam into the room. It was much larger than he expected. The sound of falling water caught his attention. He took two steps into the room. It was huge. It was at least nine feet to the ceiling, about thirty feet across, roughly sixty feet straight back and bare of all furnishings.

"Perfect." He smiled. "Plenty of room to do my ritual in here." The beam of his light glittered across a rippling surface at the far end of the long room. Water gushed musically in a restrained waterfall down a three-foot, base-relief carving in black marble outlined with hieroglyphs that seemed to be part of the back wall. The beautiful and elegant face of an exquisitely carved female goddess figure peeked through the falling water that flowed over and around perfect breasts. He could even make out the areola surrounding the erect nipples.

"Those Egyptians sure knew how to carve a woman," he mumbled in appreciation as he shined the flashlight beam all around the black marble goddess. Wings delicately folded down at her sides. Her arms were bent at the elbows with her hands lifted and clutching a loop in each palm.

"I wonder which goddess you're supposed to be?" He tilted his head to one side. "I see the wings, but you don't look like any Isis I've ever seen." His gaze dropped and he could make out the plump, pouting lower lips of her sex between her generous thighs. Water cascaded down the goddess's body and over raptor-clawed feet into a large, black marble basin sunk deep into the floor and big enough to swim in.

"Well now, an Egyptian bathtub." He chuckled. "Hell, I've seen swimming pools smaller than this," he muttered, dropping his pack to the stone floor with a muffled thump. Looking into the water, the smooth bottom was visible.

"Doesn't look too deep, and doesn't seem to have any critters swimming around," he noted. "Should be okay to swim in, and the gods know," he said with a quick, guilty look around, "I could really use a bath right now."

He dipped a finger into the water. The cool water flowed against his finger. "There's a current . . ." He looked up at the water cascading down the base-relief goddess. "Well, there would have to be, seeing as water is running into this thing and not spilling out over the edge. It has to be flowing somewhere."

The ceremonial magician stripped in record time. *I guess this'll take care of the purification part of my ritual,* he thought as he climbed nude into the cool water. *Now all I have to do is perform the spell itself.* He stared hard at the violin as he soaked.

INCANTATION

The ceremonial magician tucked his long red robes into his rope belt and away from his bare feet as he lit the seven white pillar candles, one at a time. His shadow loomed large and splintered from the multiple light sources. From his velvet belt pouch he pulled out a huge chunk of drawing chalk. Carefully he drew a huge circle, then began inscribing the complicated conjuring diagram on the stone floor within the glowing ring of candles.

Light from the Coleman camp stove flickered over the hieroglyphs and brilliantly painted carvings on the walls of the huge room he had found. The water from the fountain ran soothingly in the background.

In a strong and clear voice he called on the gods and spirits of his Arte to empower his design and witness his ritual as he drew. The archaic Latin and Arabic chant made strange echoes in the underground temple. He began to sense a vibration that resonated within his body.

He frowned as he chalked his diagram on the stone floor. In the erratic light of the candles and the cook-stove, the plain white lines seemed to be picking up the light and glowing. He could clearly make out every mark he had placed.

He continued to chant without hesitation, but his eyes grew wide as some of the inner traceries and symbols began to glow with color. Reds, blues, greens and gold began to race through his lines and glyphs as he completed them. The outer ring held a steady glow of bright white. Without stopping his incantation, he stood up and turned all the way around to look at the entire diagram. The design was definitely glowing. That had never happened in any of his previous rituals. He glanced hard at the chalk in his palm. It was stark white.

With the completion of his intricate illustration, he finished his chant. He stepped out of the conjuring circle carefully, without disturbing the chalked lines and archaic glyphs in their almost garish combination of colors. He looked back at the circle and realized that it was casting a light brighter than all the candles and his cook-stove combined.

"Fuck." he whispered, then grabbed his bag and pulled out his magical Arte book, his Grimoire, along with his silver ritual chalice and a bottle of expensive champagne. He took his violin out of the battered case that lay next to his pack and tucked it under one arm, unsheathing his ceremonial sword. Carrying everything, he reentered the glowing diagram.

Dropping to his knees in the circle, he placed his book on the floor in the exact center of the diagram. Flipping through the pages, he opened the book to the ritual he wished to perform.

He uncorked the champagne and caught the foam and some of the sparkling wine in the chalice, then tipped the bottle and filled the silver cup. Some of it ran over his hand and he sucked on his palm.

"Mmm, good stuff." Guiltily, he placed the filled chalice by his Grimoire.

Carefully observing the liturgy forms of the ritual, he stood and raised his consecrated and purified sword. He took a deep, calming breath, then pointed the sacred blade at the white ring that encircled his diagram and slowly turned in a full circle. In a resonant voice, he called out the arcane spell to raise a cone of power.

A whisper of a breeze brushed his cheek and he froze, spooked as he felt the unseen world around him stir. He heard a humming, a soft sigh that was barely a whisper of sound. At his feet, the outer ring of his diagram turned a hard gold, then became dancing flames that raced around the entire outer edge, completing the circle where it began.

Whoa. Okay, this is weird, he thought to himself. *So much for the formal invocation. I guess the spell is definitely working, but I don't remember it ever working this fast. I guess I better begin the actual spell.*

Raising his violin, he began his invocation.

"Gods and Spirits of the Ether, I ask that you grant me the inspiration to write music, for my soul is lost in the pathways of humanity and I am bereft. I ask that you show me the way back to my own soul and the music that resides in my dream within a dream."

Okay, he chided himself, *no more listening to the Moody Blues before bedtime.*

Carefully, he sat within the center of his glowing circle with his precious violin. Raising the instrument to his chin, he began to play the last song he had ever written. As he played, he poured his desire and need into his music. The song flowed from his violin, hauntingly beautiful and completely alien to this land of sand and sun.

Unnoticed, A breeze whispered through the chamber, circling from the magician in his circle of power. The candle flames danced with its passing and lightly swept the sand from the floor as it flowed outward and into the hallways of the temple. The music sailed clear and sweet, throughout the temple and the wind followed. The sound and its accompanying zephyr swept through stone and passageway, floating through room after undiscovered room.

He stopped, and the breeze fell. Echoes of his violin drifted through the stones and seemed to take forever to fade. He scrubbed his arm across his eyes, drying the tears that had dripped unnoticed down his cheeks.

He looked up as a strange howl echoed in the temple's depths, and then a powerful wind blew from the doorway and slammed into him. Wide-eyed, he noticed that the candles were not reacting, not even flickering in the strange wind. Arcane power danced on his nerves, his hair stood on end. It didn't feel angry or malignant.

Interest slithered into his mind. Something was perusing his mind and body with sexual interest, like a queen assessing a new love-slave.

The power suddenly gathered, coalesced and solidified until he could actually feel it moving against his skin. It snaked around his body, closing around his wrists in a vice-grip. His arms were suddenly jerked wide, to either side.

"Fuck!" he swore as he fought against dropping his violin. He couldn't move. His arms felt as though they were manacled with steel straight out from his sides. He wiggled his fingers. They seemed to be working just fine. He tried to stand, but his wrists felt like they were pinned to stone posts. He looked around but whatever was holding him was invisible.

"Shit! I don't believe this." He felt the arcane power slide under his loose robe with disembodied hands to explore him. He clearly felt something fondling his dick, stroking him intimately, and he was powerless to do anything. His nipples hardened and his temperature soared as his body responded to the carnal exploration.

"Fuck me! I'm getting a hard-on."

His belt loosened and his robe opened to expose his naked body as he knelt on the hard stone floor. His breath heaved as he fought the power holding him. His engorged shaft jutted upward, obscenely swollen. The head of his cock was purple with excitement, and a drop of liquid formed at the tip.

The power seized his wanton flesh and he threw his head back, feeling an orgasm rising without his control. His body convulsed and he shouted as his seed burst from his swollen cock to splatter the floor.

As suddenly as it came, the power left. The ceremonial

magician fell forward in reaction, gasping. He turned and his shoulder hit the stone floor, his violin cradled in his arms.

"Well, that was certainly fucked up," he said between pants, then rose to his knees. He looked, but there was no trace of the semen he had spattered on the floor. Carefully he placed the violin to one side, retied his robe, then grabbed the chalice of champagne.

"I better finish the ritual." He took a swallow to wet his dry mouth. "Before anything else weird happens."

Formally he raised the chalice of champagne and poured it out on the stone floor in libation, thanking the attending spirits in the archaic language of the closing ritual.

His eyes widened as the champagne soaked into the stone as quickly as it was poured from the chalice. Without hesitation, he grabbed the mostly full bottle and continued to pour the very expensive champagne on the temple floor. The bottle emptied and not a drop was left to mark the spot. He placed his fingers on the stone. Bone dry. A hard shiver raced up his spine.

He bowed formally, then picked up the silver bell that sat near his book. The sharp sweet tones from the bell marked the completion of his formal spell.

"Okay, all attendant spirits go home," he said irreverently. "And thanks for the thrill."

He picked up the sword, stood and turned in a circle to disperse the magical energy of his conjure circle. Carefully, he gave the closing benediction.

The gold light dropped from the outer ring and the colors bled away from the diagram, fading until only white chalk lines remained. The flames of the seven guttering candles that circled his chalk diagram suddenly began winking out one by one, by themselves, until only the cook-stove cast light.

Tired to the bone, he left the circle, lit a candle that would last all night, put out the cook-stove, then dropped, still formally robed, onto his air mattress. In seconds, he was asleep.

Within the depths of the temple, gentle laughter echoed softly and whispered through his dreams.

AVOCATION

He yawned and sat up in his bedding. The blue glow of his watch said it was late morning, but there was no way to really tell in the absolute darkness of the underground temple. He remembered dreaming, and he remembered that a beautiful woman had been in his dreams. But for the life of him, he couldn't remember more than that.

Yawning, he rolled off the air mattress and lit the camp light, then the small Coleman cook-stove. Breakfast could come after clean-up, but coffee came before everything.

The firelight bathed the room in soft gold as he got out of his sleep-wrinkled robe. After a quick wash, he dressed in fresh jeans that were nearly white with wear, and a loose, white, cotton shirt that he left open to the waist. He was not looking forward to the long trek back across the desert to the hotel, where the rest of the orchestra waited.

Carefully, he packed away his magical apparatus then scrubbed all traces of chalk from the stone floor. There was still no trace of the champagne he had spilled on the floor. Odder still, there wasn't a trace of spilled wax from any of the seven candles either.

"Do I really want to know?" he asked himself, then judiciously decided that he really didn't. With a mental shrug, he grabbed his supplies and started cooking breakfast.

"Mmm, smells good. Got enough for two?" said a musical female voice.

"What?" The magician turned around so fast, he landed on his butt. He blinked and his mouth fell open in shock. A gorgeous girl was standing at the doorway of the chamber.

"Oh, that was a graceful landing." She chuckled, showing an adorable dimple in a delicate and exotic face. Her eyes were onyx black, outlined in dark kohl and her lips were red as blood. Her hair was black silk, with fringe hanging straight across her brow and the rest hanging straight and fine to her hips, trimmed evenly across. Her skin glowed pale as alabaster and without a trace of tan.

Where the hell did she come from? She was the absolute last thing he expected to find in an abandoned temple, and she was smiling at him. *I didn't see anything, not even a Bedouin tent, anywhere near here.* He rubbed his eyes. *Am I still asleep?* He looked again, and she was still there.

She moved into the room with an elegance that seemed closer to dance than a stride. The blood-red T-shirt was snug against her breasts, and the generous sway suggested her lack of a bra. Her boot heels clicked on the hard stone floor. The snug black jeans she wore emphasized her rounded thighs, broad hips and narrow waist.

She raised a dark brow. "I asked if you had enough to serve two."

He closed his mouth with a snap. "Uh, yeah, sure." He grabbed the second bowl from his pile of camping stuff and shoveled instant oatmeal, thick with raisins and sweetened with cinnamon and sugar, into it. Convinced that she was going to fade into mist, proving that she was a figment of too much sun and too little sleep, he held out the bowl with both hands.

Heavy silver bracelets jingled as she bent over him to take the bowl and spoon. Only inches from his nose, her nipples stood firm against the scarlet fabric. He could feel his dick swelling in interest.

"Damn, I'm starved." She grinned broadly as she sat cross-legged. She took a bite, then another. "This is good," she said between bites. "Mm, I haven't had something this good in a long time. Thanks."

"You're welcome. It's just something I threw together," he said, breathlessly. She seemed to be real. She was so fucking beautiful. "How about some coffee? I have powdered cream and packets of sugar."

"Coffee sounds great."

"I'm, uh, Sean," he said as he poured coffee into a tin cup, handing it to her. "So, uh, how'd you get here?"

"I'm Lilli. Nice to meet you, Sean." She mixed sugar and powdered creamer into her coffee and sipped. "Mmm, this is heavenly. I live here."

"You live." He choked. "Here?" The coffee he was stirring creamer into spilled on his knee. He hissed and swore softly, grabbing for the towel lying on his pack.

Her musical chuckles became outright laughter. "Silly me." She smiled and placed her coffee cup on the floor. "You were expecting someone else?" She rose to her feet in one smooth graceful move. "Ah, I get it! You were expecting someone more like this."

Her black hair floated up in a cloud of arcane power that brought cold chills down Sean's spine. The hair all over his body suddenly stood at attention. The scent of heat and sex filled the chamber and slammed him low in the gut. A cascade of golden sparks flared in a corona around her then blazed in a blinding flash.

An Egyptian goddess in a sheer flowing gown and ornate gold collar stood in a flaming aura of power. Her long hair was ornately braided with bright gold coins and milky opalescent orbs of moonstones. Her closed eyes were heavily outlined in kohl with decorative curls, and her lids were dusted with gold and amethyst. Her lips were heavily painted and outlined in black. Her arms crossed formally over perfect breasts that were tipped in scarlet and heaved gently with her breath. Her skin was as white as milk. Her sheer white gown began just below her bosom, revealing the perfection of her form. Her long, exquisite legs ended in feet clawed like a raptor, a bird of prey.

"You have called, and I came," intoned a voice laced with eons of time and rippling with accents of languages long gone to dust.

She opened her eyes, and they were a solid onyx black with stars in their depths. She spread her hands and snowy wings unfolded from her shoulders to spread almost the full length of the room.

"Oh my God." Sean choked, then rose unsteadily to his feet, his breakfast forgotten. This had to be a dream, goddesses just didn't appear for no apparent reason, and certainly not in tight jeans. Whatever she was, his dick certainly approved. He was so violently hard he was convinced that he was going to spill in his pants.

"Goddess?" she suggested with a mischievous smile. The curve of long incisors showed over her full bottom lip.

"Goddess?" he echoed, stunned.

"Well, yes." She chuckled. "Lillith. You know, one of the Queens of the Starry Heavens, and all that." She shrugged and her breasts jiggled delightfully. She knelt on her raptor-clawed feet, and her ankles appeared to be in an odd place. Her wings folded over her back, arching high over both their heads then falling in a long graceful arch to brush the stone floor with a soft rustle for such large feathers. Her braids swung as she sat carefully on the floor in her sheer gown.

She picked up her coffee, smiling as she sipped. "Have a seat, Sean."

Sean sat, or rather, collapsed, then winced. His jeans were squeezing his dick too tightly. He sat up on his knees to give himself room. Staring at her in shock he picked up his coffee, just to have something in his shaking hands.

I called a Goddess. The thought raced in a circle in his mind. *I called a Goddess?* He sipped his coffee and grimaced. *Damn, forgot the sugar.* He turned and reached for the sugar.

He looked back at her as he stirred sugar into his cup, and discovered that she was back in black jeans and scarlet T-shirt, normal feet and no wings. He sighed in relief. *Maybe I imagined it?* She looked at him and her eyes were still pits of onyx with stars. *Maybe I didn't imagine it.*

"Wait a minute," he said as his brow creased in thought, "if you're Lillith, what are you doing in an Egyptian temple?" Sean shifted to one side, then the other, but he could not find a comfortable position with his dick that hard. "Aren't you supposed to be Assyrian or Babylonian or something?"

She laughed outright. "The Egyptians overran them so many times it's not funny. Just cause I started out there doesn't mean I stayed there. Ever notice how close Isis looks like me? Wings? Starry-night symbols? The crown and the ankh?"

"So you're Isis, too?" He sipped his coffee and found himself watching the way her long midnight hair slid lovingly across her breasts.

"Among a dozen other names as well. You called and I came. Is that so difficult to believe?"

Hell, yeah, it's hard to believe. However, his dick was having no problems at all believing that she was there, and he couldn't take the binding in his jeans anymore. He was finally forced to turn to the side and adjust himself in his jeans. He expelled a sigh of relief.

She grinned and the points of her fangs flashed with her dimple. "Like what you see?"

Sean blushed. Obviously, she'd seen that he'd had to make room for his hard-on. *Well, yeah, fangs and weird eyes aside . . ."*You're the most incredible female I've ever seen." *Jeez, I'm sharing coffee with a goddess.* "But I wasn't trying to call a goddess. The spell I did was just to get my music back."

She tilted her head to one side. "Your music?"

"Yeah. Uh." *Gods, this is painful to talk about.* "I've always had music in my head, ever since I was a kid, but lately, it feels like I'm empty inside." It had been a private battle with himself for the past year. Especially when the people he played concert violin with knew the music he had been writing over a year ago.

"What happened to your music?" she looked down at her tin cup, then back up at Sean, and her eyes were back to normal human black pupils.

"I just don't know." He shook his head in confusion. Her smile seemed to be loosening something inside him. He was still marble-hard, but he could at least hold some semblance of a conversation around his rampant libido.

"For the past three years or so, I've been playing the violin in concerts and orchestras and I love playing, but I haven't been able to write any music at all for over a year now. Sometime last year, it just . . .dried up. I set up the um, spell because I can't write music anymore. Not one completed composition. Hell, not even part of a melody."

"So you used magic?" She sipped at her coffee.

"I've been practicing magic since I found my Dad's ritual books." About the same time he found his Dad's girlie magazines. He shrugged. Magic was something he normally didn't talk about. His friends knew, but even they had no idea how deep he really was into ceremonial magic.

He swept his hands through the short blonde spikes of his hair. "Magic seems to unlock things inside me when I get stuck, and I'm pretty damn stuck, but good, right now." He looked at the stunning woman in front of him. "I've been doing small magicks all my life, but I've never actually conjured anything, or any*one*, before." He shook his head. "I was only trying to call a muse, not a full blown, all-powerful goddess."

"Hey, flattery will get you everywhere." Lilli smiled wryly and sipped at her coffee. "So you were trying to invoke a traditional muse for inspiration and ended up in my temple?" Lilli cocked her head, then leaned like a lioness on her side, her long legs stretching and her muscular thighs flexing.

"I'm here in Egypt with the orchestra and then some old guy tells me about this abandoned temple. So, I thought, damn, here's my chance to do my ritual and see if I can unlock my music." His eyes became glued to the way her jeans molded between her luscious thighs, just outlining the plump female shape hidden there. "I, uh, didn't realize that I was in anybody's temple." He swallowed. "I mean, I didn't think anyone would still be uh . . .around. Look, I'm sorry if I, uh, disturbed you."

"You haven't disturbed me, Sean." She grinned, then shrugged. "It gets boring out here after a while. No one has come to visit in a long time, and the people that do just want to take my house apart." She sighed and looked around, then sat back up.

Sean's eyes locked onto the way her breasts moved invitingly under her shirt. He struggled to bring his eyes back to her face. "Um, I was just wondering, how is it that, your being an ancient goddess and all, you're, well." He waved at her modern clothes.

"A modern girl?" She grinned at his confusion. "I live in a temple in the middle of nowhere, but I'm still a goddess. I like to keep in touch with the rest of the world, so every once in a while I go out and spend time as a . . ." she hesitated. "As a mortal."

He made a sour face, ignoring her hesitation. "I see what you mean. Not a whole lot of excitement in this neighborhood. The closest dance club is hours away, in Cairo, or Luxor. Kinda hard to show a pretty lady a good time, unless you're into camels."

"So," she pursed her lips in a sexy pout. "If you were going to show a lady a good time, what would you do?" She leaned forward. The very tip of her tongue brushed her lower lip.

"Uh . . ." Sean found himself thinking only of her full red lips. They looked so soft and succulent. So much for having his libido under control. "I, uh, well there's a candlelight dinner."

"We're off to a good start. Candlelight breakfast, at least." She grinned and leaned closer.

"Champagne." Sean tore his eyes from her mouth and focused on her incredible features. He struggled for self-control. Her eyes were pools of dark female mysteries.

"Which I had last night. Delicious, by the way." She moved a little closer.

"Yeah, and then dancing," he said softly and realized that her lips were only inches away from his. He could smell the rich exotic fragrance of sandalwood and amber laced with cinnamon and warm excited woman. Desire blazed a wildfire through him. Suddenly he could smell his own naked desire. His erection was uncomfortably tight in his jeans and thrumming in time to his pulse. He shifted to ease himself.

"And?"

Her breath stroked against his mouth. "Kisses," he murmured, focused on the red ripeness of her lips.

"I like kisses," she whispered, then pressed her rich red mouth to his.

His mouth opened in surprise and her tongue slid in to brush his. He opened wider to taste her. Warmth. Heat. She tasted of cinnamon and sugar. Need and carnal hunger hammered at him. As he sucked on her lower lip, she nipped him. The copper taste of blood bloomed briefly in his mouth.

Shit. Forgot about the fangs, he thought vaguely.

He felt her soft hand on his thigh, gripping almost painfully hard. She pulled his legs apart, making room for herself.

She surged between his legs, pressing those magnificent breasts and hard nipples to his open shirt and bare chest. He felt her hips, then her mons shifting against his restrained erection. All thought ceased. His body was a ravenous inferno for this incredible woman in his arms.

He wrapped his arms around her and hooked his legs around hers, trapping her heat against his. She moved against him, and he groaned with the delicious friction. He felt her tug the shirt from his pants, then off his shoulders. Her small hand touched his stomach, sliding up to his chest. She tugged on his chest curls, sliding her palm over his nipples. Her fingers dug lightly, and he could feel her nails scoring him. He moaned into her mouth and felt her answering moan.

He leaned forward, sitting up and taking her with him. His hands came up and cupped the globes of her ass. He dug his fingers in, to feel her muscles clenching. One hand followed the back seam of her jeans down and under to the fragrant heat of her feminine core. His fingers felt for the soft plumpness that hid her clit beneath a layer of denim. He pressed his fingers against her rhythmically. She writhed against his fingers with a small gasp, then arched her neck back, breaking their kiss. His lips sought her throat. Using his tongue and his teeth gently, he tasted and nibbled.

He opened his eyes to see a smile on her lips as he nibbled. He brought both hands up her smooth back to burrow under her shirt. He leaned forward, pressing her back against the cool floor. Limber as a gymnast, she folded back with her knees splayed and her heels by her sides.

He folded his knees under and swept his hands under her shirt, shoving it up. He squeezed and dug his fingers into their softness. Her breasts were perfect; the exact size to fit his hands. The need to taste her nipples took him and his mouth closed on her breast, tasting, licking, and sucking, first one, then the other. Her arms closed on him as he feasted. Her

145

moans of pleasure acted as spurs. He caught one nipple in his teeth and tugged. She whimpered, then grabbed his head to pull him closer.

Without thought, he slid one hand down to the button of her jeans and tugged it open. He found her zipper, drew it down, then reached into her open jeans. His fingers delved into softness.

"Damn, baby, you shave," he said in wonder. Her dew dampened his fingers.

"Do you like?" she whispered in a throaty moan, writhing as his fingers found her excited and swollen bud swimming in a pool of liquid warmth.

"Oh God, ahem . . .Goddess, yes!" He pressed her clit gently and she gasped deliciously, opening wider to his explorations.

Encouraged, he burrowed two fingers into her moist heat, seeking that sensitive place deep within. He found the soft mass of nerves and stroked. Her mouth opened wide as she arched her back in delight. She grabbed his wrist to hold him in place, pressing his mouth to her breast as she took her pleasure.

He scissored his fingers, increasing the speed and pressure within while brushing his thumb against her swollen, excited bud relentlessly.

He felt the violent tremors of her orgasm ripple through her. Her pearly essence slicked his palm, and she keened loud and long with gratification. With a grin, he pulled his hand from her pants, then licked his palm and sucked her desire from his fingers.

"Mmm. I love a considerate man," she said with a definite purr. She leaned all the way back, then stretched luxuriously on the floor, like a kitten.

"Let's get these jeans off." He pulled her legs straight so he could tug off her boots. "I want to really taste you."

"Tell you what, I'll let you take off mine." She chuckled and then sat up. "If I get to take off yours, and I get to taste you."

"It's a deal!"

"But first, why don't we make ourselves comfortable?"

"I still have the air mattress set up," he offered, looking over to the wilted mattress and its rumpled blankets on the stone floor by the flickering camp stove.

"I have a better idea." She took his hands in hers. "Close your eyes, Sean."

Sean felt the hair on his neck rise. He squeezed his eyes shut.

DANSE

Sean felt a warm wind, and abruptly, he was falling. He landed butt-first on something incredibly soft and resilient. His eyes snapped open just in time to catch Lilli as she landed on top of him.

"Whoa, hey!" They were rolling in what seemed to be, a mountain of heavily embroidered pillows of every size, shape and description. "You sure know how to get around!" He struggled to sit up. The huge, heavy framed, black marble bed they were laying on was carved with lions and owls. Sheer white silks draped and canopied the towering monstrosity.

"Well, what do you think?" She grinned as she straddled his hips.

Leaning up amongst the multitude of pillows he looked around. "Will *wow* do?" he asked, his eyes wide. "I mean, this is incredible!" He sat all the way up on the glittering pillows to take in the entire room.

The huge bed they sat on was centered in a gigantic room with tall Egyptian archways leading to a dizzying array of smaller rooms and small alcoves. The ceiling overhead was a dome of gleaming black glass inset with gold and glittering gems. Blazing torchiers were stationed in the corners of the room and the leaping flames gleamed on huge framed mirrors. Pre-Raphaelite paintings and huge medieval tapestries graced walls made of huge blocks of polished, white marble. Squinting, he thought he could make out an old Beatles poster in one of the smaller rooms.

Scattered about the corners of the rooms were massive

wardrobes oozing with clothes in exotic colors and fabrics. Comfortable chairs upholstered in velvets were grouped with other chairs so delicate, they looked as though they would shatter if you sat on them. Ornate tables and sculpted dressers were scattered with a dizzying array of statues, nick-knacks and trinkets from countries and cultures from all over the world and from every century.

"Hey, is that a computer desk over there?" he asked, pointing into a small room off one side.

"Oh, you got me!" she laughed. "I'm a chat-room junkie. I told you, I like to keep in touch."

"What have you got it plugged into? I mean it's not as if there's power or phone lines way out here." He glanced over to see her look of amusement.

"I'm on AOL: Asgard On Line. Oh, and Atlantis Internet, and then I've got an account with Heaven Link."

"Oh, that's right," he said dryly. "You're a goddess."

She rolled her eyes and threw her arms around his neck. "I just knew you'd figure it out." She smiled and pressed her cheek against his breast, rubbing her body against his in warm invitation.

"Wait a minute," he said softly. She smiled as he took her hand and lifted it to his lips for a soft kiss. "Isn't there something we're supposed to be doing?" he asked, then leaned over and lightly explored her lips with a finger. Her onyx eyes were gleaming and lovely with their exotic tilt.

"Doing?"

She opened her mouth and Sean dipped the tip of his finger in. She wrapped her lips around his digit and sucked, clamping her teeth. He groaned with the sensual feel of her damp tongue swirling suggestively against his finger.

He smiled. "Yeah, doing." She released his finger and he leaned over to kiss her mouth. She opened beneath his lips and her fingers burrowed under his shirt to dig her nails into his bare shoulders.

"Like, getting naked?" she asked against his lips.

"Oh, yeah," he said softly. He suddenly deepened the kiss, pushing her back to sit among the pillows, ravenously devouring her lips and tongue as he slid his hands under the back of her red T-shirt. Sitting up, he caught the fabric and pulled it up over her head, baring her perfect breasts to his eager gaze.

Her fingers busied themselves stripping the shirt from his shoulders, then tossing it to the end of the huge bed. His fingers hurriedly opened her jeans, then slid inside and around to cup his hands around the firm globes of her ass.

His hungry mouth took her lips once more, then he nibbled down her jaw, stroking his tongue across the pulse throbbing under the tender skin of her throat. He knelt, then swirled his tongue damply around the pale rosy nipple of her breast where he laid claim, sucking with lips and nipping with his teeth.

Her fingers worked his belt open and his fly down. He hissed in pleasure as she slid her cool hand within and found him, then softly explored his heated flesh. She leaned forward and nipped at his small and painfully erect nipples, then shoved him onto his back to pull his jeans down to his knees. His swollen cock stood at attention aggressively. He hissed as her fingers closed on him and explored his shape and length.

She chuckled. "What a very fine, um, instrument you have here."

Unconsciously, his cock pulsed in her hold, and a glistening drop of moisture formed at the tip.

"I'll be happy to play any tune you like with it," he said, groaning. He climbed up onto the bed and she released him reluctantly. Grinning lasciviously, he helped her struggle from her jeans, then tossed them to the end of her bed.

She fell back on a mound of bright pillows with her knees

splayed wantonly. The pink petals of her intimate female flesh glistened with dew. Her feminine perfume was warm and intoxicating.

"Ah ha!" he grinned as she smiled up at him. He pressed his lips to her bare mound and darted a tongue into her moist and fragrant core. She was sweet and silky on his tongue.

She sighed heavily, then gripped his hair and suddenly pulled him away.

"Hey!" he yelped, then licked her sweet essence from his lips. "I was enjoying that."

"I want you naked." Her smile was feral and hungry. "And I want it now."

He smiled ruefully, rubbing at his nearly uprooted scalp. "Your wish is my command." He tugged his jeans the rest of the way off, tossing them on the end of the huge bed. "Better?"

She nodded. "Much. Now come over here."

He crawled toward her, on his hands and knees and reached for her.

She took both his hands to hold him still. "No, don't touch me," she said softly. "I want to touch you."

He sank back among the pillows and her long nails made red lines on his stomach. He sucked in a breath. The slight sting was strangely exciting.

She mused for a moment, then gave him a serious look. "Sean, I've been thinking."

"Uh, oh." He gave her a playful flinch; partly from her long nails on his skin and partly from her sober demeanor. "Am I in trouble?"

"Could be." She looked up at him from the corner of her eye. "It has been a very long time since I've been with a man who knew me for what I truly am."

"Meaning, a very long time since you've been with someone who knows that you're a goddess?"

"Yes." She pressed a light kiss on the red welts she'd raised. "It's been even longer since anyone deliberately came seeking me." She pressed her cheek against his bare chest rubbing against the marks she'd made. "I want to gift you with my full immortal ardor." She frowned thoughtfully. "I think I said that right."

"You want to make love with me as a goddess?" He frowned. "Isn't that what we're doing now?"

"Not really." Lilli tilted her head and nibbled her lower lip. "I want to make love to you in my true form."

Sean swallowed. "You mean wings and um, claws?"

She nodded. "Yes, but only if you're willing."

Sex with a goddess, in her goddess form, he thought. *Cool!* Then, he thought some more. There were lots of stories about mortals that died seeing gods in their true forms, and most of the fatal tales were about mortal men hopping in the sack with goddesses. He wanted to ask if it was going to hurt, but he was afraid that he already knew the answer. *Shit! Never mind the pain, will I survive?*

"Oh yes, you'll survive." She chuckled as he flinched, answering his unasked question, but her eyes were very serious. "And yes, it will very likely hurt."

"Okay, I get it, telepathy too." He gave her an amused glance.

Lilli bit her lip. "Well, I am . . ."

"Yeah, I know, you're a goddess." He took her face in his palms and looked deep into her onyx eyes. "Look, I believe you already, okay?" He dropped a gentle kiss on her lips, then wrapped his arms around her in a hug. "Look, if it will give you pleasure, then I am yours to do with as you please, and hey," he added as he grinned down at her, "I get a chance to have sex with an actual goddess, the most perfect woman imaginable! So I get a few permanent scars from the experience." He shrugged. "As long as I get to live to tell the tale, I figure, so what?"

"You agree?"

"Do I get to call you *My Immortal Beloved* like Beethoven?"

"Oh, please! He was a great musician, but he was a pompous ass, too."

He choked. "Don't tell me! You and Beethoven?"

"Look . . ." She grinned and shook a finger at him. "I won't ask about your ex-lovers if you don't ask about mine, okay?"

"It a deal!" He really, really didn't want to know anyway.

Lilli grinned impishly. "And for the record, he only suspected, he didn't know for sure." Her expression grew serious. "Are you really sure you want to do this my way?"

"Hell, woman, when do we start?"

"Take my hand." It was a command, not a request.

He took her outstretched hand and felt eldritch power rippling through her fingers and up his arm as though he handled live electricity. A wind of tingling vibrancy swirled violently around them both and he watched Lilli's eyes become pits of starlit darkness. Wings of light unfolded from her shoulders.

She tugged him into her embrace. His hands gripped her winged body, brushing feathers. He felt clawed fingertips dig in. *Oh, yeah, this is gonna hurt,* he thought.

"Our journey begins with a kiss," she whispered.

His mouth opened to hers, and he felt the sharp prick of long incisors against his tongue. Her tongue captured his, then the copper taste of fresh blood flooded his mouth.

Taste of my blood, she whispered directly into his thoughts, *that we may share more than your body might normally withstand, my love.*

He swallowed instinctively and felt a cool line of liquid run down his chin.

My prey.

He felt himself lifted powerfully and swiftly into darkness on feathered wings of burning light. Her arms held him close and were unimaginably powerful. Darkness, an impression of clouds, stars and the fresh scent of night raced past his senses with eye-watering speed as they rose higher in the evening sky. I thought it was still morning?

The night is my domain, he felt her whisper. Her voice in his mind swelled in a wave of warm velvety fur that stroked him from within.

The dome of the evening sky, the veil of stars and the restless moon are all mine. All darkness is mine.

Her claws dug deep into his back, and her legs rose to wrap securely around him, embracing him and imprisoning him against the heated silk of her body. His hands sought the perfection of her breasts, his mouth sucked in the delicate fruit of her tender nipples, and she encouraged his bite. His mouth captured her breast, and he bit down with her unspoken encouragement, breaking fragile skin, tasting the sweet sharp copper of blood. He felt her lips caress his throat.

The shadows where lust and love intertwine, the inner dark of the haunted and hunted soul, the gray veils of sleep are the places where I dwell.

He felt the brush of her tongue and the edged caress of fangs. Her feminine liquid essence slithered across his thighs and belly.

Unto the gates of sleep and death.

Long fangs slid like burning knives into the column of his throat, and he choked. Searing pain screamed across his mind only to become overwhelmed by violent, blood-tinted pleasure screaming through his body.

I am Lillith, the Hunter in the Night, and you are my beloved, my prey. Her lips locked to his throat and she fed.

He gasped, shuddering as passion and carnal hunger rose in a vicious, unrelenting inferno. Independent thought became impossible as he felt her needs projected into his mind, overwhelming him to become his most abject desire. His arms pinned her to him. His hips drove upward as his aching cock sought entrance and salvation in her damp, voracious heat.

She writhed against him, and he found her moist opening. Muscles strained and he entered triumphant, then burrowed deep. She gasped and he exulted in his possession. Her clawed fingers dug into his back, her raptor's claws gouged his thighs, her damp internal heat sucking at his painfully swollen cock. She rode him, her body writhing, her nether mouth hungrily sucking at his cock as he strove to thrust in their embrace. Agony and ecstasy intertwined and became one.

Her wings brushed him, and they stopped rising. Momentarily, they held in perfect balance, the night sky all around — no up, no down — wrapped in stars and each other, writhing, gasping as he thrust and she undulated in divine lust, impaled by his flesh, locked in each other's ravenous embrace. Ribbons of blood entwined around their bodies as they clawed and devoured each other.

Her wings wrapped, enclosing them both, and they plummeted. Falling at unimaginable speed, the wind and her enfolding wings pressed against his back as she straddled him, rocking against him and taking her pleasure.

Plunging toward the unforgiving Earth, he could feel her blossoming rapture, her trembling culmination expanding as it echoed through their joined bodies and entwined souls. A tempest of growing rhapsody rose painfully in his body; they vibrated mind-to-mind, soul to soul, in perfect resonance like twinned tuning forks in their mutual intimate pleasure. An excruciating and blinding climax blazed through them and they screamed, incandescent in their exultation.

Falling, searing joy and pain took him. His liquid essence spewed into her eager heat.

She released him, separating her flesh from his. He cried out in loss and turned in his fall to face the world below. The landscape of the Earth was very close, and he could see the temple below approaching swiftly. He could see the sunlit rim of the world. It was so beautiful.

Suddenly, she recaptured him, hooking herself to his back. *Beloved,* whispered through his thoughts and the searing joyful agony of her fangs took his throat once more. Music suddenly swelled in his mind.

She spread her moon-bright wings, slowing their descent. Her arms held him against her breast, her finger claws and talons digging deep into his gouged and bloody body, slowing their fall to a soft descending glide. He could feel the pulse of his heart pouring into her body, strengthening the pounding thunder of her heart.

Am I dying? Is this death?

And still they fell.

INCANDESCENCE

The shock of landing.

His body bucked, flinching in unconscious reaction. He felt the heavy bounce of his body hitting a mattress with his face muffled in softness.

Sean jerked at the blankets he was lying face down on, sat upon his knees and glanced around. His eyes opened wide in the dim light. The room was cast in grayness, but he could still make out the furniture around him. He was in his bed at the hotel in Luxor.

"Fuck!" he swore. "Don't tell me that was all a fucking dream!" He grabbed a pillow and tossed it across the room, then flopped over onto his back.

Fire lanced him across his back. "Oh, God!" he hissed and sat up. "What the hell?" His fingers slid across his back. He winced as he encountered raised welts. He lunged out of bed and slammed the light on over the sink.

"What the fuck?" He stared in the mirror stunned. His eyes locked on a tattoo of a stylized Egyptian lioness's head biting into his shoulder. "Damn." He whistled. It was gorgeous. Slowly he turned around to see his back.

The stylized body of the lioness wrapped his entire back, the claws digging ink furrows into his opposite shoulder, down his waist and around his thigh. The tail curled around the opposite thigh. Raptor wings sprouted from the lioness's shoulders, covering his back in stylized feathers. Somehow, he knew they were owl's wings.

"So it wasn't a dream." The thread of a tune began to

whisper through his thoughts. Sean's eyes widened in the mirror as the tune began to pulse with a heavy Middle-Eastern drumbeat. His music, it was back! Sean stared at his refection as his inner music began to swell powerfully within him.

A banging noise shocked him and he jumped. Someone was at his door.

"Fuck," he swore. "I almost had that damned tune." Sean grabbed one of the small bath towels to cover his nakedness and tromped from the bright bathroom through the darkened room to the door. His foot caught on something and he tripped. The banging came again.

"Coming!" he yelled out, reached over and clicked on the small lamp on the desk. He flung his arm up over his eyes and hissed. "Shit! The light wasn't this bright this morning, they must have changed the bulb on me."

Sean turned to look at what he had tripped over. His foot was caught in the strap of his Arte bag. His camping equipment was jumbled in a heap in the middle of the floor on a big pile of sand.

The knock came again only this time, it sounded like someone was actually kicking the door. He stared at the floor for a moment, then ran to the door. He unlocked the door and found the hotel manager staring at him.

"Can I help you?" he said and flinched back from the light in the hall — damn, it was bright.

"Sir, I realize that this is the middle of the night, however your car is in the middle of the parking lot and it is blocking our guests. Could you move it please?"

"Um, sure," Sean said in some confusion. What the hell was going on? "Let me get some clothes on, I'll be right down."

Sean shut the door in the manager's face and ran for the bedroom. His clothes were scattered all over the room and everything was dusted with fine sand. He bit out a curse, pulled his car keys and more sand from his jeans pocket, and ran to get something clean from his drawers instead.

Sean's booted toe tapped to an inner rhythm as he descended to the hotel lobby in the elevator. The new tune was still with him. His shoulders and back itched under the soft cotton of the T-shirt.

One of the hotel staff met him in the lobby and walked out into the huge parking lot. Sean found his jeep sitting cockeyed on a huge pile of sand right in the middle of the main lot, as though it had been dropped there. He did not want to think on how it could have gotten there, but he suddenly suspected why he didn't remember the drive back.

EPILOGUE

"Hey are you ready yet?" A fist banged the door of Sean's tiny dressing room. "We got a concert to put on!" It was the distinct voice of his drummer, impatient as always. The smell of clove cigarettes was thick in the cramped room, and thicker out on the dance floor of the Goth club.

"On my way!" Sean shouted back. He shrugged into the silky black shirt, but left it unbuttoned. He was going to take it off during the first song anyway to show off the tattoo. The stylized Egyptian art would go perfectly with the first song from the new album. It was the first piece he'd written after his one-year dry spell.

"You know," yelled the drummer through the door, "you would have been done already if you had gotten here during the day—with the rest of the band!"

"Yeah, yeah, whatever." Sean grumped as he slicked his hair back with gel. There was just no way to explain to the guys that he'd come out of Egypt with a problem with daylight. Thank God for sun block! He grinned in the mirror as he absently tucked his sunglasses into the back of his shirt, hooking them on the collar. They thought the dark glasses were just so he could look cool. Even some of the stage lights burned his sensitive eyes. Long incisors peeked over his bottom lip, and he automatically adjusted his smile to hide them.

He hurried out of the narrow room and down the hall to ram into a small and soft body. "Oh, sorry!" he apologized, then stopped in his tracks.

"Oh! Hey!" she said. The Goth chick was stunning; exotic

onyx eyes outlined in heavy black kohl, long blue-black hair brushing her hips, tight black jeans, a glittering red T-shirt, no bra.

"Hey, wait!" he called as she turned away. "Don't I know you?"

"Maybe," she grinned, turning back. "Tell you what," she dug into her jeans pocket. "If I miss you after the concert, here's my e-mail. Drop me a note and we'll chat."

"Hey, um." he said, taking her card. "You wanna go to breakfast after the concert?"

"Maybe," she smiled, turning away again.

He hurried to catch up to her retreating form. "Hey, I'm Sean!" he called after her.

"I know," she said, and disappeared from view.

He glanced at her card. "Lilli," he read. "What a weird e-mail address."

Everyone knows that a child's laughter makes fairies, but Captain Houk comes from a far older century, and he remembers what breaks them: Carnal Knowledge.

THE PIRATE'S PIXIE

Present day, New York City, in the late spring . . .

"*LOS ANGELES, California (CNN) — A man and his parrot were rescued by a U.S. Navy frigate off the coast of Costa Rica last week, after being adrift at sea for almost four months in a crippled antique sailboat. The captain claims that he was treasure diving when his antique craft was blown off course . . .*"

Captain James Aloysius Houk scanned the morning paper's headlines while stalking back toward the small breakfast table by the balcony. His oriental-style midnight blue satin robe whispered over his black silk pajamas with his strides. He pushed the neat tail of his blue-black hair over his shoulder, and it fell to his waist. Modern fashions be-damned, his hair was his one true vanity, and he would not think of cutting it. A smile curled his lip, and his black mustache twitched. The modern women seemed to like it.

The nineteenth-century hotel suite he currently occupied was tastefully appointed with rich carpeting, polished brass, and graceful velvet furnishings. It did not have quite the eighteenth-century elegance that he was accustomed to, but he found it comforting after a fashion. It was as close to home as he would get in this twenty-first century.

The newspaper rustled as he laid it across the table. The view from the balcony was the broad green sward of New York's Central Park, but the skyline rising behind it was disconcerting. He supposed that he would never be comfortable

163

around buildings that touched the sky.

He sat down at the table and pushed his breakfast tray to one side with his left hand to make room for the paper. He stared at his palm. It still surprised him to see his hand rather than an enormous hook. He shook his head and turned to the ornate birdcage sitting only inches from his coffee cup. "Even with the identification you fabricated, the news reporters persist in spelling my name wrong."

The tiny female sitting on the cushion on the bottom of the cage shook her head, then flipped a long lock of pale gold hair over her bared shoulder. "I told you that would happen if you used your real name, Captain." Her voice was melodious and quite lovely for such a small throat.

"Why so you did, Belle. So you did . . ." Houk swept a finger across his black mustache and smiled tightly. "However, my name is the one thing I can claim as truly mine, and I have no desire to give it up."

"I'm happy that you're settled on dry land, thrilled that you have a nice place to stay and tickled pink and purple that you get to keep your true name." Briefly, her hands knotted in the ragged handkerchief she persisted in wearing for a dress. "Now, what about me?"

Houk peered down at the paper. "You? For some reason, they see you as a parrot."

She sighed and rolled her eyes dramatically. "I told you, adults see what they want to see, not what's there. Now quit avoiding the subject!"

"And what subject would that be?" He turned a page of the newspaper.

"The subject is me; still being in this cage!" She scowled, her leaf-green eyes bright with anger. "I kept my side of the bargain." The rainbow-hued wings sprouting from her shoulders fluttered briefly at her back, bathing her in golden light. She floated up onto her feet as delicately as a ballet dancer.

"When are you going to let me go?"

Houk's mustache twitched as he pursed his lips. "This twenty-first century is full of so many marvels that trap the unwary: television, microwaves, ATM machines . . ." He lifted his cup and sipped at the rich coffee. "I will set you free as soon as I am satisfied with my new situation."

"I gave you knowledge of the twenty-first century, and you're rich from your cursed pirate gold!"

Houk shot a narrow glare at her. "That gold was in my ship when you carried it and my person off to your fairy tale island. It belongs to me!"

"Fine! You have it, it's yours." The fairy grabbed the bars and rattled her cage ferociously. "What more do you want from me?" The cage rocked and slowly lifted from the table in a shimmer of golden dust.

"Belay that." Houk casually reached out and set his hand down on the top of the cage, forcing it back down onto the tabletop. "You will cause yourself harm."

The fairy struggled briefly, then sank to her knees at the bottom of the cage. "I want to go home."

"Home to where, Belle?" The captain lifted his chin and his lip curled. "Your fairy tale island no longer exists, you let it sink into the sea."

"There wasn't any reason for it to be." She set her delicate chin on her knees. "The boys left."

"Did you never think that perhaps that island was my home, too?"

She scowled. "I made it for the boys, not for you!"

Houk's fingers curled on top of the cage and his knuckles whitened. "Then why the hell did you keep me there? Do you have any idea how many times I tried to leave, only to find that damned island dead ahead?"

She looked away. "I couldn't make a villain smart enough for the boys. I needed a real adult."

"I'm flattered that you thought me a worthy villain for a pack of half-wild children." Houk's voice dripped with sarcasm. "And as usual, you did not bother to spare a thought for my sanity when you decided to dismantle your fantasy island." He scowled ferociously. "I awoke to find that my moronic crew and all the other superfluous inhabitants of your fantasyland had disappeared overnight!"

She locked her arms around her knees. "They weren't real."

"I gathered as much," Houk said dryly. He gestured with the coffee cup in his right hand. "There wasn't enough sense among them to fill this cup." His brows lowered. "But I was real."

"I took care of you. You never aged and you never died . . ."

"Took care of me?" His cup slammed onto the saucer. "I lost a hand!"

"I gave it back!"

"How generous!" Houk rolled his eyes and sneered. "The brats finally leave and I get to have my hand back." He pulled his hand from her cage and tightened it into a fist. "Did you never think in all that time, that I might need it?"

The pixie turned away. "I'm sorry."

"You're sorry?" Houk leapt from his chair and slammed his fist on the table, making the cage jump. "Sorry doesn't begin to fix what you did to me!" He snatched his fist back and turned sharply away, locking his hands behind his back. Damn his short temper. Thank God he had his hand back or real damage would have been done. He had always been a little too free with that vicious hook.

She looked up at him. "If you're so mad at me, then why did you take me with you?" She pressed her face into her knees. "Why didn't you just let me fade with the island once you were free?"

"Free?" Houk turned back to the fairy in the cage. "Free to go where? What life I might have had is dead and dust!" He pointed a long finger at her. "I spent two hundred years in your make-believe prison, fairy. You owe me an entire life! You will go free when I am satisfied that your debt to me is paid in full!"

She grabbed the bars. "What do you mean: a prison! I made that island a paradise!"

The captain sneered. "A paradise for a pack of pre-adolescent boys. For a grown adult, it was living hell."

"What?"

"There was not one anatomically correct female on that island."

"So?"

"Because of you . . ." He leaned forward on his elbows and peered intently into the cage. "I haven't had sex with something other than my right hand in over two hundred years."

The fairy scooted as far back from the captain's hot gaze as she could. "Sex?"

"Yes, sex!" Houk snorted. "Even the brats finally left your paradise to get laid!"

"That's not true!"

"It is true, you little fool!" Houk rolled his eyes. "That's why one of those pests brought that half-grown chit back with him. He was hoping to have something interesting to play with." His lip curled. "But you wouldn't let her stay."

Her eyes brightened and tears fell from her eyes. "I rescued him, he was mine!"

Houk continued as though she hadn't spoken. "I'm guessing that he started flitting between worlds to play with her there, but every time the brat revisited the real world, he aged. When he finally achieved adolescence and discovered what his dick was actually for, he grabbed all the other pests, told them what they were missing and they all took off after him."

She shook her head. "No, that can't be it . . ."

He sighed. "You blind and stupid child . . ."

"I am not a child!"

"Really?" Houk's black brow lifted and a smile curled his lip. "Do tell."

She turned her back on him. "I haven't been a child for long time."

Houk leaned closer to the cage. "I find myself curious. Are you then an adult?"

She lifted one shoulder in half a shrug. "For a pixie."

"You mean there is a difference?"

She snorted. "Of course! For one thing, I'm bigger."

Houk shrugged. "I really wouldn't know as you are quite small compared to me, and I have never seen another pixie."

She looked over her shoulder at him and gave him a smug smile. "An immature pixie can't make whole islands, not the kind that people can actually live on."

Houk's brows rose. This was interesting news indeed. Perhaps there was hope for a more personal revenge after all. "Then you were a full adult when you carried me off?"

She turned away and crossed her arms over her chest. "An immature pixie can't lift a whole ship."

Houk pursed his lips. This was getting more interesting by the moment. "Well then, since you claim that you are an adult, and considering the nature of your so-called paradise, did you never find your island a bit simplistic?"

She shrugged and peeked over her shoulder. "I couldn't really add anything interesting, the boys would have gotten hurt for real." She dragged a toe across the cushion. "And I did make it for them, so I couldn't really change it."

Houk thoughtfully scrubbed his chin with his hand. "Out of curiosity, how long did you have all those brats to yourself on the island before you brought me into your little fairy tale?"

She ducked her head. "A while."

Houk grinned. "Well now, the truth at last."

She turned and glared at him. "What truth?"

Houk leaned back in his chair and folded his arms. "You brought me in because you were bored." He lifted his chin and a smile curled his lip. "I wasn't there for those brats of yours, I was there for you!"

"What?" She whirled around and stomped her foot. "I was not bored!"

"Oh, really?" He dropped his chin and lowered his brows, but his smile remained. "Then why is it that you seemed to find your way to my ship on almost a daily basis?"

She hunched her shoulder, then lifted her chin. "I had to make sure that you were okay, too. You were real, like the boys."

"Mother of Heaven save me . . ." Houk dropped his elbows on the table and sighed. "Belle, the island is gone, the fairy tale is over. There is absolutely no one left but you and I. What is so very terrible about admitting that those brats occasionally became tiresome and you simply needed another adult to speak to?"

She folded her arms and turned her head. "I loved my boys."

Houk nodded. "As any parent loves their children, no matter what kind of pest they are in actuality, but even they need adult company." He leaned forward and folded his hands together. "Admit it, you came out to see me because you needed the occasional respite, and an adult mind to converse with." He snorted and his mouth tilted up in a tight smile. "Roughly about once a day."

She gave him a tight smile. "I came out there because you caused as much trouble as they did."

Houk's brows rose. "Ah . . ." He slowly sat back in his chair. "Then I was just another form of entertainment for you, all be it of a more mature variety?"

She nodded. "Sure."

Houk pursed his lips and tilted his head casually. "Then might I assume that you collected me in particular because you found my person interesting?"

"Yes." She winced and abruptly blushed. "Uh, no! I meant I just kind'a found you, and well I ah . . ."

"Took me." Houk's brows rose in polite inquiry. "Then you didn't find me interesting?"

"Well, yes, I did!" She bit her lip and ducked her head. "I just . . . Well, you looked the part." She shook her head in obvious confusion and groaned. "I told you why I brought you to the island. I needed . . ."

"An adult to play villain." Houk nodded sagely and bit back a smile. "So, I looked the part. Might I assume you found me a rather attractive pirate? Dashing, perhaps, even somewhat handsome?"

She rolled her head back and groaned. "Okay, yes. I thought you were rather a nice-looking pirate, so I brought you back to the island." She dropped her chin and glared at him. "To be the pirate."

"I see." Houk leaned back in his chair and picked up his coffee cup. "So you did not want, say, an ugly pirate?"

She jumped back and shook her head. "No! Absolutely not!"

Houk sipped at his coffee. "Most pirates are, you know. Quite ugly. In fact, I don't believe I was quite this, virile?" He raised a dark brow. "When I began as your pirate." He examined his coffee cup and glanced only briefly at her. "In fact, I do believe I have quite improved over the years." He shrugged casually. "Not that I mind."

She just stood there staring at him. Her eyes wide and her lips parted as though she'd been caught doing something naughty.

Houk sipped at his coffee and smiled. Who would have thought a pixie could blush so charmingly? In fact, her cheeks were getting pinker by the moment. He turned to his paper and didn't even look up when the little pixie suddenly collapsed in a small huddle of knees, wings and natty handkerchief.

He turned the page of his paper. So, she *had* been making improvements on his appearance. He had suspected as much, but it was nice to have blushing confirmation.

He almost laughed out loud. The little terror had a . . . What was the modern term? Oh, yes, a crush. The pixie had a crush on him. Well then, if she was mature enough to have developed a crush and two hundred years was a long time to have such feelings, then she was more than ripe enough to respond to seduction. He tapped his finger on the page and grinned broadly. In fact, since she had been changing his appearance to suit her own personal taste, how could she possibly resist?

He turned the page of his paper. The question was; how did one begin to seduce someone who had no knowledge of sex?

An advertisement caught his eye: Escort Service. His brows rose as his twenty-first-century knowledge filled in the blanks. Well now, there was an idea. He was more than ready to break his long celibacy but had been leery of the women that had so blatantly approached him. A woman for hire was another story entirely.

He glanced briefly at the huddled pixie. And what better way to introduce someone to carnal knowledge than with a demonstration?

Houk carefully wedged the pixie's cage within the curio cabinet in the living room. "Remember, Belle, no one can hear you, because in this century only I believe in fairies."

The pixie frowned. "Why do you keep calling me Belle? That's not my name!"

"I prefer to call you by something a bit more elegant than that childish name the brats gave you." He smiled. "Belle means beautiful."

"It does?"

Houk nodded. "In several languages." He checked the lock on her cage. "Be good." He smiled as he closed the glass door on the curio cabinet, enclosing the birdcage behind mirrored glass. He whistled as he strode into the master bedroom.

"Captain! What are you up to now?" The pixie grabbed the bars of the cage and jerked on them. It didn't budge. The cage was wedged in tight, and the oak cabinet was too large for her to even shift without completely covering it in fairy dust.

"Curse that pirate! He doesn't make any sense! Why did he put me here, of all places?" She frowned as she stared through the wide-open bedroom door. She had a grand view of his four-poster bed. "What? Does he want me to watch him snore?"

The chime to the door made her jump.

The captain strode from the bedroom wearing nothing but the black silk bottoms to his pajamas. His feet were bare, as his entire upper body. He had pulled his blue-black hair from its binding and it swung in waves to his waist.

She'd never seen him so . . . naked. He had always been completely dressed. She watched in fascination. His entire body rippled with muscle. He reminded her of a great hunting cat in motion. Black curls fanned across his muscular chest and speared downward to his waistband. For just a moment, she wondered what she would find if she followed that trail into his pants.

Houk opened the front door.

"Hi, I'm Julie from the escort service."

He smiled and stepped back. "Ah, yes. Please, come in."

A female walked in. She was nearly as naked as he was. Boots stretched up to mid-thigh nearly reaching the hem of a skirt that didn't quite cover her bottom. Her shirt was too snug and cut too low to completely contain her breasts. Golden waves tumbled past her shoulders. She smiled with lips as red as blood.

Huh? The pixie frowned. *What was she doing here?*

Houk closed the door. "I'm pleased to meet you, Julie. I'm James." Casually, he walked all the way around the girl, circling her like a beast measuring his prey. His eyes narrowed, and his smile broadened.

Julie smiled. "Do you like what you see?"

Houk pursed his lips. "Very much so."

Julie tilted her head thoughtfully. "You're the guy I read about in the paper, the one that was lost at sea for months, right?"

Houk nodded. "I'm afraid so."

Julie set her purse down on a small table by the leather sofa. "In that case, you probably need it pretty bad. Do you want to get started right away?"

Houk stopped his circling and dropped his chin, pursing his lips in a slight pout. "Would it be too much to ask?"

She shook her head. "Not at all. You're quite a hottie, so it'll be my pleasure."

His brows shot up. "A hottie?"

"Oh, yeah." Julie licked her lips and reached for the hem of her shirt. "I haven't seen a man as fine as you outside of the movies." She pulled her shirt over her head and tossed it on the floor. Her breasts were full and round and completely naked. She reached up and tugged her pink nipples. "Come and get it, sailor."

"Don't mind if I do." He reached out and cupped her breasts. He tugged on her nipples and licked his lips. "Very nice."

Julie sighed and pressed into his palms. "Oh, you have good hands."

A groan escaped Houk's throat and he knelt to take a nipple into his mouth. He suckled like a starving man with loud slurps of obvious enjoyment. His arm closed around her waist, pulling her closer to his mouth.

"Oh yeah, God, your mouth!" Julie lifted her short skirt, baring her butt. "Your mustache tickles!"

Houk slid his hand down and cupped her bare butt cheek. He squeezed, then slid his hand between her thighs.

"Oh yeah, that's the spot." Julie whimpered. "Keep that up and I'm gonna cum on your hand."

Houk lifted his lips from her breast. "I'm afraid that I do not have much control. It has been too long."

"That's okay." She smiled. "You have a whole hour, so go ahead and get off now. I'll suck you back to life for the next go around."

Houk smiled up at her. "Do you mind?"

"Are you kidding?" She smiled. "I'm ready for you right now."

Houk stood. "Very well, then." He tugged at the drawstring on his bottoms. The silk slid to the floor.

"Uncircumcised?" Julie licked her lips. "Now that is a lovely view."

The pixie gasped. She'd never seen anything like this. On an island full of boys, she knew a dick when she saw one, but she'd never seen one so . . . enthusiastic, or so large. The whole thing was swollen and a deep purple, and curved stiffly upward with the cap poking past its sheath.

Her breasts suddenly tingled and ached. The pixie looked down inside her dress. Her nipples were hard and swollen. She stared at herself in dismay. This was not a good sign, not for a fairy. She looked up and discovered that Julie was completely naked but for her tall boots.

Julie gently pushed on the captain's chest. "Sit down, handsome, and I'll do you on the couch."

Houk dropped down on the couch and laughed. His cock rose hard and smooth against his belly. "You'll *do* me?" His voice was husky.

Julie set her hands on his shoulders and grinned. "Oh, yeah." She climbed onto the couch and straddled him on her knees. She tipped forward and presented her nipples to his lips.

Houk took the bait and sucked a nipple into his mouth, then wrapped one arm around her waist. He grabbed his shaft and pushed the head forward, rubbing against her slick and spread flesh.

The pixie frowned. What the heck were they doing?

Houk grabbed her butt with both hands and shoved her down onto him. He groaned as his cock disappeared.

The pixie tilted her head. Where had his dick gone? Was it actually in her? An odd throb started deep in her belly. Something she'd never felt before.

"God! You're big!" Julie moaned. "Oh, yeah, this is going to be a good fuck."

Houk released her nipple with a wet pop and sank his fingers into her butt cheeks. "Have I told you that you have a superlative ass?"

"Thank you, James." Julie grinned and rolled her hips. "I'm glad you like it." She pushed with her knees and his dick slid partway out. "I'm rather fond of this big fat cock myself." She sat down hard, burying him back in her body.

Houk arched back on the couch. He sucked in a breath and cupped his palms under her spread cheeks. "Damn! I'm sorry, but I simply must fuck you."

Julie moaned. "Do your worst, James, I can take it as hard as you can give it."

Houk smiled. "Music to my ears, my dear Julie." Houk held her still and bucked his hips, driving his cock up, and up, and up into her body hard enough make sharp slapping sounds against her ass. He grunted with the impact.

"God, yes!" Julie writhed and moaned as he pounded into her. "Don't stop! Don't stop!"

Houk looked past her shoulder and stared straight at the golden cage hidden behind the mirrored glass. A smile of pure malice curled his full lips as he fucked the lovely girl in his arms.

The pixie couldn't tear her gaze from the two on the couch. She felt her pulse leap in her throat and couldn't take a full breath. His dick *was* in her—and the girl obviously liked it there. Her nipples burned. She rubbed against them, but it didn't make the ache go away. It became uncomfortable to sit with her knees together. She spread her knees and discovered moisture wetting her thighs. She explored the moisture with her fingers and discovered the swollen nub at the top of her cleft. It was aching in time with her nipples. She pressed her fingers against it to relieve the ache, but something coiled tight in her belly instead. Sensual pleasure bloomed. A sense of danger bloomed with it.

Suddenly, Julie wailed. "Oh, fuck, I'm cumming!" Her whole body tensed. She gasped and hissed. "Shit!" She moaned and fell forward to rub her breast against the Captain's broad chest. "Oh, that was good. Your turn, handsome."

Houk licked his lips. "I want to cum on your tits," he husked.

Julie grinned. "My tits are yours to cum on, James."

"In that case . . ." Houk pushed her to the side, laying her down on the couch. "I shall take you up on your kind invitation." His dick slid from her body, glistening with damp. He set one leg on the floor straddling her hips and arching over her body. He spit on his palm, then grabbed his swollen shaft. He jerked on it with hurried motions.

Julie writhed under him. "That's it, oh, yeah, cum on my tits, handsome."

His mouth opened as he gasped for breath. "Fuck . . ." Every muscle in his body tensed. He bared his teeth and groaned. "Oh, fuck . . ." A stream of white cream burst from his dick and spattered across her belly and breasts.

Julie smeared his cream across her breasts with her hands. "Oh, yeah, that feels so good!"

In her golden cage, the pixie came up on her knees as her fingers moved on her private flesh. Her other hand tugged on her aching nipples. She closed her eyes and bit her lip to still her whimpering cries. Pleasure boiled within her and tightened to a delicious crisis. Abruptly, her wings began to beat, and her magic rose within her, echoing the climb toward climax.

I have to stop!

She didn't want to stop. The cresting waves of pleasure promised a unique and unknown fulfillment that she simply had to have . . . But her magic was swelling toward a ferocious crescendo. Something was about to happen, something huge and terrifying.

I have to stop now!

She pulled her hands away from herself and grabbed the cushion under her, gasping for breath. She had no idea what had been about to happen, but she knew for a fact that her doom lay in giving in to that delicious and threatening delight.

The sound of enthusiastic moans caught her attention and she opened her eyes.

Julie sat up on the couch, her breasts still wet with cum. She had the captain's dick in her mouth and she was licking and sucking on it with noisy enthusiasm.

Houk tossed his head back and groaned. "You delightful

creature!"

Julie released him from her mouth and wiped her hands across her lips. "Told you I'd bring you back to life."

"So you did." Houk grinned. His cock arched up toward his belly, wet with saliva. "Now then, dear Julie, would you be so kind as to bend over the arm of the couch?"

Julie rose to her feet. "I'd be delighted to, James." She turned and walked around the couch with just a bit more wiggle in her butt than strictly needed to be there. She bent over the couch's arm, pressing her hands into the seat cushions. "Will this do?"

Houk shifted Julie's haunches a few degrees then spread her legs a bit wider. He looked over his shoulder at the curio cabinet where the pixie was hidden. He smiled. "Perfect." He stepped away.

The pixie swallowed hard. She could actually see the girl's spread cleft. It was deep pink and shiny with moisture.

Houk set one foot up on the arm of the couch.

In that position the pixie had a completely unobstructed view of his cock pointing straight at Julie's pink flesh. She also had a rather interesting view of Houk's muscular ass and the plump roundness of his ball sack at the base of his cock. For no apparent reason, her mouth watered.

Houk squeezed one of Julie's ass cheeks while holding his cock positioned with his other hand. "Are you ready for me, my sweet confection?"

Julie looked over her shoulder and smiled. "If I get any more ready I'm going to drip on the carpet!"

Houk licked his lips. "Exactly what I wanted to hear." His thighs and butt flexed as his cock pressed into her. The girl's flesh opened, stretched and swallowed the rigid cock. Slowly it disappeared into her body.

Julie moaned.

The pixie's mouth opened in shock. So that's where the

dick went. Her fingers traced her own mysterious flesh and she discovered the opening to her own body. She slipped a finger within and wondered what it would be like to have a cock in there.

Houk groaned and pulled his cock partway out. The girl's flesh stretched around him as he retreated. He shoved his cock back in, her flesh puckering as it swallowed his cock. He pulled out, then back in, then out . . .

Julie moaned. "Don't tease me, James! Fuck me!"

"As you wish." Houk increased the speed of his thrusts. He used his entire body to pound into the delighted girl. Sweat formed on his back and dripped. His breath came in soft pants.

The pixie's throat tightened and her mouth dried. Her body gave a hard throb. *I am not going to touch myself.* She closed her eyes and jammed her hands under her arms. Her nipples throbbed angrily. *I won't! I won't! I won't!* She tightened her knees, but her secret flesh only pulsed more intensely.

The sound of damp flesh striking damp flesh was loud.

Julie gasped. "Oh, God! I'm gonna cum!"

"Good girl!"

The pixie peeked and immediately regretted it.

Houk grunted as he slammed into her, driving the girl into the seat cushions and shaking her entire body with every thrust. "Cum for me, Julie, cum on my cock and make me feel it."

The pixie closed her eyes and turned all the way around, but her mind's eye filled in all the blanks to match the wet fleshy sounds she was hearing.

She felt her power surge. This time there was no stopping her body's hunger for forbidden pleasure, she was going to reach climax. She shook her head in denial even as her body pulsed toward the precipice. She didn't want her life to end just yet! Tears formed in her eyes. There had to be some way to stop her doom!

In sheer desperation, she tossed a pinch of her own pixie dust over her head and willed herself into a deep sleep that only morning sunlight would draw her from.

Houk pounded into Julie's tight cunt with criminal satisfaction. The enthusiastic little whore was worth every penny he'd paid. If his revenge on the pixie hadn't been so damned all-consuming, Julie would have been an excellent choice to keep his bed warm.

"I'm cumming!" Julie writhed and bucked under him. "Oh, shit, oh, shit . . ." Her breath caught. She stilled, then shivered hard. A howl escaped her throat, announcing her fulfillment. She bucked and moaned, shaking with erotic tremors.

It was the most beautiful thing he'd seen in two hundred years—a woman's joyful climax. He groaned as her body pulsed like a wet velvet glove around his cock. He felt his balls tighten with imminent release. "Fuck!" He thrust hard, burying his cock, as deep as he could go. Intense pleasure boiled up his cock and spewed into her trembling body. He thrust again to prolong the delight of his climax. Groaning, he thrust once more, using her body to squeeze the last of his load into her.

He pulled from her limp and sated body with a heartfelt groan of satisfaction. Laid at last! He cupped her ass cheeks and spread them. His cum oozed from her swollen and well-fucked cunt to slither down her thighs. Triumph burned in his blood.

The pixie was next.

He glanced over his shoulder at the curio cabinet. Had she been able to resist masturbating to her own doom?

Julie moaned. "You are one hell of a fuck, James." She

wriggled until she lay sprawled on her back with her legs still splayed wide over the couch's arm. "I think I'll stay here for just a minute if you don't mind." She chuckled. "I honestly don't think I can walk just yet."

"Now that is quite a compliment." Houk dropped onto the couch next to her and stroked the pale gold curls from her brow. "You were quite wonderful yourself. Thank you."

"No, James, thank *you*." Julie smiled with eyes dilated wide from her pleasures. "Let me know if you ever need company again. Fuck the agency, I'll do you any time you like." She turned her head and kissed his palm, surprising him. "You are a perfect gentleman."

Houk smiled and shook his head. "I assure you, I am not a gentleman."

An hour and a half after she arrived, Julie left with a distinct wobble in her walk and a grin on her lips.

Houk closed the door and shook his head. It was nice to know that although out of practice, he hadn't lost his touch for pleasing women. He turned to look over at the curio cabinet. Had the foolish pixie taken the bait? He strode for the cabinet and pulled open the glass door.

The pixie was a tiny stillness at the bottom of the cage.

His heart stuttered in his chest. Good God! Had he killed her? According to what he had been told long before he had been stolen away to the island, carnal knowledge was the only way to render a pixie harmless, but it wasn't supposed to kill them!

He scooped her up and pulled her from the cage with trembling hands. Her long golden hair flowed through his fingers. Her shimmering wings were as ephemeral as a rainbow. Her chest rose and fell in deep even breaths. He sighed in relief. She was only sleeping.

A rich sweet musk rose from her body.

His brows shot up. "Well now . . ." He bent over her and sniffed. The perfume rising from her body was unmistakable. She smelled of feminine arousal. He grinned. Oh, yes, she took the bait all right, but why was she asleep? Was this supposed to happen?

The glitter of shimmering gold caught his eye. She was covered in pixie dust.

His lips curved into a bitter smile. The smart little chit must have put herself to sleep before she reached climax. It was a valiant effort on her part, but there was no way in hell that he was letting the little bitch loose while she still had the magic to destroy him. He shook his head. He'd simply continue with her carnal education until she masturbated to her first orgasm — and her doom.

Speaking of masturbation . . .

Impatiently, he tugged the old handkerchief from her delicate form. Her glorious body spread across his palms and there was nothing childlike about it. The view took his breath away. His gaze swept across her full breasts, her narrow waist, her gently rounded belly, her broad and womanly hips, and the apex of her plump thighs with avaricious delight. He could feel her ridiculously round bottom against his palm. She was built to please a man — a human man. He smiled. "My dear Belle, I am afraid that your doom has definitely come upon you."

He pulled the cage from the curio cabinet and carried it and the pixie into the bedroom. He set the cage on the dresser right in front of the mirror then gently placed the sleeping fairy back on the cushion. He crumpled the old handkerchief in his palm, then stuffed it into his robe pocket.

He locked the cage and yawned. He needed a shower and then sleep. Morning would be soon enough to continue tormenting the pixie with carnal knowledge. Sooner or later, lust would drive her to masturbate. Once she reached climax, her magic would evaporate, and she would become mortal and human flesh.

He grinned. God, he couldn't wait! He'd been dying to fuck that perfect little body for over a century. By the time he was done with her, she wouldn't have a hole that didn't have cum in it.

The pixie stirred from sleep in a pool of bright sunlight. It was right in her eyes. She moaned and turned over on her belly.

"Sleep well?" Houk's voice held lazy amusement.

The pixie groaned. "Like the dead." And as far as she was concerned, she was more than willing to go on sleeping, too. Her breath stilled. Something wasn't right.

She swept her hand across the cushion and found a bar. Okay, so she was still in the cage, she could feel the cushion under her. Then she realized that she could feel the cushion along her entire body. Her eyes popped open. Her dress was missing. She glanced around. It wasn't anywhere in the cage.

She lifted her head. The cage had been moved from the cabinet to Houk's bedroom. She was on his dresser facing the foot of his bed with a very close view of Houk lounging upright against the headboard with a newspaper strewn across the covers. His broad furry chest was completely bare above the covers.

She scowled. "Houk, where is my dress?"

"The handkerchief?" Houk turned a page of his paper. "I have it."

"Give it back!" She sat up with her arms over her breasts. "It's mine! My boys gave that to me!"

"Actually, it belongs to me." Houk snorted. "The brats stole it." He raised his chin. "That was the last actual handkerchief I had from my former life as a privateer. Did you never notice the monogram? They were my initials."

The pixie winced. "I . . . I can't read."

Houk nodded sagely. "That can be remedied."

"Houk, I'm naked!"

"So I see." His gaze raked her nude form and a predatory smile graced his lips. "You're quite lovely, did you know that?"

The pixie sputtered. He thought she was lovely? Well, he was rather nice to look at, too, but she wasn't about to tell him that. Not to mention that looking at him was stirring all those strange feelings again. She turned her head away. "Would you please find me something to wear? And get yourself dressed!"

"I prefer you in the nude."

The pixie fisted her hands. "Well, I don't!"

"Then, I guess you'll have to expend some magic and make something to wear."

She leveled a glare at him. "You know I damn well can't do big magic in this cage! I have to be in flight to do something like that!"

Houk shook his head slowly and tisked. "Then naked you shall remain."

"Oh, you stinking pirate!" The pixie dropped down flat and howled while pounding the cushion with her fists and kicking her feet.

Houk smiled. "Such a child-like display, while vastly entertaining in your current state of undress, is very unbecoming in a young lady."

The pixie raised her head. "I'm not a young lady, I'm a pixie!" She thumped the cushion with her fist. "Will you get dressed?" She couldn't take much more of all this naked nudity.

Houk folded the newspaper and set it to one side. "Unfortunately, I cannot. At least not just yet."

"Why not?"

Houk caught the edge of his blanket. "I have to do something about this first." He pulled the blankets away with a dramatic flourish. He was utterly naked. He spread his legs, giving her an unobstructed view between strong thighs of the entire length of his profoundly erect cock rising proudly above his plump ball sack.

The pixie choked. "Didn't you wear that thing out last night?"

Houk laughed. "Such is the nature of a man's cock." His eyes narrowed. "Every morning in fact, without fail."

The pixie winced. "It looks painful."

"It is quite the opposite, but it can be inconvenient at times." Houk smiled slyly. "Perhaps I should have kept Julie overnight to take care of this for me. She so enjoys her work."

The pixie swallowed as every memory from last night crowded into her head. A seditious coil of excitement tightened in her core.

"Irregardless, it is a simple matter to take care of oneself." Houk spit on his palm and wrapped his hand around his erection. He stroked himself, pulling the sheath down to expose the purple head. He groaned. "As hard as I am, this will not take long." He slid his hand up, then down with a firm grip.

The pixie flinched back. He was going to make that white creamy stuff, that cum come out of him again. "Houk! What are you doing?"

He smiled broadly. "Masturbation." His ass flexed as he stroked his cock. "The proper application of one's hand on one's privates coupled with the stimulus of a fine imagination." His eyes narrowed. "Or a lovely view." He licked his palm and squeezed the purple head of his cock. He groaned. "Would you like to know what delicious little fantasy entertained me for the past century or so?"

"No, I don't!" The pixie tightened her arms around her

breasts and shook her head.

Houk licked his lips. "One morning, a very long time ago, I discovered you bathing in a pool of morning dew, naked, and unimaginably exquisite. Your nipples were hard little pebbles and your cleft was as pink as a rose." He took a deep breath. "Since that moment I have been imagining what it would be like to have you full sized and spread beneath me."

What? The pixie stared. He had seen her? He wanted . . . her? Her core gave a vicious pulse. A spot of moisture smeared her thighs. She gasped and bit her lip to keep from touching herself.

Houk smiled and his eyes were as hot as a furnace. "I have been unable to think of anything other than your sweet body, and what it would be like to fuck it ever since."

"Stop! I don't want to hear any more!" She turned her back on him and found herself facing the mirror. She could clearly see Houk tugging on his cock and her own naked breasts tipped with flushed and hardening nipples.

Houk's smile was hungry. "You can cover your ears if you like, but you cannot hide that luscious body from me, not anymore."

"You're awful!" She closed her eyes, but she could still hear his hurried breaths and the slapping sound of his hand working his cock.

"I have been a villain for over two hundred years. Some habits take time to overcome. Now where was I? Oh yes . . ." His breathing quickened. "I imagined spreading the petals of your tender sex and tasting the sweet salty dew of your arousal with my tongue."

The pixie's breath caught, imagining his head between her spread thighs, his long silky hair spilling over her, his tongue on her secret flesh, licking the tiny nub at the top of her cleft.

"I imagined filling my hands with your breasts and sucking on your pink nipples."

The pixie squeezed her breasts with her arms. His mouth would be hot and wet; his teeth would pinch deliciously. Her nipples burned.

Houk groaned. "I imagined pushing my cock into your tight, wet cunt."

The pixie whimpered. He'd be big and hard. Her empty core clenched in demand.

Houk gasped for breath. "I would fill my hands with your plump ass and fuck you; rocking your body with my thrusts as your hips bucked against mine, fucking me just as hard." He moaned. "God! How I would fuck the living hell out of your tight wet cunt."

The pixie looked helplessly into the mirror.

His hand moved with frenzied speed on his cock. Every muscle in his body tensed. His masculine nipples were hard nubs. His eyes blazed with sensual heat as he stared at her. "I could just hear your cries as you came under me; your body trembling and squeezing my cock with your exquisite climax. And then I would shove my cock as deep as it would go and fill your hot little cunt with my cum."

He choked. "Oh, yes, that did it . . ." He reached under his pillow and pulled out a small square of linen. He wrapped it around his cock and tugged. His throat released a deep groan and he threw his head back. "Oh, yes, oh, fuck!"

Cream erupted from his cock and spilled over the linen in his hand, spattering a long stream on his belly. "Ah, that's much better." He continued to tug, milking more cum from his cock and sighed. "Quite a load, too." He mopped the cream from his belly with the small bit of cloth and sat up. "Now that my balls have been emptied, I can take my shower, and get some work done." He got up and tossed the soiled cloth to the end of the bed. He chuckled as he walked into the bathroom.

The pixie stared at the abandoned cloth. She sucked in a

sharp breath. It was her dress.

Houk came out of the shower with a towel wrapped around his hips singing a ditty that she had heard the pirates sing before:

If all the young lassies were bells in the tower,
And I was a sexton; I'd bang on the hour!
Roll your leg over, and roll your leg over.
Roll your leg over! It's better that way!

The pixie hadn't known that the song was so . . . sexual.

Houk pulled a black suit from his closet. "Out of sheer curiosity, Belle, what do you muse on when you masturbate?" He pulled off the towel and picked up the trousers.

The pixie scooted back to the far side of her cage. "I don't!"

"You don't?" Houk shrugged into a silvery silk shirt, then turned to the mirror by the closet door to button it. "You do not imagine anything at all?" He picked up a long black tie and skillfully knotted it around his collar.

"No!" She shook her head. "I don't—whatever it is you said it was . . ."

"It is called masturbation." He tucked the tails of his shirt into his trousers. "When you touch yourself to reach orgasm." His smile was sly.

The pixie shook her head vigorously. "No—no, I don't do that at all!"

"You do not masturbate? Not ever?" Houk's brows rose as he sat down on the bed to put on his socks then his shoes. "Why ever not? I find it very relaxing."

"Because . . . Because it's not something fairies do!"

"No?" Houk picked up the double-breasted jacket and shrugged into it. "How dull."

The pixie shivered. He was taunting her deliberately. He

was trying to do something, and whatever it was, it was working. She had never been so confused and so frightened in all her life. "Why do you hate me so much?"

In two strides, he was at the side of her cage.

The pixie huddled as far from him as she could.

"I do not hate you, Belle." He sighed and shook his head. "My lust is far too strong to ever hate you." He straightened and lifted his chin. "But, I am very angry with you, and I will have my revenge, pixie."

"Why don't you just kill me?" The pixie felt the tears start in her eyes. Just like her island, she really didn't have a reason to continue. The boys she had lived for were gone. "You can, you know. I'd . . . I'd let you."

"Belay that right now!" Houk grabbed the cage with both hands. His mouth was white as he scowled down at her. "I have never had a wish for your demise. Your downfall, yes, but I would never seek your death!"

"I don't mind, really." The pixie closed her eyes. "Without my boy . . ."

"That brat never knew what he had." Houk sneered. "Even if you wore mortal flesh, that brat would still seek out someone his own age to play with. He is a boy, and boys know nothing of love."

The pixie blinked up at him. Her heart thumped oddly in her chest. "Love?"

Houk released the cage as though it burned his hands. He picked up the brush on the dresser and proceeded to ruthlessly bind his long hair into a neat tail.

The pixie tried to understand the sudden and raging confusion tearing through her heart. "Houk?"

"Yes, Belle?"

"What did you mean: love?"

Houk sighed and set the brush down. He bent and set both hands on the dresser, staring hard at the floor. "In case you haven't noticed, I have been in love with you for over a hundred years."

"But that's impossible!" The captain couldn't love her — they were enemies!

Houk laughed, and the sound was bitter. "Tell that to my heart, because it refuses to listen to me." He looked over at the cage. "When you began to tear apart the island, I knew, of course. I knew that the stupid boy had abandoned you, taking the rest with him. I knew that I was free to go finally. I also knew that I could not continue my life without having you nearby." He groaned and straightened. "I put you in a cage and took you with me because I could not bear the thought of never seeing you again."

The pixie tilted her head in confusion. "But you're mad at me."

"Oh, yes, indeed." Houk nodded and laughed. "You have no idea just how angry I am. But I do not hate you."

The pixie hit the cushion with her fist. "Houk! You are not making any sense!"

Houk shook his head. "Love, as a rule, does not make sense." He pushed away from the dresser and straightened his jacket. "When you decide that you want to masturbate, please wait for me. I do not wish to miss your moment of climax. I am guessing that it will be a sight to remember forever."

The pixie cringed. Not that again . . ."Wait, where are you going?"

"I will be back in a few hours." Houk picked up a pair of sunglasses. "I am going to talk to a few lawyers and businessmen about my gold." He came back to the cage and carried it out to the curio cabinet. Gently, he wedged the cage within.

Houk paused before closing the glass door. "Belle, when you gave me knowledge of this century and all its rather interesting inventions, did you realize that you gave me knowledge of the entire century?"

The pixie bit her lip. "Is that bad?"

Houk chuckled. "Considering that this is the beginning of the century, not at all. It gives me a distinct advantage in investment."

The pixie frowned. "Huh?"

Houk smiled. "All you need to know is that you have provided very well indeed for my future."

The pixie shrugged. "Oh, okay."

Houk left the cabinet open and returned with a tiny child's tea service. He opened the cage and set it within. "Here is your breakfast."

"Great! Thanks!" The pixie grabbed for the teapot full of orange juice and the hunk of toast slathered with honey.

Houk shook his head and lifted a cautionary finger. "No masturbation until I get back."

The pixie scowled at him. "Do you mind? I am eating!"

Houk laughed as he closed the cabinet door.

She watched him leave with a briefcase in one hand and a silver-handled cane in the other. She knew for a fact that the cane contained a long and deadly blade. She had made it herself from his cutlass. He was a pirate after all, and no pirate ever walked without his sword.

The pixie awoke to the sound of the front door opening. She had fallen asleep out of sheer boredom.

Houk closed the door behind him, whistling a jig slightly off-key. He strode in with a light step, dropping his briefcase and sword cane on the leather couch then picked up the telephone. He smiled as he ordered dinner. He resumed whistling and walked straight into the bedroom. He opened his closet, pulled off his jacket, and hung it neatly, then continued to get undressed.

The pixie's brows rose. Houk was in a good mood. Maybe he wouldn't bother her with more of that sex-stuff.

And yet, some sneaking part of her rather hoped he would.

Well after dinner, Houk carried the pixie's cage into his bedroom. He set the cage on the dresser and shrugged out of his black robe, baring his broad shoulders, muscular chest and the silk bottoms to his pajamas. He hadn't bothered with the shirt. "I am pleased to see that you have gotten quite used to your own nudity. Are you ready to masturbate for me?"

The pixie gasped. "What?" She hadn't actually gotten all that used to being without her dress, but she had figured out how to drape her hair over her breasts. However, it itched when she pooled it in her lap, and she kept forgetting to keep her knees together. "I am not going to . . . to . . ." She winced. She couldn't say it.

"Masturbate? Why ever not?" Houk pulled back the covers on his wide bed. "I merely want to see what you look like when you reach climax." He dropped onto his stomach and rolled around until he faced the foot of his bed. He set his chin on his hands and bent his knees, kicking his feet lazily in the air. He smiled.

The pixie tilted her head. It was a rather silly pose for the former pirate.

"I showed you mine. Several times, in fact. Why don't you want to show me yours?"

She winced. "Because . . . because . . ."

"Don't tell me you've never done it before?"

"Uh . . ." The pixie bit her lip. "No."

"Why not?"

The pixie glared at him. "Because it's dangerous."

"Dangerous?" Houk rolled his eyes. "Belle, no one ever died from masturbation."

"They didn't?"

Houk fell over laughing. He grinned at her while lying on

his back. "No, no dear girl, masturbation is not fatal in any way, shape or form." He raised his brows. "Why would you think it was dangerous?"

The pixie closed her arms around herself. "Because I feel this big, big surge of magic when I do it. It scares me. A lot."

Houk rolled back over onto his stomach and set his chin down on his hands. "Hmm . . . This sounds serious. Perhaps you should tell me more. What else do you feel?"

The pixie pulled her knees up. Should she tell him? Did she dare? She winced. Since when was she this afraid of Houk? Since when was she afraid of anything? She was acting like a little coward. It was embarrassing, yes, but that's all it really was.

"Come on, Belle, I can't help you if I don't know." Houk's voice was gentle, soothing, and he looked so sympathetic.

The pixie looked down at her knees. "Well, my nipples tingle and ache."

"And?" His voice was encouraging.

The pixie swallowed. "And there's a fluttering really low in my belly."

"And?"

"And I get all wet." Her voice was barely a whisper. Damn, this was really, really embarrassing.

"Where? Where do you get all wet, Belle? Show me."

A small squeak escaped her throat. "Show you?"

Houk snorted. "For goodness sake woman, it's not as if I don't know what a cunny looks like."

"A . . . cunny?"

"It's the more genteel term for cunt, your lower privates. The modern vernacular is pussy. I know you had a nice clear view of Julie's cunny last night."

The pixie's memory provided a nice clear image of Julie's pink flesh and Houk's cock driving into it. She swallowed. "Oh, that . . ."

"Spread your legs, Belle, and show me where you get all wet."

The pixie tightened her knees. "Do I have to?"

Houk sighed. "I need to see what you are talking about to help, Belle. Open wide and show me your pretty little cunny."

The pixie nibbled on her bottom lip. Did she really want to do this?

Houk raised a black brow. "Belle, have I ever lied to you? In all my years as the villain of your fairy tale island, have I ever lied?"

The pixie winced. "You haven't always told the entire truth . . ."

Houk raised his chin. "But, I have never once lied."

The pixie shook her head. "No. No, you've never actually lied."

Houk lowered his brows. "I have no wish for you to come to harm. Do you believe this?"

The pixie nodded. She believed him. For some reason, she knew that Houk did not want to hurt her. Scare her? Yes, absolutely! Embarrass her? Without question! But, hurt her? No.

Houk dropped his chin on his hands. "Belle, believe me, touching yourself will not hurt you in any way."

The pixie sighed and set her hands on her knees. She spread her legs open and moved her long hair out of the way. She turned away and closed her eyes.

"Belle?"

"Yes?" She opened one eye. His gaze was focused between her legs. He was staring. Her cheeks filled with heat.

He looked up at her face. "Belle, use your finger and show me where you get wet."

The pixie licked her lips and pointed.

"Ah . . . I see." He nodded. "Tell me, what else do you feel when your cunny grows wet?"

The pixie winced. She knew this wouldn't be the end of it.

In for a penny, in for a pound . . ."It throbs."

"What throbs?"

"The top part."

"That top part of what?" His voice radiated pure patience.

The pixie lightly touched the nubbin of flesh at the very top of her cleft. "This right here."

"Oh, I see." Houk nodded. "That is your clit."

The pixie blinked. It had a name? "Oh . . ."

Houk nodded. "Your clit is very sensitive and an important part of sexual pleasure." He raised a brow. "Now then, what makes your clit throb, and your nipples ache, and your cunny get wet?"

The pixie frowned. "When you did all that stuff last night and then this morning."

"I see." He nodded. "Then I think I know exactly what the problem is."

The pixie bit her lip. "Okay . . ."

He smiled. "Belle, those are all symptoms of lust."

"Lust?" The pixie tilted her head. "Is it serious?"

Houk's smile broadened. "No, my dear. Your cunny grows wet when your body is preparing for sexual penetration."

The pixie sucked in a sharp breath. "Penetration?"

"Yes." Houk nodded. "All those feelings happen when your body is asking for a nice hard cock to come into your body and fuck you. When you are properly fucked, your clit is also stimulated. Fucking will bring you to climax, or orgasm. As you are too small for a man's cock to fuck you, your only relief for lust is masturbation."

The pixie shook her head. "I can't, it makes all these big feelings tighten up in me, and my magic feels like it's going to boil over."

"It's supposed to." Houk nodded sagely. "That's what an orgasm feels like. There is a buildup and then an extremely pleasurable release."

"Really?"

Houk shrugged. "That's what orgasm feels like to me. In fact, there is no greater pleasure in the world than orgasm. Once my cum erupts, I feel quite relaxed." He set one arm down on the bed. "Julie came several times and thoroughly enjoyed every one."

"Oh, yes . . . I guess so." Julie had certainly looked like she had enjoyed it.

Houk leaned up and propped his chin on his hands. "Now then. Are you feeling lust right now?"

The pixie shrugged. "Not really." That was not quite truthful. There was a slow simmer going on, but it wasn't anything like last night or this morning.

Houk sighed. "Unfortunately, I am." He sat up and rearranged himself until he was perched on the foot of the bed. His silk bottoms had a profound tent. "Seeing your deliciously round breasts and your pretty pink cunny has stirred me quite a bit." He looked down at himself. "As you can see, I am suffering quite badly from lust." He tugged on his drawstring. "And I will not be able to sleep properly until I do something about it." He stood up and let the silk bottoms fall to the floor, revealing the strong column of his erection.

The pixie swallowed hard. "Are you going to . . . to masturbate?"

Houk smiled as he sat back down on the bed. "Yes, I am." He spat on his palm and pushed the sheath down, uncovering the swollen head of his cock. His lids drooped a little and his cheeks flushed. He groaned. "Let me know if you want to masturbate, too." He leaned back on one elbow and licked his lips. He closed his palm around his shaft and slowly drew his hand up, then down. He sighed. "Mmm . . . This feels wonderfully pleasurable."

The pixie felt her breath catch and her pulse leapt in her throat. Her nipples tingled as they came to attention. Warmth spread through her and pooled low in her belly.

Houk smiled. His lips seemed redder and fuller. "Squeeze your breasts, Belle. Make your nipples nice and hard for me."

Unable to resist the tempting persuasion in his voice, or the restless excitement suddenly running rampant through her body, the pixie cupped her breasts and squeezed them. Electric heat sparked and burned. A soft moan escaped her throat.

"Oh, yes . . ." Houk's groan echoed her. "Your nipples, tug your hard little nipples."

The pixie caught her nipples in her fingers and tugged. She was jolted with a warm curl of delight that spiraled straight down to her core. She rubbed her palms against them, making the delicious feelings spread.

"Your cunny is getting wet, Belle. How does your clit feel?"

The pixie automatically explored her cleft and discovered moisture. Her clit was hard and swollen. She pressed it with her dampened fingers and gasped. It pulsed hungrily and insistently. She simply had to press and rub some more.

"That's it." Houk sat up slowly, his hand working his cock with slow deliberation. A bead of moisture formed at the tip. "Lay down, Belle, it's easier if you lay down on your back and keep your knees up."

The pixie fell back onto the cushion and her knees splayed wide. She could still see his hand working his cock. Her gaze locked on that strong hard length. Her fingers rubbed across her moist flesh while her other hand rubbed and squeezed her breast. The delicious spurts of pleasure from her breast and her clit met in the middle and coiled together. Soft whimpers came from her throat. Her hips moved restlessly, then found a rolling motion that seemed to feel natural and increased the warm feelings of gathering heat.

Her magic sparked and coiled with her delight. Fear washed through her. "It's starting again," she whimpered breathlessly.

Houk licked his lips and his eyes seemed to darken. "Relax," he said in a calm even tone. "You are simply approaching climax. You will be just fine. I'm right here." He stood up at the foot of the bed.

She pressed with her heels and arched her back, lifting her bottom from the cushion to let her wings have room to flutter. Golden light radiated from her skin with her wing-beats. Her fingers moved with frantic haste. Her hips trembled in time with her fingers. Delight sparked throughout her body. Something began to swell in her core, something huge and momentous. A soft whimper escaped. "It feels so big."

"Orgasm does. Keep going, Belle, let yourself go and cum for me."

She moaned and writhed. It felt so good, it felt so scary . . . She felt her breath trying to still in her throat. She moaned with fear, but the heat and pleasure were too much to resist. The rising tide suddenly crested, and she stilled.

"Don't stop, Belle, keep going. You're right there." He opened the cage door. "Don't worry, I'll catch you."

Her fingers moved and she toppled. Heat fire, release . . . explosion. She wailed and bucked, ripped apart by the intense tide of incredible glory. Golden light burst around her.

It was happening! Houk shoved his hands into the small cage and scooped her up at her moment of incandescence. Power slammed through him, burning through his body. He shouted as the writhing pixie in his hands began to swell and expand. He barely made it to the bed when Belle suddenly became a solid armful of woman. Her wings still graced her shoulders, but they were tiny flecks of rainbow. Unlike the rest of her, they had not grown.

He rolled her on her back and shoved her long hair from her cheeks. Her lips were rosy pink and parted on a soft gasp.

Her leaf-green eyes were dilated wide with the pleasure still burning through her.

There was no time to lose. He only had moments; she could still return to being a pixie if he did not act quickly. He covered her lips with his and kissed her, claiming her mouth as he raised her knee and settled between her thighs. His cock brushed against her moist cleft, and his balls tightened. He gasped and grabbed for control.

She whimpered and writhed under him, fighting the kiss.

He angled his head and took her mouth more fully, tasting her, tasting the arousal on her tongue. He cupped her soft breast and squeezed, willing her rise back into desire, into arousal.

She stilled, and her tongue brushed against his. She moaned softly and lifted under him, pressing her moist flesh against the heat of his cock.

That was all the encouragement he needed.

He slid a hand between them and took his cock in hand. He rubbed the swollen head against her wet flesh, searching for her opening.

She moaned in his mouth and lifted against him, hooking one leg over his back. Her arms closed around his shoulders.

He found her and pressed. She was small and tight. He knew he was going to bring her pain, but he hoped to fire her arousal high enough to drown the pain of her soon to be sundered maidenhead. It was going to take every skill he had to bring her to climax quickly. He groaned as the head of his cock spread her and made room for itself within. He nearly came right there.

He released her mouth and latched onto her nipple, sucking strongly and insistently. Her nipple was velvet on his tongue and tasted of rich desire.

She gasped and arched under him, clearly enjoying his mouth on her breast.

He cupped her ass and raised her, then bent his knees. He thrust hard, taking her swiftly. He felt her resistance and shoved past it, sundering her innocence and sheathing himself fully in her body. She was a wet velvet fist around his cock. He groaned.

She arched and wailed.

He bit down on her nipple, deliberately confusing her pain with a bright bolt of pleasure. He held still, fully sheathed in her body, and slid a hand to where they were joined. He felt the heat of her flesh stretched tight around him, and shuddered. He moved to the swollen clit at the top. Dipping his fingers in her moisture, he rubbed the tiny nubbin.

She bucked.

He sighed. She was still very much aroused. He moved his mouth to her other breast and attacked the hard nipple with his tongue and teeth. His fingers rapidly stirred her clit while keeping her pinned on his cock. She squeezed him so hard, it took all his concentration not to pump hard and fill her with his cum. Her pleasure had to come first. If he took her carelessly, all would be lost.

He felt her body moisten and flutter around him. She was coming around . . . He continued sucking and nipping on her nipple while rubbing on her clit. Moisture slithered past his lodged cock.

She moaned softly and rocked under him.

He nearly wept with relief. She was ready for her first fuck. Sweat dripped from his brow. He withdrew slowly, only a little, then pushed back in.

She raised her hips to meet him.

He groaned with the pleasure of her moving under him. He withdrew, drawing more of his cock from her, then shoved back in a little more swiftly, a little harder.

She groaned and arched to meet his thrust.

Yes . . . He shoved both hands under her ass and angled her for better penetration. He thrust slowly into her, timing his thrusts to match her body's movements, following her lead. Her body would tell him exactly how much, how fast and how hard he had to ride her to take her to a swift climax.

He groaned as he took her. His balls were painfully tight with the need to release. His control hung by a thread. It would not take much to lose it — and lose her in the process.

She rocked under him, encouraging him to take her faster, harder . . .

He released her breast and gasped for breath. It was time. He wrapped his arms tight around her waist and rolled, bringing her atop him. He raised his knees and her feet tucked under his ass, bringing her more tightly down on him.

Her head came up in surprise. Her hands splayed in his chest, unerringly finding his nipples and jolting him with bolts of electric delight. She looked down at him in drowsy bewilderment. "Houk?"

He swept a hand across his damp brow and smiled. "James, call me James. Fuck me, Belle, ride me hard and make me cum."

She shifted atop him and bit her lip. She was moist and very close. He could feel it in the trembling flesh that gloved him.

He reached up and cupped her full breasts because they were simply too beautiful to resist. He caught her nipples and tugged.

She leaned forward onto his hands, pressing her clit against his pubic bone while shifting his cock within her. She moaned and rocked. Her hands found his shoulders and her fingers dug in. Sharp little nails scored him. She rocked and lifted, then fell and rocked again.

He stared up at her. She was glorious in her lust. He grunted as her pace increased until she rode him far harder than he had planned to ride her. Her appetite was incredible.

However, his stamina was severely under-practiced. If she kept that up, she was also going to kill him for sure.

He gasped as his balls tightened a notch more. He was losing it . . ."Belle, hurry. I'm going to cum very soon."

As though his words were spurs dug into her flanks, she gasped and her breath stilled. Her body trembled around him, she was there; she was falling . . . He could hear the whir of her tiny fluttering wings. She screamed as she came spectacularly apart around him.

At last! Orgasm took him in a violent shattering storm. He caught her, dragging her down onto his heart and holding her tight. He howled from the strength of his climax, bucking hard up into her as his cum pumped from his balls into her hot wet depths. Her tight body squeezed him dry.

She writhed in his arms shuddering and gasping as her pleasure continued to rampage through her. A ball of golden light formed on her back where her tiny wings fluttered frantically on her shoulders. The light generated by her tiny wings expanded to blinding brilliance. It exploded.

The air was suddenly full of whirring, whizzing, laughing balls of light. Hundreds of them spun around the room.

She cried out and collapsed in his arms. Her tiny wings were gone. She was fully human, at last.

He brushed her golden hair from her brow. "Look, Belle, turn and look what you made."

Her eyes opened partway drowsy with pleasure. She turned and looked over her shoulder. She sighed. "Oh, pixies!"

James nodded and smiled. "They say that a child's laughter makes pixies, but in Cornwall, where my Nana came from, there is another way."

The pixie groaned and shifted as she drifted up from sleep.

Such a strange and exciting dream . . . She snuggled back down, hoping to recapture it. She moved her hands and discovered the pillow her head resting on and the blankets she'd been sleeping under. *Huh?*

Her eyes snapped open. She blinked, then frowned. *Where am I?* She could see that she was in Houk's bedroom, but the angle was wrong, and everything looked out of proportion. Her heart stuttered in her chest. Her fingers explored the sticky wetness smearing her thighs. She was in Houk's bed, and his cum was seeping from her cunny. She reached behind to touch her shoulders. Her breath stilled in her throat. Her wings were gone . . .

Something large, warm and solid moved against her back.

She squeaked and rolled away.

An arm looped around her waist and pulled her back tight against a warm, breathing mass . . . with an erection. A kiss brushed her shoulder. "And just where do you think you are going?"

She twisted sharply to look behind her and landed flat on her back. Houk's handsome face rose above her. His jaw was dark with morning stubble. He braced himself on his elbows, warm and gloriously naked. His long black mane spilled across her shoulders. She could feel his cock brushing enticingly against her stomach. "Houk?"

"James." He smiled at her with half-lidded eyes. "We have become intimate, Belle." He leaned down and his lips brushed hers in a delicate kiss. "Call me James."

"In . . . intimate?" She licked her lips where he kissed her. His rich masculine scent washed over her.

"Oh, yes, very intimate . . ." He smiled and his hand slid down her side then over her hip. "Very intimate indeed." His palm brushed her belly.

"Wait!" she grabbed for his hand, stopping him. "What are you doing?"

"At this very moment?" His lips curled in a feral smile. "I am seducing you." His lips sought her breast and he stroked her nipple with his tongue.

Seduce? She sucked in a sharp breath. Her nipple tightened under his wet mouth. Erotic heat pulsed with awakening hunger. She tried to pull her fleeing thoughts together. She grabbed his long hair and tugged his head up. "I meant, why are you doing all this?"

"Why?" He grinned. He twisted his hand from her grasp and delved between her parted thighs. "Because I have a painfully hard cock and desperately want to fuck you." He brushed the plump outer lips of her cleft, then explored the tender folds of her wet flesh. "You're already wet, you're ready for me . . ."

"Damn you, pirate! That's not what I meant at all!" She grabbed his wrist, but he caught hers instead. "Hey!"

He pinned her wrist over her head. "Enough of that, Belle." His eyes narrowed. "Your body is more than willing."

"First, tell me why!" She twisted under him and shoved his shoulder with her free hand. "I don't understand why I'm big like this, like you are. What have you done to me?"

He grabbed for her other wrist and pinned them both over her head. "Pixies are creatures of innocence. Carnal knowledge is a pixie's doom." His hips flexed and his cock surged against her belly. His mouth set in a cruel smile. "It renders them human."

She stilled utterly. "What?" It came from her lips as the barest of whispers. "You made me *human*?"

He shook his head and delivered a smug smile. "No, Belle, I am only a man; I have no magic. You chose to be human."

She shook her head. "But I don't want to be human."

"Don't you?" He took her mouth in a demanding kiss.

She couldn't stop the sudden hunger that rose in ferocious answer. A moan escaped her throat and she parried his tongue with her own. His cock shifted against her stomach. She pressed up against his warm length. Her thighs parted in invitation.

He released her mouth and his lip curled. "I think you desperately wanted to be human — for me. I think you love me." He dropped his head and captured her nipple. He sucked hard, then tugged with his teeth.

I love . . . Houk? She gasped and arched her back, pressing her breast tighter to his mouth, scorched by the bolts of fire that stabbed straight down into her core. Her heart thumped and ached in confusion. What she felt for Houk was so different from what she felt for her boy. She loved her boy and had jealously watched over him, but her boy had never stirred her heart or her body with such overwhelming fear, desperation, confusion and . . . hunger. Was this love?

A long finger surged into her body and pressed something deliciously exciting within her. Her hips bucked in time to his buried finger.

He released her breast and rose over her. "There, you see? You want *me*." His eyes blazed with possessive heat as his fingers curled within her, driving her to writhing madness. "You want my cock in your cunt, so you made yourself human — for me." He found her swollen clit and stroked it.

Heat pulsed and gathered in a tight coil. She writhed under him and cried out.

"You had me for over two hundred years, Belle." His hand cupped under her knee, encouraging her to lift and open for him. "Now I have you." He settled between her thighs and his cock nudged, then pressed at the opening to her body. "And I will never let you go." He grunted and surged within.

She gasped with the invasion. He was thick and hot, stretching her to accommodate him. She moaned and twisted under him, pinned by the weight of his body.

"God, yes . . ." He slid his hands under her thighs and sat

up, pulling her until her back arched from the bed. He spread his knees, pulled back and thrust, and thrust . . . He groaned. "God, you feel so damned good!"

At this angle, his cock struck that sweet delicious spot within her with every stroke. She cried out, helpless to resist the onslaught of wave after hammering wave of pleasure.

"Cum for me, Belle," he gasped out. "I can't wait, and I want to see you cum while I fuck you."

Her breath stilled and her toes curled. Climax hovered on the threatening edge. She twisted, unable to fall.

"Now." He licked his thumb and stroked her painfully swollen clit. "Cum now!"

His touch scorched through her, pushing her over the glittering edge. She fell and exploded in a howling blaze of shuddering glory.

"Yes!" He threw back his head and pounded into her writhing body. Abruptly he froze, buried to the hilt. His breath exploded out of him and he thrust. "God!" He thrust once more, then fell on top of her to take her lips. He pressed her open and sucked her tongue into his mouth, stealing her breath in a deliberate act of carnal possession.

She moaned into his mouth as his cock pulsed in her body. He was right; she did want him enough to become a human woman, but *love*?

Houk slid from the bed, completely at ease with his nudity. "Out of bed with you."

She grabbed the sheet, rolled over and groaned. "After all that? Do I have to?"

"Yes, you do." He caught her around the waist and pulled. "We have much to accomplish today."

She squealed as she was dragged from the bed. "Houk!"

"James." He set her on her feet in a tangle of sheets. "Call me James." He tugged the sheet from her and left it on the floor. "Into the shower. Now." He caught her by the shoulders and turned her toward the bathroom. "You stink of sex."

"I stink of you!"

"Why, yes you do." He dropped a kiss on her brow.

She let him propel her into the bathroom, and then into the glassed-in shower stall. "You are a pain in my ass."

"You have no earthly idea." He grinned as he turned on the water.

She let herself be shoved under the water and groaned as she stood under the spray. The hot water felt heavenly. "I ache all over."

He reached past her for the soap. "After the way you rode me last night and then how you came apart this morning? I find myself quite unsurprised." He caught her shoulder and turned her toward the wall. "Put your hands on the tiles and I will bathe you."

She frowned at him. "I can bathe myself, thank you."

"But I am bathing you at the moment." He moved her thick mane over one shoulder. "Hands on the wall. Now."

She scowled. "Houk, I am not one of your crew, I don't take orders from you!"

"I am well aware that you are not one of my crew. I just finished fucking you." His brows lowered. "But you will follow my orders, and my name is James."

"Follow orders? Like hell!" She turned to shove past him. "Houk."

He grabbed her and shoved her face first, tight against the wall, using his size and weight to keep her pinned. His lips brushed her ear. "Continue along those lines and I shall be more than delighted to spank that saucy ass of yours." His hands cupped her round cheeks.

"Spank me?" She looked over her shoulder at him. "You're not serious?"

"Absolutely." His gaze was steady and ruthless.

She bit her lip. He was serious.

He smiled. "And then I will part those rosy, freshly spanked cheeks . . ." His soapy finger slid down the wet seam of her butt to circle the tight rose of her anus. "And shove my cock right up your tight little ass."

Her eyes opened wide. "You'll do what?"

"I will spank you and then fuck you up the ass." He raised a black brow. "Care to test me?"

"I . . ." Her breath stilled in her throat. His finger was pressing against her anus. He would do exactly as he said, and she just knew it would not be something she would enjoy.

"Now then . . ." He smiled, but his eyes were hot with aggressive challenge. "What is my name?"

She turned away, clenched her jaw and held her tongue.

He pressed his slick finger directly on her anus and began to push. "My name, Belle. What is it?"

"No." She closed her eyes and struggled to keep him out of her butt.

"Yes." His finger wiggled just a little and slid right in. He shoved until his middle finger was buried to the knuckle.

She gasped, mortified. His finger was in her butt!

"Mmm . . . You are rather tight." He chuckled softly. "When I shove my big thick cock up there, it's going to stretch you wide open." He wriggled his finger. "And when I fuck your sweet ass . . ." He pulled his finger part way out and shoved it right back in, then out, then in . . . illustrating what he intended to do. "My cock will stretch your anus so wide; my cum will roll right out of it."

She shivered and bit her lip to hold back her moan. His invading finger was embarrassing, but it didn't actually hurt. His huge cock would be another story entirely.

His lips brushed her ear. "Belle, my name. What is it?"

She cringed against the wall. She hated giving in on

anything, but she really hated giving in to Houk.

"Belle?" He pressed a second soapy slick finger to her anus. He twisted his wrist and the second finger pushed past her anus and into her ass.

She came up on her toes and moaned. His two fingers were uncomfortably tight.

"I will keep adding fingers to your ass until I get an answer out of you. Take your time. Eventually my cock will harden enough to shove in there, instead."

She tried to twist away but he had her pressed tight against the wall. "Damn you, Houk!"

"Bad girl." He pressed a third finger against her anus. "This one is going to hurt."

She couldn't take a third finger; she was aching from the two already in her. There was nothing she could do. He had her. "James."

He chuckled softly in her ear. "Yes, Belle?" He shifted the fingers in her ass but did not pull them out.

She whimpered. "Your name is James."

"Why, yes, it is."

Blasted pirate! What more did he want? She clenched her teeth. "Damn it, James, get your fingers out of my ass!"

"Say: please."

She choked. *Please?*

"You are running out of time; my cock is definitely getting hard."

She pressed her head against the tiles and groaned. *Did this never end?* "James, please get your fingers out of my ass."

"Certainly, Belle." He pulled them out.

She moaned and shivered in relief. Or was it disappointment? He was confusing the hell out of her and somehow, she just knew it was deliberate.

"Now, are you going to be good so I can bathe you?"

"Fine, sure, whatever." She wasn't in the mood to keep

fighting; at least not at the moment.

"Excellent." He tugged her back by the hips and positioned her with her feet splayed and her hands against the wall. "As long as you remain obedient, all things will go well for you."

"Obedient?" She turned to watch him rub soap on a cloth.

"Absolutely." He smiled the stepped behind her. "This is a very dangerous century, Belle." He began scrubbing her shoulders with the cloth. "You are not a pixie anymore, so you will need protection and care."

She grit her teeth. "I'm not helpless!"

"You are a small female without magic. Compared to me, you are quite defenseless." He dragged the cloth down her butt and knelt to scrub her flanks. "That reminds me, do you have any of the twenty-first-century knowledge that you granted me?"

She lowered her head. "No."

"I thought not." He stood back up and wrung out the cloth and draped it over the bar along the side of the shower. "First, we will need to get you a legal identity, then we shall have to do something about your lack of an education." He reached for the soap and lathered his palms.

"A legal identity? What for?"

He reached around her and cupped her breasts with his soapy palms. "So I can marry you, of course."

She stilled in shock. "Marry?"

He chuckled and his hands roved over her breasts and belly, covering her in soap. "It is what two people in love do. They get married, they have children . . ."

"Houk . . ."

He stilled and his cock nudged her butt. "Who?" His voice was dangerously calm.

She hissed. He was hard and he most definitely would shove that thing right up her ass. "James."

His soapy hands moved across her belly, but his cock

stayed positioned in the crease of her butt. "Yes, Belle?"

She took a deep breath. "James, I don't want to be married."

He stepped closer and pressed against her back. "I'm afraid it's far too late for both of us." His fingers moved lower, slipping between her thighs to soap her cleft. "You have ruined me and we must both pay the consequences."

What the hell was he up to now? "Ruined?"

"Oh, yes." His voice caressed her ear. "I am hopelessly in love with you, and completely ruined for anyone else. So, you must marry me, it's the honorable thing to do."

He was hopelessly in love with her? He had said it before but . . .

His fingers slid over her clit. "No one else will ever make me happy."

She shuddered under his rubbing fingers and came up on her toes. She couldn't think past the tight coil of heat building in her core and the words: 'hopelessly in love.'

He pressed his hips against her butt and his cock nudged between her splayed thighs His shaft rubbed up against her dampening cleft. "See what you have done?"

She looked down and saw the head of his cock poking out between her thighs. "But I don't . . ."

"You don't love me?" His hands closed around her breasts. "Oh, but you do." He pinched her nipples.

She gasped as erotic fire raced from her nipples to her core and bucked. His cock nudged against the hungry mouth of her cunny. She didn't think, she simply pressed back against him.

He groaned and his hands closed on her hips. "You drive me to madness, Belle. I simply cannot resist you." He thrust, taking her in one hard lunge.

She gasped as he filled her, coming up on her toes in exquisite delight. She did want him, in her body and in her life.

Perhaps she did love him after all.

He set a hand on the shower wall and locked an arm around her waist. "You are mine!" He thrust hard, again and again, imprinting his possession on her body and her soul. His panting breaths were loud in her ear. "I will never let you go. Never."

She moaned as he took her, his thrusts driving her toward a sudden and brutal climax. Ferocious pleasure rose in a menacing tidal wave. She gasped for breath and cried out.

"My name. Say my name, Belle." His thrusts increased in speed slamming into her with frantic force. "I want to hear it as you cum with my cock in your cunt."

She wailed as her climax took her and tore her apart in his arms. "James! Oh, God, James!"

He shouted and closed his arms tight around her, locking her to him. His cock pulsed deep within her body. He shuddered with the last of his climax. His breath was harsh as he whispered in her ear. "I would die without you."

She trembled, limp and sated in his arms. "James?"

He panted against her shoulder. "Yes, Belle."

"I think you may be right." She felt a sharp, stabbing pain in her heart. "I think I do love you."

He turned her to face him. Water from the shower dripped down his cheeks like tears. His smile was blinding. "Of course you do. And you will marry me." He took her lips in a gentle kiss.

She opened for him and kissed him back as the shower's spray washed her tears away.

Finally clean and wrapped in a towel, Belle stepped out of the bathroom on wobbly legs. She loved Houk . . . no James, and she was going to marry him. She shook her head. How could she live as a human without a trace of magic?

A twirling mote of gold light in one corner of the room, very close to the window, caught her eye.

A pixie? Tugging the towel around her, she climbed up on the bed and stood up on the mattress. She held out her palm. "Hello?"

The light buzzed around the room then circled her palm and landed. It was a tiny figure, more wings than manikin with a tuft of bright gold hair.

"Hello! Hello!" The little voice rang like a small bell.

"A bright shiny day to you," she said softly. She smiled. *Was I ever this small?*

Suddenly the room was full of tiny golden lights all calling out in voices that chimed.

"Hello!"

"A bright shiny day!"

Several landed on her arms, her shoulders, and on top of her head. She giggled, and the room filled with the tinkling laughter.

A masculine chuckle came from behind her.

"Oh!" She turned, and the pixies launched from her in a scatter of golden motes.

James smiled as he lounged against the doorframe with a towel knotted around his hips. "I leave you for only a moment, and already you are into mischief."

She grinned, even as tears filled her eyes. "They're pixies!"

He nodded. "Of course they're pixies." He held out his hand.

Belle bounced from the bed and rushed over to take his hand. "I haven't seen that many in one place for years, and years, and years!" She wiped at the tears in her eyes.

James brushed at her tears with his thumbs. "According to my Cornish Nana, when a pixie falls in love and loses her wings, all her lost magic shatters into new pixies. The world may have lost you, but you have given a very jaded world a fresh taste of magic." His lips brushed hers. "Come, it is time to dress and greet the twenty-first century."

On a white-hot summer day in the garden of the only Angli-can Church in New York City, the pixie known as Miss Belle Tinker by her New York state driver's license became Mrs. James Belle Houk. The church had been James's idea, not hers. She would have been perfectly happy with a Justice of the Peace, but James was incredibly old-fashioned for someone possessed of twenty-first-century knowledge.

The small ceremony was closely witnessed by both of James's black-suited and blank-faced lawyers. The disreputa-ble and nattily attired gentleman who had arranged for her new identity stood on the far side of the church's fence with a foolish grin on his face. A tiny golden mote flitted around his hat. Apparently, he believed in fairies.

No one else seemed to notice the whizzing golden lights flitting among the flowers.

Her fairy tale gown shimmered with rainbow hues as she gave her vows. James held tight to her hand and smiled broadly, dressed in a snow-white frock coat and broad-brimmed hat festooned with white feathers. His silver-han-dled sword cane was looped over his arm, a pirate and a gen-tleman to the end.

He kissed her lips at the end of the ceremony and whis-pered. "Belle, where are your shoes?"

She pouted up at him. "They pinch."

"Belle, you cannot walk around barefoot here, the ground is dangerous."

She grinned. "Then I guess you'll just have to carry me."

James scowled playfully. "Wench." He leaned over and scooped her up into his arms.

She laughed as he carried her out of the church garden and set her in the limousine. "Where to now, Captain?"

James raised a black brow as he slid in beside her. "Now? I take you home."

Belle frowned. "But I thought we were leaving the hotel?"

James grinned. "I have a wedding present for you."

Belle was immediately distracted. "A present? For me?"

James nodded. "I bought you a home."

"A home? Really?"

"Of course, it is traditional for the bridegroom to provide for his wife. Once we change at the hotel, we will go straight to the airport."

"We're going by plane? Where is it?"

He leaned back on the leather seat. "First things first, Belle." He pulled his coat away from his lap then reached for the buttons over the firm bulge in his pants. "These breeches are decidedly tight."

Belle frowned. "James, what are you doing?"

"Preparing myself for your gratitude." He pulled out his cock and groaned. "Down on your knees and thank me properly for my gift, Belle."

Belle bit her lip. "You want to fuck here?"

He stroked himself, pulling the sheath down and exposing his cock-head. He smiled broadly. "I want your mouth."

Belle swallowed. "My mouth?"

"It's called fellatio. I want to fuck your mouth."

She eyed his cock. He wanted to spill his cum in her mouth? She cringed. "Uh . . ."

His brows lowered. "If you prefer, I can take your ass instead once we get to the hotel."

"No, thank you!" She dropped to the floor with undisguised haste. Her layers of skirts filled the floor and spilled on the seat behind her. She focused on the rigid column of his cock. The flared head was deep purple, and the veins were pronounced. Her panties dampened with eagerness and regret that he didn't want to fuck.

"Pull down your gown, I want to play with your nipples as you suck me."

She frowned up at him. "That's a lot of demands for a bit of gratitude."

"It is a very large present." He raised a black brow and smiled. "And I expect a lot of gratitude for it."

A large present? Belle blinked. "Oh."

He nodded and pushed forward to the edge of the seat. "Good, now pull down that gown and get up here."

"Aye, aye Captain." She pushed her hair behind her and tugged the bodice of her gown down, exposing her full breasts.

He smiled. "What a lovely sight." He spread his satin covered knees. "Bring them to me."

Belle set her hands on his knees and came up between them with her lips parted.

"One moment."

She stopped and looked up at him. "What?"

His grinned as he reached into his coat pocket. "I have something to entertain us both, while you suck me off." His hands closed on her breast. A gold chain fell from his palm. "As sensitive as you are, I think you will find these very interesting indeed." He trapped her nipple then fastened a tiny clasp on it.

Belle hissed as lighting lanced from her nipple to her core. "God! What is that?"

"The same as this." He caught her other nipple and set the tiny clasp on the other. The gold chain hung between them. He looped the chain around his finger. "They are called nipple clasps." He tugged.

Belle whimpered. The little clasps bit into her with a demonic jolt that burned straight to her clit.

"Pull up your skirts, Belle."

She could barely think past the pulsing in her nipples and

her clit. "What?"

"I want you to masturbate as you suck me."

She scowled as she tugged her skirts up from under her knees. "Anything else?"

He tilted his head and pursed his lips. "I'm sure I can think of something."

She rolled her eyes and sighed. "Knowing you . . ."

He cupped a hand over his ear. "Is that a complaint?"

Yikes! Her last complaint about his sexual demands had gotten her tied to a chair with a vibrator. She shook her head. "No!"

"Good. Do it."

She shoved her hand down into her panties. She parted her outer lips to find her clit hard and hot. She stroked it with her middle finger and bit back a moan.

"Now, Belle, give me your mouth and begin by licking me. All of me."

She leaned forward and stroked the hard column of his cock with the tip of her tongue. He tasted cleanly of soap and smelled of male musk. She stroked up to the top and ran her tongue around the flared head. A touch of salty musk bloomed on her tongue. Intrigued, she stroked the plum crown and tasted more of him.

Between the sensual curls of warmth spiraling from her fingers on her clit and the taste of aroused male on her tongue, her mouth began to water.

He sighed. "Mm, very nice." His eyes closed and he shifted lower on the seat. "Make sure you lick everything and do not forget my balls."

She explored his entire length, making his cock gleam wetly then crouched down to taste the plump muskiness of his balls.

The chain tightened.

Her breath exploded out of her. The tugging on her nipples

increased the ache in her clit. If that kept up, she was going to cum and fast.

"Keep licking."

She dove between his thighs and laved his balls with her tongue. She drew one into her mouth and gently sucked on it, exploring its shape and taste, then released it to suck on the other.

He groaned. "Remind me to teach you how to give a rim job."

She nearly smiled as she stroked the underside of his balls with her tongue. She had discovered what a rim job was quite by accident from a friend on the Internet. There was no way in hell she was going to remind him to teach her how to lick his anus. She nibbled just a bit. Reminder or not, knowing him, she'd end up doing it anyway.

He hissed and tugged on her chain. "Up! Get up and give me your mouth!"

She came up between his knees and opened her mouth. She licked the top of his cock, then closed her lips around him.

He threw his head back and groaned. His hips bucked, plunging his cock deeper into her mouth. "Suck it!"

She sucked as he thrust halfway into her mouth, nearly choking her. The sound of wet suction and his panting groans filled the car. Her moans joined his as he tugged her chain and her fingers danced on her clit. She was going to cum very soon . . .

He caught the back of her head. "Deeper!"

She tried, but when he struck the back of her throat, her body wanted to gag.

"Swallow your spit."

She swallowed.

He pushed, and his cock slid deeper into her throat. "Yes!"

She couldn't breathe and whimpered in alarm.

He let her come up and she sucked for air.

"Keep swallowing and you'll take more of me." He pressed the back of her head.

There was no help for it. She had no desire to have him ram his cock up her ass. So far he had only used his fingers, but sooner or later . . . She swallowed and took his cock into her throat, then again, and again, coming up briefly for short breaths.

He arched his entire body as he fucked her mouth. "I'm nearly there . . ." He used both hands and held her down and grunted as he thrust.

She whimpered as his cock thrust into her throat. She couldn't breathe . . .

"Yes!" He pulled her partway up.

She drew in a breath around the cock in her mouth. His cock pulsed on her tongue and thick salty liquid sprayed from it. He was cumming in her mouth.

"Swallow it."

She closed her eyes and swallowed. There was a lot of it. Some of it slid past her lips and down her chin. She had to swallow a second time to get it all down, then a third to clear her mouth.

He released her and she sat back. She wiped her mouth with the back of her hand and glared at him. "That was nasty."

"Is that so?" James smiled as he tucked himself back into his trews. "You still have one last hole to fill, Belle."

She turned away. Would he never stop with the ass-fucking thing?

He caught her chin and turned her to face him. "Do you have any idea how beautiful you look with my cum dripping from your mouth?" He leaned forward and lifted her up onto his lap. He pressed a kiss to her lips. "I love you, Mrs. Houk. Thank you for making me a very happy man."

Belle blinked back sudden tears and curled her arms around his neck. "I love you too, James."

The limo rolled to a stop.

James tucked the chain into her dress and pulled her bodice over her breasts. "Time to change for our trip home, Belle."

"Are you going to take those off me?"

He smiled. "Not just yet."

The hotel room held an open trunk ready to hold their wedding clothes. Belle guessed that the rest of their baggage had already been sent to the airport. Their traveling clothes were laid out on the bed in the master suite.

Belle reached behind her and suddenly realized that she could not get to all the tiny buttons of her wedding gown. It was far too snug to pull up over her head or down past her butt.

James grinned as he shrugged out of his frock coat. He set it neatly in the trunk. "Do you need help getting out of that gown?"

Belle turned to face him in complete disarray. "Yes. Too many buttons."

He dropped his waistcoat in the trunk and held out his hand. "Come."

Belle turned her back on him and his fingers made short work of her buttons.

"There, set it in the trunk when you have it off, but do not dress just yet." He caught her chin and turned her to face him "And do not remove the clasps on your nipples."

She sighed and nodded. "I'll leave them on."

"Good." He released her chin and stepped over to sit in a chair.

She pulled the gown down and off. James was still playing games. Honestly, just how much sex did one man need?

Barefoot and clad only in the tiny silk panties, she laid the frothy mass of shimmering silk over his seventeenth-century finery.

James stopped in the process of peeling off his stockings. His buckle shoes were already in the trunk. His black brows lowered. "You didn't wear your stockings, either?"

Belle winced. "The belt thingie that holds them up is uncomfortable!"

He pulled off his other stocking and jerked at the pearl buttons on his shirt. "Belle, I told you to wear them."

She folded her arms across her chest and immediately dropped them with a hiss. The sudden contact with the gold clasps had made her nipples throb viciously. "I didn't want to." She set her hands on her hips instead. "I'm wearing the damned panties!"

"I wanted the stockings on you for a reason." He stood up and pulled off his shirt. His muscular chest flexed. "You realize that now you will have to be punished?"

Belle's mouth fell open. "Punished?"

He scowled. "I don't have time to bugger you properly. I'll have to save that for when we arrive at the house." He unbuttoned his snug breeches. "However, we have plenty of time for a spanking."

"A spanking?" Belle backed away. Her heart pounded in her throat. "You're not really going to spank me?"

"Absolutely." He stalked over to the trunk, superbly nude and bristling with affront, he dropped the last of his clothes in the trunk. All that was left of his wedding finery was the black ribbon in his hair. "I should have spanked you a month ago after that fiasco in the park."

"Hey! The pixies decided to make the carousel horses gallop through the park, not me!"

James lifted his chin. "But they would not have thought of it if you had not made that comment about them being trapped by the poles."

Belle winced. Actually, she had said something a bit more specific, but she was not going to tell him that. Thank God they were leaving town before he heard about the lions in front of the New York public library.

He closed the trunk and sat down on it. He patted his knee. "Come here."

Belle had no interest whatsoever in going over there.

He frowned ferociously. "Do not make me chase you. I chartered a private plane, and I still have enough rope to tie you naked in the cargo hold."

Belle swallowed. He had tied her to the foot of the bed last time. The time before, he had tied her spread-eagled across the table. Then there was the chair and vibrator incident. He was always careful to ensure her comfort, so to speak, but personally, she was getting a little tired of being tied up. Recently, he had developed a fascination with Japanese rope bondage. God only knew what he would do with her this time.

"Now."

She inched toward him. "Must you spank me?"

He nodded. "You disobeyed. You must be punished." He held out his hand. "The faster you lay across my knees, the faster it will be over."

"Promise?"

He nodded. "I promise. Time is something we do not have much of." He wiggled his fingers. "Come."

She cringed and set her hand in his.

"Good girl." He tugged, and she fell forward into his arms. In less than a breath, he had her positioned face down across his knees. He tugged her panties down and sank his fingers into her butt cheek. "Why must you always disobey? You know how much I enjoy punishing you."

Oh, God, he'd asked her a question. That meant he wanted

an answer, and she had better make it good. "Um, because I love you?"

"Good answer. For that, you only get ten smacks."

"Ten!"

"Would you rather have the twenty I originally planned?"

"No, thank you!"

"Are you sure?"

She nodded. "Oh, yes! Quite sure!"

"Very well then . . ." SMACK!

She flinched at the crack, then gasped as her right butt cheek heated and burned. "Shit!"

"Language, young lady. That gets you an extra."

"What?"

SMACK!

She yelped then writhed. Both cheeks were burning. "Damn it, that hurts!"

"It's supposed to; you are being punished." He chuckled. "You may scream if you like. I'm sure that the staff is used to hearing your screams by now."

"You stinking . . ."

"Yes?"

She cringed. Now was definitely not the time to vent her temper. "Just hurry it up, will you?"

He leaned over so she could see his grin. "As you wish."

SMACK! SMACK! SMACK! SMACK! Each blow came on one cheek, then the other.

She shouted on the last one and couldn't stop herself from bucking across his knees. Her butt was one mass of heat. On top of that, her nipples were throbbing from the pounding. Worse of all her core was throbbing with hungry interest. She could feel moisture dribbling from her cunny. She had no clue why it was happening, but if he kept smacking her butt, she was going to climax.

"I don't know about you, but I am quite enjoying myself."

Belle panted across his knees. "Oh, gee, that comes as a huge surprise." She turned to glare at him. "How do you expect me to sit on the plane ride after this?"

"You should have thought of that before you chose to be disobedient." He smiled as his hand rubbed her fiery cheek.

She hissed. His hand felt like sandpaper on her raw butt.

He slid a finger down the seam of her ass and delved into her cleft. "My goodness, you are wet. I do believe that you are wetting my knee. You must be enjoying this as much as I."

She groaned. He'd noticed her strange excitement. It figured. "Tell that to my sore butt!"

"Don't mind if I do." He leaned over her and applied his mouth to her cheek.

She sucked in a sharp breath. His tongue made tingling swirls and the wetness felt almost chilling on her hot skin. Her mind locked on his tongue. She suddenly wished with all her heart that he would apply it to her wet cunny. A moan escaped her throat.

He bit down.

She yelped. His teeth felt like sharp fangs.

He sat up. "Only five more to go."

She groaned. "Great."

SMACK! He rubbed his palm across her.

She released a soft yelp, then groaned. His hand felt like it was covered in needles on her burning butt. She couldn't stop herself from rolling her hips.

SMACK! He dug his fingers into her cheek.

She yelped a little louder and bucked across his knees. "Easy with the claws!"

He snorted. "They're my fingers."

"Not from this end!"

"Really? How about from this end?" He slid a finger into her cunt. He chuckled. "You are certainly churning butter in there, all smooth and creamy."

She moaned. It felt so good, her thighs opened all by themselves. She lifted her butt to get more of him.

He curled his finger, and his thumb brushed her clit. "Are we getting close to climax?"

She whimpered as everything coiled tight and jerked back against his hand. Just a little more and she would cum . . .

"Ah, I see that we are." He pulled his fingers away. "Too bad for you."

She collapsed and moaned in frustration.

SMACK!

She yelped and nearly came right there. She was so close to climax that the vibration from his hand on her butt jolted her clit. On top of that, the rocking of her body jolted her pinched nipples, sending a spear of erotic heat straight to her throbbing clit. A few more strikes and she would cum. "Again!"

"Again?" He laughed out loud. "Your word is my command."

SMACK!

Her clit pulsed ferociously in time with her nipples, sending her just a tiny bit closer to the edge. She writhed. "Again!"

SMACK!

Her breath stilled in her throat and her toes curled. She was right there. One more would send her over. She couldn't find the breath to ask for it.

"All done."

Her breath exploded from her lungs. "No!"

"No?" He laughed out loud as he lifted her from his knees and set her up on her feet. "I am truly sorry, but your spanking is over."

Belle stood on shaking knees, panting for breath. She was so close to climax that her core was tied in knots. She cupped her breast and squeezed her thighs, but it did nothing to relieve the vicious ache.

He raised a black brow. "How close are you?"

Normally she would think twice about answering him. He had a nasty habit of turning everything inside out. But right at that moment, she was too close to the edge to care. She moaned. "I'm right there. One more smack would have done me."

"I see." He smiled and his eyes heated. "Lie down on your back and spread your knees. Now."

Belle dropped to the floor and hissed when her butt made contact with the carpet. She lifted her butt from the floor and groaned.

James got down on his hands and knees between her splayed thighs. "I expect a thorough show of gratitude for this."

Belle bit her lip and whimpered. "Anything! Anything! Just make me cum!"

He chuckled and dropped to his elbows. "I will remember that." His lips brushed the inside of her thigh.

She stared in shock. "What are you doing?"

He smiled. "Cunnilingus."

"Huh?"

He wrapped his arms around her thighs and grinned broadly. "Fear not, you will quite enjoy it." He dropped his head and his mouth made contact with her mound. Then his tongue swept her from anus to clit.

Her body jolted viciously. She gasped. "Oh my god!"

His mouth fastened on her cunny and proceeded to feast with greedy slurps and loud suction. With careful and de-monic precision, he sucked and nibbled on everything but where she needed it most—her clit.

She howled and bucked with insanity. She was so close to the edge that all it would take is the lightest touch, which was precisely what he denied her.

He slid his long middle finger into her core. He pulled it right back out and pressed against her anus. Before she knew quite what had happened, his finger was sliding up into her ass while his index finger worked its way into her hungry core.

She writhed in a confusion of mixed signals. Her core was delighted by his entry, but her anus was not.

His tongue lightly tapped her clit.

The air went clean out of her lungs and her body arched, shoved straight onto the razor edge of explosion . . .

He chuckled and it was an evil sound. His lips closed on her neglected clit. He focused his tongue on her and fluttered it.

Her toes curled sharply, and her hips came right off the floor. She burst in a howling firestorm of merciless and blinding release. She screamed.

Neverona was a green jewel floating in the wide blue of the Caribbean ocean. A pair of mountain peaks climbed at the north end and white beaches stretched around a lovely cove at the south.

Belle stared out the plane's tiny window. "You bought an island?"

James nodded. "Can you think of a better place for us to live? There's a manor house very near the cove and a small airport further inland."

Belle looked over at the pirate in his black Armani suit. "James, that must have cost you a fortune. You didn't use all your gold, did you?"

James shook his head. "Fear not. I barely touched the wealth I currently possess." He grinned. "Because of your gift of twenty-first-century knowledge, I was able to invest very wisely indeed." He tilted his head. "It was quite comforting to discover that business is still conducted pretty much in the same fashion as it was in my day. And I have a distinct advantage."

"What's that?"

James grinned broadly. "I am a genuine pirate."

That was the understatement of the universe . . . Belle looked out the window. "Do you think the pixies will find the island?"

"They have succeeded in finding every other place we have gone to, no matter how far," he said dryly. "I doubt we will escape them even here."

Belle chuckled. James loved to complain about 'the little pests,' but he had never gone out of his way to drive them off. He was obviously as pleased with their existence as she was. She bit her lip. The world needed a touch of magic.

A line of palms waving on the beachfront caught her gaze. "You know, I didn't realize how much I missed our island." She turned back to kiss him on the cheek. "Thank you."

James patted her hand. "I'm glad I could please you." He caught her chin in his fingers. "I do love you, Belle."

Belle felt her heart thump. She would never get tired of hearing him say that. Her boy never had, not once. She leaned across him and took his mouth in a kiss designed to curl his toes. "I love you, too." She whispered against his lips. "Even if you are a codfish."

He raised a black brow. "That will get you a spanking, Belle."

She grinned. "I should hope so!"

He caught her around the waist and pulled her onto his lap. "Consider it a promise." His smile was pure pirate.

ABOUT THE AUTHOR

For me, writing is more than a passion; it's an *obsession*. The stories crowd into my head. I write them down so I can get some peace. Where do I get my ideas? Rampant curiosity. I play the game of 'What If?' with everything I encounter. Everything I do and everything I see triggers a story to be told. I am a voracious reader of Romance, Science-Fiction, Fantasy, Horror, and Erotica, so naturally, my stories follow along the lines of what I like to read."

Morgan Hawke has been writing erotic fiction since 1998. She has lived in seven states of the US and spent two years in England. She has been an auto mechanic, a security guard, a waitress, a groom in a horse-stable, in the military, a copy-writer, a magazine editor, a professional tarot reader, a belly-dancer and a stripper. Her personal area of expertise is the strange and unusual.

Ms. Hawke maintains a close and personal relationship with her computer and her cat.